THE UNENDING CHASE

Also by Cap Daniels

THE
UNENDING CHASE

CHASE FULTON NOVEL #4

CAP DANIELS

ANCHOR WATCH
PUBLISHING
** USA **

The Unending Chase
Chase Fulton Novel #4
Cap Daniels

This is a work of fiction. Names, characters, places, historical events, and incidents are the product of the author's imagination or have been used fictitiously. Although many locations such as marinas, airports, hotels, restaurants, etc. used in this work actually exist, they are used fictitiously and may have been relocated, exaggerated, or otherwise modified by creative license for the purpose of this work. Although many characters are based on personalities, physical attributes, skills, or intellect of actual individuals, all of the characters in this work are products of the author's imagination.

Published by:

ANCHOR WATCH
—— PUBLISHING ——
** USA **

13 Digit ISBN: 978-1-7323024-5-7
Library of Congress Control Number: 2018911401

Cover Design: German Creative

Dedication

This book is dedicated to...
My dear friend, mentor, teacher, and sometimes tormenter, Leo,
who is the real-life inspiration for the fictional Leo in this novel.

To list Leo's titles, degrees, licenses, and certifications
would consume this page and still be incomplete.

To adequately catalog his attributes as a man of impeccable character,
astonishing capability, boundless knowledge, and unequalled wisdom
would be impossible.

Leo taught me to fly airplanes without looking out the window,
but that doesn't scratch the surface of the countless lessons he taught me
about how to live life without limits and to constantly strive to improve
in everything that I do, competing only with myself and demanding
more of myself than others could ever expect.

Special Thanks To:

My Astonishing Editor:
Sarah Flores – Write Down the Line, LLC
www.WriteDownTheLine.com
Sarah's tireless efforts to make me a better writer never cease to amaze
me. She is a brilliant teacher, inspiring source of constant encouragement, and astonishing talent when it comes to turning my work into
palatable fiction. Without her, my work would be unreadable.

Explosive Ordnance Disposal Technician:
"Boomer" (Real name withheld upon request)
His patience with my ten thousand questions about how explosives
can actually work under water was a testament to his calm, deliberate demeanor.

Master Instructor Dan Lennon and the dive professionals of Rain-
bow Reef Dive Center in Key Largo, FL:
Their knowledge and experience were invaluable in creating the
technical diving sequences in this novel.

Medical Editor Judson Moore, M.D. –
Orthopedic Surgeon Extraordinaire:
Although Dr. Moore is a wizard at repairing the damage humans do
to their arms, wrists, and hands, his guidance and direction on how
to properly inflict injury during the interrogation scenes in this
novel was invaluable.

The Dive Medical Officers and Hyperbaric Medicine Specialists at
the University of Alabama Birmingham for whom I have unending
admiration and appreciation:
Following a scuba diving accident in 2014, the physicians at UAB
not only saved my life, but also restored me to full strength through
prolonged recompression therapy. My experience with those amazing professionals during that terrifying period of my life is the inspiration for many scenes in this novel.

Table of Contents

1

The Wrong Team

Exhaustion overtook me, and I collapsed to the wet, hard-packed sand of the eastern shore of Cumberland Island off the coast of Georgia. Every inch of my body ached, and my head throbbed in time with my heart, as it seemed to be making great efforts to leap from my chest. The sun peeked over the horizon of the eastern sky and the Atlantic Ocean lapped gently at the beach. Sweat poured from my mosquito-ravaged body, and my last ounce of strength washed away with the tide.

The pounding in my head morphed into a rising crescendo of intense, thundering beats. Not only could I hear the approaching thunder, but I could feel it in every muscle of my body. It grew louder and stronger until there was no choice left but to open my eyes and see, feel, and hear anything other than the relentless, inevitable pounding. I gasped and instantly drew myself into a ball as a bounding herd of wild horses galloped around me, enveloping me in their advance, their hooves bouncing off the wet sand, and their nostrils flaring.

After having survived countless encounters with Russian assassins doing their best to end me, the thought of my end coming beneath the hooves of a horde of wild horses sent the last energy within me escaping as uncontrollable laughter. As quickly as they'd arrived, the horses disappeared, continuing their irrational sprint down the beach as if pursued by some invisible predator. I had been spared.

In my exhaustion, I'd forgotten about the horses. Cumberland Island was home to a herd of nearly two hundred feral horses; the descendants of those brought to the island in the sixteen hundreds by European explorers and settlers.

The last several hours of my life had been spent scouring the island for Captain Ekaterina Norikova, the Russian SVR officer whom I'd known as Anya Burinkova. I'd loved her once, and despite the deception, there remained some part of me that always would.

I'd fallen hook, line, and *gruzilo* for Anya, especially when she'd supposedly given her life working with me to save my former college baseball coach's daughter, Skipper, from a Miami porn producer. Only weeks after Anya's supposed death, I'd received a mysterious call from a man named Michael Anderson, a Russian illegal who'd escaped U.S. custody and kidnapped Skipper. He demanded that if I ever wanted to see her alive again, I would face him in the middle of the night where he was holding Skipper on Cumberland Island.

I'd dropped everything and put myself and Clark Johnson on the island as quickly as possible, where we not only found Skipper bound and gagged, but where we also found Michael Anderson's body with Anya's fighting knife sticking out of his back.

Skipper had said, "It was her, Chase. It was Anya."

I'd given up believing Anya was dead sometime before that night, but thinking she'd beaten me to Cumberland Island and killed Skipper's abductor minutes before I'd arrived was almost unfathomable to me.

I'd sent Clark and Skipper back to the mainland in the boat we'd used to race to the island. Skipper needed a doctor to make sure she wasn't hurt. I had remained on the island, consumed by my insatiable desperation to find Anya Burinkova before she could disappear again.

I searched every inch of the island throughout the darkness of that long night, running at a breakneck pace until I fell onto the sand, completely spent. The sun had broken across the eastern horizon, and I'd found no sign of Anya or any boat that may have brought her to the island. There was no other way to get to Cumberland Island—except by helicopter.

As I lay there, desperately trying to muster the strength to continue the useless search, my phone chirped.

"Yeah."

"We're back," said Clark Johnson.

Clark, a former Army Ranger and Green Beret, now worked for the same agency that employed me as a covert operative. Our skill sets complemented each other perfectly, and we'd become not only brothers-in-arms, but also lifelong friends. He was the closest thing I'd ever have to a brother.

"I'm on the ocean side. I'm not sure where, but I think I'm on the north side of the entrance to Christmas Creek. The surf is light over here. You won't have any trouble landing or getting off. Is Skipper okay?"

"Yeah, she's fine. Just some scrapes and bruises. She's with me. We'll be there in ten minutes."

I hung up, relieved to hear Skipper wasn't hurt. She'd been through more than any twenty-one-year-old girl deserved. She was tough, but at that point, I didn't know just how tough she actually was.

"Chase, get up. Let's go. Chase!"

I opened my eyes to see Clark standing over me, kicking my boot.

I scrambled to my feet and dusted sand from my clothes. "I'm sorry, man. I didn't mean to fall asleep. I'm spent."

"Come on. We'll get you some grub and a shower. It looks like you could use both. I take it you didn't find Anya."

"No," I admitted. "No sign of her anywhere."

"That's what I figured," he said, helping me into the boat.

He shoved us off the beach, and we powered away through the light surf and back around the north end of the island. After a short ride, we pulled alongside the old wooden dock at the Jekyll Island Club and crawled out of the boat.

Clark gave me a hand up. "This is the first place you and I ever met. Remember?"

I smiled through my exhaustion. "Yeah, I remember. You were standing right over there, hitting on Anya, and I was trying to decide whose side you were on."

"I wasn't hitting on her," he protested.

"Yes, you were. You hit on everybody."

Instead of a wasted effort to defend himself further, he changed the subject. "Let's get you inside and cleaned up."

We mounted a golf cart and headed for the hotel.

Skipper slid her hand into mine. "Are you okay, Chase?"

"Yeah, I'm fine. I've just been chasing a ghost at a sprint for the past seven hours. How about you? Are you okay?"

"Yeah, I'm fine. Thanks for coming for me. It's pretty much becoming a regular thing, you rescuing me."

I shook my head. "I got there too late this time."

Skipper stared at her shoes. "I know you don't believe me, but it was her."

"I believe you." I squeezed her hand then pulled Anya's knife from my pocket.

Skipper looked at the knife with a blank expression.

"It's Anya's knife," I said. "She left it intentionally for me to find. Did she say anything to you?"

She shook her head. "No, she only spoke in Russian to the guy. I mean, I guess it was Russian. It sounded like it."

I wrapped the knife in the rag and stuck it back in my pocket.

"Do you remember what she said?" I asked, hoping she could remember any of the sounds. If she could get close, maybe I could piece it together.

"It sounded like, 'Will she bite these common tees.' I know that sounds stupid, but she said it to him over and over. Then she stabbed him twice in the chest. I'd never seen anything like it. She moved so fast. It was like she was possessed or something. It was scary, even though I knew she was saving my life. Then he fell by the fire, and she looked straight at me. She looked the same as when the two of you pulled me out of that house in Miami, but she was like, cold and focused or something. And then she stabbed him again, right in the back, then took off running. It freaked me out. I mean, why did she leave me there tied up? Why didn't she cut me free?" Her hand trembled in mine.

"Tell me again what she said. Try to remember, and try to say it just like she did."

"I don't know, Chase. It just sounded like, 'Will she bite these common tees.'"

"Could she have said, '*Vy oshibayetes' v komandè*?'"

"I don't know. Maybe. It kinda sounded like that."

"Was she saying it to you or Michael Anderson?"

"Oh, she was definitely saying it to him. She never even looked at me until after he was dead. So, that thing you said. What does it mean? What do you think she said?"

"I think she said, 'You're on the wrong team.'"

2
A Brand-New Man

Clark was right, as usual. A shower, a meal, and a few hours of un-interrupted sleep made me feel like a brand-new man. Jack Ford, the operations manager of the Jekyll Island Club, granted us the use of a pair of adjoining rooms on the second floor of the glorious old hotel. The Club and Jack had a long and storied history of coopera-tion with the organization for which Clark and I worked. Theirs had been a relationship of mutual benefit for decades. When the Club needed a favor, regardless of the magnitude, we'd always said yes. When we needed anything the Club could provide, Jack Ford always rolled out the red carpet.

I'd been recruited into the agency on the hallowed grounds of the Club by a collection of seasoned operators with heroic and larger-than-life histories of their own. Ace, a former fighter pilot; Beater, a Naval Academy graduate and intelligence-gathering leg-end; Tuner, the father of acoustic signature identification; and Dr. Robert "Rocket" Richter, also a fighter pilot and key player in the early days of manned supersonic flight alongside Chuck Yeager. They were the four men who plied me with expensive scotch and Cuban cigars, took me sailing on the most magnificent sailing yacht I'd ever seen, and asked me to give up life as I knew it and dedicate myself to the service of others. Their question and my answer had changed my life forever.

Dr. Richter had been my favorite UGA psychology professor and the man who led me into the hands of the other three who recruited me into the service of my country as a covert operative. I had those men to thank, or perhaps to blame, for what my life had become.

I had accomplished very little compared to the men who'd led me into this life. I'd killed a notorious Russian hitman and his twin brother on my first real mission out of training. I'd rescued my coach's daughter from a series of bad decisions. That mission was personal and not associated with my employment with the agency. I'd successfully lured a notorious Russian colonel, Victor Tornovich, into the open and ended his meteoric rise up the SVR ladder, but I didn't feel like I'd done anything to measure up to the accomplishments of men like the four who'd recruited me, and men like my partner, Clark Johnson.

The time was coming for my agency to expect more of me. I wanted to earn my stripes and prove I was worthy of the company I kept, but I was consumed with the singular thought of finding Anya, as I'd come to believe she was still alive.

I met Clark and Skipper in the dining room for an early dinner. The maître d' sat us at a private table near the back of the ornate room so we could talk without curious guests listening in.

"So, tell me what's on your mind, Chase." Clark raised his eyebrows and stared at me over his water glass.

"You know what's on my mind," I told him. "I have to find her."

He closed his eyes and swallowed a mouthful of spring water. "You're only going to find her if she wants to be found."

"She may not want me to find her, but I know for sure that she wants me to know she's still alive. If she didn't, she would've snuck in, killed Michael Anderson, and silently slipped away, leaving no trace. But that's not what she did. She stared straight at Skipper, making sure she recognized her. And on top of that, she left her knife sticking out of his back—specifically for me to find."

"You may be right, but why? Why wouldn't she just kill him, cut Skipper free, and wait for you?"

"I don't know. Maybe she's afraid."

Clark laughed. "That girl ain't afraid of the devil, let alone any- thing on Cumberland Island. What could she possibly be afraid of?"

"I think it all depends on her status," I said.

"Her status?"

"Yeah, her status. If she's running from somebody, she may be afraid I'll turn her in. She has to know I'm pissed about the whole ordeal. Maybe she's afraid I'll hand her over to Langley."

Clark shook his head. "I don't know, Chase. There are too many unanswered questions. Too much we don't know to be making those kinds of assumptions right now."

"I guess you're right," I admitted, "but here's what I think hap- pened. I think the CIA pulled her out of that VA hospital in Miami and saved her life just so they could interrogate her. I think she killed the agents who were guarding her in that safe house and then flew their helicopter out of there."

Clark subconsciously nodded as I spoke. "All of that is possible, I guess, but how did she know where Anderson and Skipper were? And more than that, if she was still working for the Russians, why would she kill him? Why kill Anderson? He was red commie to the core. You don't get more loyal to the Kremlin than him."

"I don't know," I admitted, "but I believe it was her. I believe Skipper's story, and I believe it was her knife. There aren't ten knives like that in the world."

"Okay. Let's say it was her. What now?"

"I've got to find her."

Clark shook his head. "You know as well as I do that if she wants you to find her, she'll come to you. You said it yourself. She's a lot better at this than you."

"Yeah," I said, "but is she better than you?"

"Maybe," he said quietly.

Out of the blue, Skipper opened up. "I have two things to say."

She had our attention.

"First, thank you for believing me. I know it was her. And sec- ond, I want in."

"What do you mean you want in?" I asked.

"I want to go to that school. You know, The Ranch or whatever. I want to do what you do."

"No!" Clark and I yelled out.

"It's not up to either of you," she said confidently.

"You don't get to walk up to the gate and just say, 'I want to be a spy, so let me in.' That's not how it works."

"Okay, Chase. Tell me how it *does* work."

Silence filled the air, and I returned Clark's gaze. Neither of us knew what to say.

"Well," Clark said hesitantly, "they come to you. You don't go to them."

"So, maybe that's how it worked for you two, but how do you know that's how it is for everybody?"

"It's not just that, Skipper. You have to have something they want. Clark was a Green Beret and—"

"And what were you? Did they need baseball players with broken hands? Is that what you brought to the table?"

She was right. I'd never stopped to question why I'd been recruited. I had nothing to offer except my bloodline. My parents had apparently been successful agents, and after their murders, I became an orphan with covert ops in my blood.

"I was a psychologist, and an athlete, and. . . ."

Clark gave me a look that said shut up—the one he always sent my way when I was about to say something I shouldn't. Maybe I'd one day learn to heed his glare, but Skipper needed to know the truth.

"My parents. They weren't just missionaries." I paused, cleared my throat, and locked eyes with her. "They were operators like me. They were murdered in Panama not long before I met you and your family. That's how I became an orphan and how I ended up at UGA."

Skipper sat dumbfounded and silent.

I continued. "It's in my blood. They recruited me because they knew I'd want to fight back against the people who killed my parents, and they used that to recruit me."

I could see her eyes begin to moisten as she considered what I'd said. "I didn't know," she whispered.

"I know," I said. "There was no way you could have known, but that's not the point. The point is that you have to have something they want. You have to bring something to the table, and it's not easy. It's not something you want to go through. And it's not something I want you to go through."

She licked her lips. "Think about that, Chase. Think about what I've been through and what I've survived. Think about what I've seen, and heard, and experienced with you. I'm a survivor and a fighter, and you know it."

"Yeah, but—"

"No," she demanded. "But nothing. Let me finish. I can run boats, I can dive, I can shoot, and I'm in great shape. You or Clark can teach me to fly. I'm smart and resourceful, and I'm not afraid. What am I supposed to do? Just go to school and become a teacher or a nurse or whatever and pretend I don't know what goes on behind the scenes in the real world? Huh? Is that what I'm supposed to do? Is that what you want?"

"No," I admitted. "You're right. You are a survivor, and you're tougher than anyone I know, but—"

"No buts, Chase. It's what I want."

Clark stood up from the table and walked away.

"Where's he going?" she asked.

"I don't know. He does that when he needs to think . . . or poop."

She giggled. Part of her was still a little girl, but she was right. She was smart and tough, and because of the people who'd hurt her, she had enough anger and hatred brewing that she could become a dangerous weapon with the right training.

Clark reappeared. "Okay. Listen. You don't know what you're asking." His tone was a fusion of overprotective big brother and drill sergeant. "The Ranch is no joke. If you go there, they're going to beat you into the ground and make you hate everything about life. You're not ready for that."

"Yes, I am" she demanded.

"No, you're not," he said. "You don't have any idea what happens in that place. I know you've been through some shit, but not like what they're going to put you through up there. You'll wish you were dead before you make it out of there."

She locked eyes with him and set her jaw. "I've already been in a place just like that. I wanted to die every day, and I would have if you and Chase and Anya hadn't found me. So don't tell me about wanting to die. Don't try to describe Hell to me. I lived there, and there's nothing they can do to me at The Ranch that can compare to what I've already been through."

"Don't interrupt me again," he insisted, unfazed by her rant. "I'm going to teach you to fight. Chase is going to teach you to think, and we're both going to teach you to turn out the lights for people who've overstayed their welcome on the planet. You're not going to The Ranch. You're going to our training grounds, and you're going to work for and with us. If, after that, you still want to go, I'll do everything I can to get you in . . . as long as Chase agrees."

I hadn't expected that, and I wasn't sure what to say, but both Skipper and Clark were waiting impatiently for something to come out of my mouth.

"Are you sure they're going to let us do that?" I asked.

"Who's going to stop us?" said Clark. "We can do whatever we want. We're way overdue for a new mission. It's coming. When we get an assignment, if both of us believe Skipper can be of some value, she can go with us. But not before we train her. We won't ask. We'll just do it."

Skipper stared at me, waiting for me to say yes.

"Where's Tony?" I asked.

Tony was Clark's brother and Skipper's boyfriend. He was an active duty Coast Guard rescue swimmer. I couldn't imagine him letting her get kidnapped by Michael Anderson. He would die before he let anyone hurt her.

"He's TDY to San Juan for a few weeks," she said.

"What kind of temporary duty assignment is that?" I asked.

"There was a helicopter crash," she said, "and they lost two rescue swimmers while we were home visiting my folks. He got called away to fill in for them until they can find permanent replacements."

That explained why Tony hadn't fed Michael Anderson to a wood chipper or shark when he abducted Skipper.

"Does he know you're all right?"

"Yeah. I called and told him everything. He was pretty mad, but not at me."

"Your decision to work with us affects him, too," I said.

She frowned. "Yeah, I know. We've talked about it before. Tony's like you guys—he doesn't think I'm ready."

"It isn't that you're not ready," I said. "You just don't know what you're asking."

"So, what about Clark's idea, then?"

I gave in. "Okay, we can train you, but I'm not taking you with me on my next mission if I don't think it's safe."

She raised her eyebrows. "When have you ever been on a safe mission?"

I threw my crumpled napkin at her, and she batted it out of the air before it hit her face.

"Now I see why you were just a catcher and not a pitcher," she said. "That was weak."

3

Penny for Your Thoughts

Sufficiently recuperated and recharged, I was ready to fetch my beloved boat, *Aegis*, a fifty-foot custom sailing catamaran I'd left in Norfolk, Virginia. She was in the capable hands of Penny Thomas, a woman I'd met in Charleston, South Carolina, who'd been sailing with two friends aboard *Crude Awakening*—a boat that could've been *Aegis*'s twin. Their boat looked so much like mine, in fact, Colonel Tornovich's men had sabotaged it, thinking they planted their explosives on my hull. The explosion occurred offshore, sinking *Crude Awakening* and leaving her owner, Teri Huddleston, in the hospital with some pretty nasty burns. The boat ended up on the bottom of the North Atlantic, but Penny, Teri, and Teri's husband, Kip, all made it out alive. Teri's burns were healing nicely, and she was already out of the hospital and shopping for a new boat.

Penny and I had become . . . well, what we had become wasn't well-defined yet. Clark, and Fred, the psychiatrist, had encouraged Penny and me to spend quality time together so I could clear my head after losing Anya. It was working, and I was thoroughly enjoying my time with Penny, but I had no idea where the relationship was headed or how long it might last.

I dialed Penny's number and waited for her to answer.

It went to voicemail. "This is Penny. I'm doing something more important than answering the phone, so leave a message, and I'll call you back . . . maybe."

That's pure Penny.

"Hey, it's Chase. I just wanted to check in and let you know everything is okay, and we'll be headed back to Norfolk later today. Give me a call when you can. Oh, and I'm sorry for running off the way I did, but it was an emergency, and . . . well, I'll tell you about it when you call."

I'd told Penny bits and pieces of what had happened with Anya. What I told her was the truth, but not the whole truth and nothing but the truth, so help me God. The life I led didn't mix particularly well with full disclosure. I'd told her I was a freelance writer, and she pretended to believe me. If she and I were going to continue our—whatever it was—sooner or later, I'd have to tell her something closer to the truth.

My phone chirped, and I stuck it to my ear. "Hello?"

"Hey, Chase. It's Penny. I'm sorry I missed your call. I was a little busy. This boat is a handful by myself, but she sure is fun to sail."

I pictured Penny at the helm with a jib sheet in one hand and the wind blowing her long hair wildly around her head.

"I have faith you can handle anything *Aegis* can throw at you."

She let out a scoffing sound. "Yeah, I know I can, but it's still easier with some help."

"Well, we'll be heading back to Norfolk in the next twenty-four hours, so you'll have some help soon."

"There's no need to go back up there," she said. "*Aegis* and I are headed south."

"What?" I was surprised she was doing more than just taking *Aegis* out for a day sail on the Chesapeake.

"Yeah, we're headed south. I told you I was going to bring her to Charleston if you didn't come back soon. I got tired of waiting, so we're offshore and making fourteen knots. I'm planning to make Hatteras or Ocracoke tonight."

"It sounds like you have everything under control." I tried to sound unconcerned.

"Oh, yeah. Everything's cool. The weather is good, and *Aegis* and I have really started to bond. I just don't want to sail through the night single-handed. I'll get some sleep around Hatteras and get started again when the sun comes up."

"I have an idea," I said. "How about I meet you in Wilmington tomorrow night?"

"Okay, that sounds great. I'll be the hot chick with the sexy catamaran."

I laughed. "Yes, that's exactly what you'll be."

"Oh, how'd your emergency writing assignment go?"

"Oh, uh . . . Pulitzer material. I'll tell you all about it tomorrow night."

"No, you won't," she said. "But it's okay. I'm sure you'll tell me the truth someday."

I grimaced. "You're a lot smarter than you want people to know."

"I know," she said. "See you tomorrow night."

I didn't realize she was serious about bringing *Aegis* back to Charleston by herself, but I wasn't surprised.

I shared my plan with Skipper and Clark.

Skipper landed her hands on her hips. "So, who's Penny?"

Clark wasted no time. "Penny's his girlfriend."

"She's not my girlfriend," I protested half-heartedly.

Clark glared at me. "You're sleeping with her. You're letting her take your boat out alone. And you blushed when I called her your girlfriend, so I'd say she's your girlfriend."

"We're just—"

Skipper jumped in. "Don't, Chase. I get it. I'm sure she's great. I can't wait to meet her, but please tell me she isn't tall, blonde, and Russian."

Clark laughed. "Two out of three ain't bad."

I gave up my protest.

We rented a car and drove back to St. Augustine to pack up some clothes for Skipper. I rented her a room in a bed-and-breakfast until we could find her a more permanent living arrangement.

I'd come to love St. Augustine. Something about the city was so alluring to me. I felt at home in the Municipal Marina, and I enjoyed everything about America's oldest city.

* * *

"I've got an idea," Clark said as he crammed a piece of French toast into his mouth.

Skipper and I waited for him to swallow and announce his idea.

"Why do you do that?" she asked. "Why do you start a sentence and then shove something in your mouth?"

Clark made a show of slowly chewing and finally swallowing the syrupy toast.

"It's called a dramatic pause," he said in his best British accent. "I'm a thespian at heart, don't you know?"

I held up my hands in mock surrender. "Hey, your sexual preferences are none of our business. I just want to hear your idea."

"You're funny," he mumbled through a mouthful of coffee. He wiped his mouth. "How about we rent an airplane, and I'll drop you off in Wilmington. And then Skipper and I can start her flying lessons while you're bringing the boat back down with Penny."

Skipper's eyes lit up. "Yeah! Let's do that."

We'd let her do a little flying in the King Air over the past few weeks, and she was already showing great potential to be a good pilot. Clark was a certified flight instructor, so he could have her soloing in a matter of days.

Skipper's eyes were wide, and a girlish grin of anticipation locked on her face.

"Sure," I said. "That sounds like a good plan. She's got a lot to learn, and we might as well start with the simple stuff, like flying."

She ran around the table and hugged me as if she were eight years old and I'd just bought her a pony. She had no idea how much work learning to fly would be, but her enthusiasm was beautiful.

We finished our breakfast, and I made a few calls, trying to locate an airplane that would be suitable for Skipper's training. There were plenty of Cessna 172s and Piper Cherokees that could be rented by the hour, but their schedules kept them booked up, limiting the time they'd be available. I finally called Jack Shipley, a pilot I'd met at the

St. Augustine airport. He owned a Bonanza and shared my love of sailing.

"Hey, Chase! How are you?"

"I'm doing great, Jack. Listen, I hate to bother you, but I'm looking to teach Skipper to fly. Do you know of any available planes?"

"Who?" he asked, clearly confused.

"Elizabeth," I said. "The young lady I told you about who needed a ride to see her parents in Athens."

"Oh, sure. I remember. So, you're going to teach her to fly?"

"Yes, sir. It looks like it. I'm looking for something we can rent for maybe a hundred hours or so."

"A hundred hours? What the hell are you going to need a hundred hours for?"

"We don't just want to teach her to fly. We want to take her all the way through commercial multi-engine, so we want something simple to start with, and then we'll build a little time and move up to a complex."

"Ah, gotcha," he said. "How about a Cessna one-eighty-two Skylane? I've got a friend who lost his medical certificate—heart attack—so he can't fly anymore. He's going to have to sell his one-eighty-two. It's just sitting in the hangar. I imagine he'd be willing to rent you a block of time in it, but he'd rather sell it to you, I'm sure."

"That sounds perfect," I said. "Can you set up a time for us to take a look at it?"

"There's no need to set up a time. He lives right by the airport. Come on out here. We can take a look at it now if you want."

"We'll be there in less than an hour," I told him.

I filled Skipper and Clark in on the plan to see the Skylane. Skipper twitched with evident excitement, but Clark wasn't convinced.

"Are you sure a Skylane is the best option to start?"

I shrugged. "It's not optimum, but I can't find a simple airplane that's not booked up."

"Sure," he said. "Let's go take a look. Maybe we can make it work."

Jack led us to the hangar where we met Cliff Fowler, a retired airline pilot who had to be approaching ninety.

"So, you're looking for something to learn to fly in, huh?" he said.

"Yes, sir. This young lady is just dying to learn, and we can't find another airplane that's available for as much time as we need. We want to fly every day if the weather permits." I tried not to let him see I was sneaking a look inside his hangar.

"Well, come on in and look at the old girl. She's just sitting in here waiting to die . . . like me. She needs to be flown."

"They all do," I said, following him into the hangar.

"She's a little dirty, but other than that, she's in pretty good shape. She's a nineteen-eighty-four R model. I bought her new, and she's lived in this hangar since she left the factory in Wichita. I put a little over three thousand hours on her, and I put a new factory Lycoming O-Five-Forty in her about six or seven years ago. There's less than five hundred hours on the new engine, and the prop was rebuilt last fall, so it's got less than twenty hours on it. Everything works the way it should—or at least it did the last time it was flown. That must have been about, oh, maybe a month ago."

The airplane was pristine. It was obvious the old man took a lot of pride in her. I could only imagine how devastating it would be to have the flight surgeon tell me I could never fly again.

Clark went to work flipping through the maintenance logs while I inspected the airplane. She was flawless.

"Take it around the patch a time or two if you want. I'm sure she'd love the exercise," Cliff said.

"Why don't *you* take us for a ride?" I suggested. "After all, she is your airplane."

Cliff bowed his head and pointed to his chest. "Oh, I can't. The flight doc says my ticker's no good for flying. Bastards yanked my medical."

Clark connected the tow bar to the nose gear and looked up. "Come on, Cliff. My medical is good. I'll sit in the right seat, and you can show us how your old girl flies. I think that might do your ticker some good."

Cliff stared at Clark for a long moment. "Thank you."

We pulled the Skylane from the hangar, did a thorough preflight inspection, and climbed aboard—Skipper and me in the back, and Cliff and Clark up front.

Cliff took the controls, and we spent an hour in the air above St. Augustine, listening to his stories and watching him enjoy flying his airplane.

Back on the ground, I started the negotiations. "It's a beautiful airplane. You've clearly taken very good care of her. As we said before, we need to teach Skipper how to fly, and we need to build some time toward her commercial ticket."

Cliff grinned at Skipper. "I remember when I was her age. The Great Depression was trying its best to kill everybody, and all I could think about was doing anything other than chopping cotton and hoeing corn. Then, the Nazis and the Japanese stirred up enough trouble to get me off the farm and into the navy. I'd never seen an airplane up close 'til they sent me off to flight school. Flying made a good life for me."

I didn't know what to say, so I just listened.

He ran his arthritic hand over the propeller and sighed. "Those days are over, but it's been a good ride for an old man. I've flown everything I wanted to fly, short of the Space Shuttle. I guess it's time I come to terms with leaving the sky to young folks like you."

"I'd like to hear about the planes you've flown over the years," I said.

Cliff repositioned his false teeth. "I'd like to tell you about those planes and the things I've seen, son. Do you want the airplane?"

"I'd like to rent it for a hundred hours or so," I said, glancing over the plane again.

Cliff shook his head. "I'm not interested in getting into the airplane rental business. There's too much liability and insurance to deal with, and I'm an old man. I just want to watch Jeopardy and read Hemingway."

"How much?" I asked softly.

He patted the cowling with his aged hand and looked over his pride and joy. "One seventy-five."

One hundred seventy-five thousand dollars was well above what I thought the airplane was worth, and Cliff must have seen that on my face.

"For all of it," he added.

"All of what?" I asked.

He waved his wrinkled hand at the hangar. All of it, son. The airplane, the tools, and whatever else is in there. I own it all, and I'll take a hundred and seventy-five thousand for everything. Have you got that kind of money? It's worth a good bit more than that, so the bank will be glad to carry a note for you if you've got a job."

"I have a job," I told him. "And we can afford the airplane without getting the bank involved, but I'd like to make a counteroffer."

He shook his head. "I can't take any less than that for it, son. That's a bargain because I like you and your friends, and Jack Shipley speaks highly of you."

"My offer isn't for less, Cliff. It's for more. I'll pay the one seventy-five for the airplane and hangar, but I want to buy some of your time, too. We're going to have questions about the plane until we get to know her, and you know more about her than anyone else. I'd like to call on you when we have questions, and I'd like you to tell me about flying in the war."

"Wars," he corrected me. "Plural . . . wars. I flew in the second World War, Korea, and Vietnam."

"Then I'll give you ten thousand dollars if you'll agree to answer the phone every time we call. What do you say, Cliff?"

"I'll have to decline your offer, son. I won't live long enough to make that a good investment for you, but I will answer the phone every time you call, and in return, I'd like you to come by every now and then and have a drink with an old man. It'd be nice to have the company."

I stuck out my hand, and he shook it as if he were twenty years old.

"Oh, yeah. And one more thing," he said.

"Name it."

"If it wouldn't be too much to ask, I'd like to fly with you from time to time. You know, just as a stroll down memory lane."

"We wouldn't have it any other way, Cliff."

He smiled, exposing a mouthful of brand-new dentures that made him look like Gary Busey's grandfather.

"As much as it pains me to say it, we're going to need a lawyer to write up the deal and write a deed for the property," he said.

"A necessary evil, unfortunately," I agreed. "If you have an attorney, I'll be more than happy to pay his fee if you'll arrange for him to take care of the paperwork. In the meantime, I'll find a mechanic to conduct the pre-buy inspection, and we'll close when you're ready."

"It's been a pleasure, Chase. I'm happy to see my airplane going to a good home."

I gave him my contact information, and we shook hands again.

"Oh, I almost forgot," I said. "I need to be in Wilmington this evening. With your permission, I'd love to use the airplane. Clark will fly it back home tonight after dropping me off . . . if that's okay with you."

The old man licked his lips. "Forgive me for being cautious, but I'd like to have a little cash to firm up our deal before you take the airplane anywhere."

"Of course," I said. "I understand completely. I'll go to the bank now and meet you back here in an hour."

"That'll do just fine," he said with a slight nod.

We left the airport and headed for the bank. I drew ten thousand dollars in cash against my Cayman Islands account and the rest as a cashier's check.

Cliff wasn't expecting the full amount, but I knew it would set his mind at ease letting us use the airplane for the hop to Wilmington. He presented me with the keys and had his attorney, who was coincidentally also his daughter, draw up a simple contract. We signed it with Clark and Skipper as witnesses. I was the proud new owner of N682CF and considered it serendipitous that Clifford Fowler had the same initials as me. November-six-eight-two-Chase-Fulton had a nice ring to it.

4

And a Dog

The flight to Wilmington was perfect. My new airplane behaved just as advertised, and we made the trip in less than two and a half hours with Skipper at the controls and Clark in the right seat.

When we landed, Clark checked his phone, closed his eyes, and sighed. "Where's your phone?" he asked.

"It's in my pocket. What's wrong?"

"See if you missed a call."

I pulled the phone from my pocket and listened to my missed message.

"Chase, it's Dominic. We have a job for you. Call me right away."

I knew the reason for Clark's sigh. "It was your dad," I said. "He has a job for us."

"For us, or for you?" asked Clark.

"He didn't say, but I'll find out."

Dominic—my handler and Clark's father—answered on the first ring. "Chase, thank you for getting back with me so quickly."

"I was in the air, Dominic. I'm sorry I missed your call."

"It's okay. We have a mission. Where are you?"

"I'm at the airport in Wilmington."

"Delaware or North Carolina?"

"North Carolina. I'm picking up my boat and bringing her back to St. Augustine."

Dominic spoke as if he were thinking aloud. "Wilmington to St. Augustine . . . that's about three hundred miles. So, you'll be home day after tomorrow?"

"Maybe," I said. "But it may be the day after that, depending on the wind and weather."

"That's perfect," he said. "I'll meet you in St. Augustine in three days with a package. Is Clark with you?"

"He is," I said.

Clark was trying to listen in.

"Good. Have him there, as well. This job may require more work than you're capable of doing alone. I'll see you in three days."

I was left standing on the tarmac, staring at my phone.

"What did he say?" demanded Clark.

"We have a mission."

"We?"

"Yes, we," I said, relieved.

"What is it?"

I closed my phone and shoved it back into my pocket. "He didn't say. He just said he'd meet us in St. Augustine in three days."

"That's it?" he asked.

"Yep, that's it. I'm going to grab a cab and head to the marina."

I pulled a card from my wallet and handed it to Clark. "Here. Use this for fuel and whatever you need. I'll see you in a couple days."

Skipper hugged me. "Thanks for the airplane."

"It's not yours," I said playfully.

"Oh, I didn't mean that. I just meant thank you for buying it so I can learn to fly. I won't let you down. I promise."

"I know you won't. You never have. And the plane is as much yours as mine. Enjoy her."

"Do I get to name it?" she asked.

I laughed. "Of course you do."

She hugged me again, and I headed off for the terminal.

There was a taxi waiting, and I made it to the marina just in time to see Penny motoring up as I walked onto the boardwalk.

She laid the big boat alongside the dock like an old pro, and I secured the lines to cleats. She shut down the engines, bounded off the boat, and then leapt into my arms.

"I've missed the crap out of you, Chase Fulton. Are you okay?"

I grinned. "Yes, I'm great. And I missed you, too, Penny Thomas."

She kissed me and hissed, "Feed me. I'm starving."

"As you wish," I said, leading her up the ramp toward the bustling streets of Wilmington.

We had dinner and small talk about what she'd done while I was gone and her trip down the coast. As always, she was full of energy and excitement, so I listened while she talked incessantly—mostly between bites, but not always.

We finished dinner and headed back for the boat. Holding hands, we strolled as if we had no particular place to be.

"Can we get a slip so I can shower and run the air conditioners tonight?" She batted her eyelashes at me.

"Does that ever work on any man?"

"It works on *every* man. Even you, big boy."

"Of course we can get a slip so you can shower." I held my nose, feigning disgust. "You could certainly use one."

The harbormaster rented us an end mooring since he didn't have any slips wide enough for the catamaran. He charged us ninety dollars and said we'd have to be gone by nine a.m. because he needed the space for a private yacht scheduled for a mid-morning arrival. I paid him and moved the boat to the end of the floating dock.

After I'd connected the shore power and water line, Penny promptly fired up the air conditioners then disappeared into the head for her long overdue shower.

I sat at the navigation station, remembering how I used to anxiously await Anya's post-shower arrival. Her hair would be wet, and she'd rarely be wearing anything other than a towel draped across her shoulders.

Penny was beautiful and funny, but she wasn't dangerous. She'd be a great girlfriend for a major league baseball player, which is what I should've been, but fate dealt me a different hand.

How long will I be able to keep my secrets from Penny? How long will she let me keep lying to her?

She soon emerged from the head wearing a University of Georgia T-shirt and nothing else. She sashayed up the stairs to the main salon, smiling a seductive, sultry smile, and staring straight at me.

"Where'd you get that shirt?" I asked, trying not to smile.

She pulled at the shirt and looked down. "Oh my. This isn't my shirt at all. What was I thinking?"

She pulled the shirt over her head and let it fall to the deck. She was a remarkable woman and impossible to resist.

Anya who? So what if Penny isn't dangerous? She is stunning.

* * *

The next morning we were up with the sun and headed south out of the Cape Fear River and back into the North Atlantic. The northeast wind made for a nice August day of sailing under the coastal Carolina heat.

We settled into our cruising routine and set the autopilot. If God ever created the perfect day for sailing, that was it.

I stood on deck with one arm wrapped around the mast, letting the sun beat down on my skin and the fresh salt air bathe my nostrils. I had a feeling of peace; a feeling of being right where I belonged.

"When are you going to tell me the truth?"

I closed my eyes and sighed. "The truth about what?"

"The truth about you," she said. "You're no writer. You're a cop or something. Writers don't get emergency calls and disappear for days at a time."

Can I tell her the truth? I trusted her with my boat. Why can't I trust her with the truth?

She forced a smile and offered me a way out. "It's okay. I understand. It's some kind of secret squirrel stuff, and you can't talk about it."

I licked my lips and started to speak, but she stopped me.

"If it's this hard to tell me the truth right now, then don't. Just don't tell me any more lies. Okay?"

I reached for her hand and led her back to the cockpit. I sat on the settee, and she sat on my lap with her beautiful freckled face inches from mine.

"I'm not a writer, and I won't lie to you anymore."

She pulled off my UGA baseball cap and placed it backward on her head. She was adorable and irresistible. We kissed softly until the radar alarm yanked me from my stupor.

I stood and immediately scanned the horizon for other boats. The radar hadn't lied. We were on a collision course with an enormous motor yacht plowing through the waves from the southeast.

"That must be the yacht that needed our spot back in Wilmington," I said.

"Who cares?" said Penny. "Wilmington is behind us, and we're the stand-on vessel."

She certainly knew her maritime law. The rules of the road on the water dictated that sailboats under sail were usually required to maintain course and speed, while the more maneuverable motor vessel did whatever was necessary to avoid a collision.

What is *supposed* to happen isn't always what happens on the water, or anyplace else for that matter. That day was no exception. The yacht continued powering straight toward us.

I disengaged the autopilot and picked up the VHF radio mic. "Black motor yacht, twenty-five miles south of Cape Fear, this is the sailing vessel *Aegis* on channel one-six, over."

I waited impatiently for the captain of the yacht to answer. I was lifting the mic back to my lips when the radio crackled.

"Sailing vessel *Aegis*, this is the motor vessel *Moscow Mule*. We're bearing away to starboard. Sorry for the scare."

"No worries, Captain," I said. "I would've missed you had it become necessary."

I watched the bow of the yacht turn ever so slightly to the east and resolve our imminent collision. I recognized the yacht as it came abeam.

"*Moscow Mule*, SV *Aegis*, go up to sixty-eight," I said into the mic.

"*Aegis*, *Moscow Mule* on six-eight, over."

"*Moscow Mule*," I said. "You didn't happen to buy that boat in Miami, did you?"

"We did, *Aegis*. Do you know the boat?"

Anya had killed the Russian oligarch and billionaire, Dmitri Barkov, aboard that boat, and I had helped her strap diving weights to his body and send him to the bottom of the Straits of Florida. I had commandeered that boat and traded it to my handler, Dominic Fontana, for *Aegis*. It had a new paint job and some exterior modifications, but it was undoubtedly Barkov's former yacht.

"I don't know the boat, but I did see her in Miami. She's beautiful. Congratulations on the acquisition," I said into the mic.

"Thanks, *Aegis*. Enjoy your cruise. *Moscow Mule* will be standing by on one-six."

"I'm not going to ask," said Penny. "That way, you won't have to lie to me, but the look on your face says you know a lot more about that yacht than you're admitting."

As I'd promised, I didn't lie. I just smiled.

We sailed into Winyah Bay, southeast of Georgetown, South Carolina, and dropped anchor in the same spot we had anchored on our northbound leg a few days before, but somehow, it had felt like years.

I secured the deck and inspected the rigging as Penny vanished into the interior. When I'd finished my work, she reemerged on deck with a pair of cocktails and a cigar.

"You've been snooping around in my humidor, I see."

"Not snooping," she said. "Just exploring."

I punched the cigar and toasted the end, filling the air with the beautiful smell that can only come from true Cuban leaves.

Penny watched me enjoy the cigar. "I think that's sexy."

"You think what's sexy?" I asked.

"A man smoking a cigar and drinking the old-fashioned I made for him."

I lifted my tumbler. "You made me an old-fashioned?"

"I did."

I looked through the glass at the ice cubes suspended in the golden whiskey. "Here's to beautiful women who know how to make a good old-fashioned."

She raised her glass. "And here's to sexy men who know how to drink them. Cheers."

We drank and watched the pelicans dive on baitfish in the shallows.

"What are you doing?" she asked with surprise in her voice.

I hadn't realized that I was stirring my cocktail with the butt of my cigar, just like Padre, the old man who'd told me about my father in Charleston. I pulled the cigar from the whiskey, placed it in my mouth, and savored the taste.

"I saw an interesting old man do this a while back, and I guess I just picked it up. I didn't realize I was doing it."

"You do that a lot, you know?"

"Do what?"

"You get that pensive look, and you're a thousand miles away. I'd love to know where you go in that head of yours when that happens."

"I'm sorry," I said, a little embarrassed.

"No, don't be sorry. It's part of who you are. Never apologize for who you are."

I dipped the cigar back into the whiskey and then handed it to her.

Her smile was innocent, and her eyes were curious as she reached for the cigar. She held it between her thumb and index finger. "What am I supposed to do with this?"

"You're supposed to put it in the corner of your mouth and forget who you are for just a moment." I nodded my encouragement. "Go ahead. Give it a try. You might be surprised."

"I've tried a cigar before, you know."

"Not like that one," I said. "That was grown in a field where tobacco has been grown for five hundred years from seeds that can trace their ancestry back to the days before Columbus ever laid eyes on Hispaniola. And on top of that, that particular cigar has been soaking up the best old-fashioned I've ever tasted."

She tried to suppress a smile, but Penny wasn't very good at suppressing anything, especially an emotion. She slid the cigar between her lips and closed her eyes. She exhaled a cloud of smoke that danced around her head like a fog rolling in off the ocean.

I reclined back in my seat. "I see what you mean."

"What?" she said. "What do you see?"

"I see what you mean about that being sexy. I've never wanted to be a cigar, but if I could be yours, I might not mind so much."

"You're a funny boy." She seductively played with the cigar before slipping it back into my cocktail. I enjoyed the show and let myself forget about everything else in my world.

I pulled the cigar from the glass and took a long drink. "It's going to happen again when we get to Charleston."

She nodded. "It's going to *keep* happening, isn't it?"

"Yeah. I'm afraid so."

"Whatever you do . . . is it dangerous?"

"Sometimes."

"I thought so."

She walked around the table then sat on my lap. She seemed to enjoy nestling herself onto my thighs, and she'd be getting no complaints from me.

"You're a complicated man, Chase Fulton . . . if that's really your name."

I sighed. "That's really my name, but it doesn't matter."

"What do you mean it doesn't matter? Of course your name matters."

"It doesn't matter because I'm the last of us. Both of my parents and my sister are dead. My father had a brother, but he died in Vietnam, and my mother had a sister, but she never had any children. I'm the last remaining Fulton in my family."

"Do you want children?" she whispered.

I took a long, slow draw from the Cohiba and considered the question.

"I don't know. Maybe someday. But certainly not now."

"I do," she said. "I want a boy and a girl and a black lab."

I played with her hair and tried to count the tiny freckles on her nose and cheeks.

"Do you kill people?"

Her question hit me like a truck. I was terrified. *Yes, no,* and *I can't tell you* were the only possible answers. Two of those meant *yes,* and the third was a lie. I chose a fourth option.

"Sometimes."

"Bad people?"

"Yes."

"I thought so. That's where you go, isn't it? That's where you go when you stare off into space."

"Probably," I admitted.

"Is it hard?"

It should be hard for humans to take the lives of others, but it wasn't hard for me. It was sometimes troubling afterward, but the act itself wasn't hard.

Don't lie to her, I told myself.

"No, it's not hard. I've been well trained, and I believe in what I'm doing."

She ran her fingers through my hair—a habit she had that I'd come to thoroughly enjoy.

"Are you ever scared?"

"I'm scared right now," I admitted.

"Why?"

"What I do is necessary and important, but it doesn't mix well with the two-kids-and-a-dog lifestyle."

She tilted her head and pressed her lips to mine in a long, tender, exquisite kiss.

"I'm not asking you for two kids and a dog right now. Right now, all I want is to finish our cigar and cocktails, and for you to take me to bed."

5
Sister?

We sailed into the St. Augustine Inlet and down the Matanzas River without any more uncomfortable conversations. The weather was perfect, and *Aegis* continued to impress.

Penny looked like a bright-eyed child taking in the Castillo de San Marcos and the sites of Old Town St. Augustine. "Is this where you live?"

"Sometimes," I said. "I live wherever I drop the anchor, but I like this town. If I had a real home, this is probably where it would be."

I radioed the Municipal Marina and asked for a slip, hoping number seven was still empty, but no such luck.

"Hey, Chase. Welcome back. There's a trawler in seven, but you can tie up behind Earl at the end. She scared away the last guy we put behind her."

Earl at the end was a sixty-something, Oompa-Loompa-looking woman who was the best diesel mechanic in St. Augustine. She and I had become friends while I'd been a resident of the Municipal Marina, and it had become our custom to flirt incessantly with each other at every opportunity.

Penny deployed the fenders, and I laid *Aegis* alongside the dock, just behind Earl's boat. Penny leapt to the dock and began tying up just as Earl came waddling toward us. She stopped a few feet away from Penny, eyeing her up and down. "Oh, you're new."

Earl crawled aboard *Aegis* and grabbed me in one of her famous bear hugs. "I knew you'd be back, stud muffin. You just couldn't stay away from momma, could you?"

"Hey, Earl. You know I can't resist you. I just had to come back."

Penny was standing on deck, laughing. I had intentionally left out any warning about Earl. I thought it would be fun to see her reaction, and I was right.

"I knew it!" said Penny, feigning anger. "I knew you were too good to be true. She's your wife, isn't she?"

I shrugged and tried to play innocent.

"Oh no, honey," said Earl. "He ain't my husband. He's my boy toy. I don't mind sharing him, just as long as you keep your hands off them diesels. I'll kick your ass over them engines."

Penny couldn't hold back her laughter. "I'm Penny."

"Nice to meet you, Penny. I'm Earline, but you can call me Earl. Everybody does. I'm the resident fix-it-when-it's-broke girl and part-time supermodel. It's good work if you can get it."

"It's nice to meet you, Earl, and I promise to keep my hands off the diesels, but I can't make the same promise when it comes to Chase."

"Oh, don't you worry about stud muffin here. He's plenty enough man for both of us."

"Don't I know it?" said Penny.

Earl laughed. "Are you back to stay, baby boy?"

"No, unfortunately, it's just a temporary stop. I have a new assignment. I'm just here for a meeting to get the details."

"Assignment . . . piffle," Earl huffed as she waddled away.

Penny chuckled. "Well, that was interesting."

"Yeah, *interesting* is an excellent word for Earl," I said.

Penny watched the overweight, under-tall, sixty-something woman. "You didn't really . . . with her. Did you?"

In my best Vanna White Wheel of Fortune pose, I pointed at Earl. "Come on. Look at her. How could I resist?"

Penny playfully jabbed at me until her mock attack ended with her arms hugging my neck. "Thank you for bringing me here. I can't wait to check out the city."

"I didn't bring you here. You brought me. I was just along for the ride, but you're going to love St. Augustine. We'll get cleaned up and go to dinner if you'd like. Do you salsa?"

She stepped back, put on her best Cuban seductress face, and danced around the cockpit.

"Okay, clearly the answer is yes, you salsa. There's a great club just a couple blocks away. I'm a terrible dancer, but we're going to have some fun, you little Havana hottie."

We showered, changed and headed up the ramp to Avenida Menendez, the riverfront street in Old St. Augustine. It was bustling with tourists wearing ridiculous hats and sporting sunburns galore.

We walked north toward the Castillo de San Marcos before turning left on Cuna Street. I wanted Penny to see the old fort while the sun was still up.

"That's gorgeous!" Her eyes were wide, and she was grinning like a kid staring through a candy store window.

"Yeah, it's pretty impressive. The Spanish built that in the late sixteen hundreds. I think it was started in sixteen seventy-two and finally finished around sixteen ninety-five, but I'm not certain. We can do the tour tomorrow if you'd like."

"I'd love that," she said, unable to take her eyes off the three-century-old stone fort.

Winding our way through the narrow streets of Old St. Augustine, we came to the parking lot for the Columbia, my favorite restaurant in the city.

"What's going on over there?" Penny said, pointing through the trees lining the eastern edge of the parking lot.

I peered through the trees and saw a man shoving a young woman against the wooden fence. The woman was cowering and begging the man to leave her alone.

"Stay here," I said, "and get ready to call the police if I can't get this guy calmed down."

"Chase, don't get involved. I don't want you to get hurt."

"Just get ready to call the cops if it becomes necessary. I'll be fine."

I waded through the banyan trees, keeping my approach slightly behind the man to keep as much tactical advantage as possible.

I glanced back to see Penny frowning and standing at the edge of the pavement with her cell phone in her hand. As I turned back to face the quarreling couple, the woman let out an abbreviated gasping scream as the man drew a switchblade knife from his pocket and thrust it toward her throat.

Great, a knife fight. That's what I need.

I picked up a heavy stick about the size and shape of a baseball bat and quickened my approach. I couldn't let the man cut the terrified woman.

She let out another choppy scream when she caught a glimpse of me approaching with the stick raised over my head. Instinctually, she yanked away from the man and staggered backward, ultimately falling to the ground, flat on her back.

I came down hard with the stick, landing the blow an inch above the attacker's hand, breaking his wrist, and sending the switchblade tumbling to the ground. The man reeled in surprise from being blindsided, and he grunted an agonizing groan from the pain of the broken wrist. He raised his left hand in front of his face and assumed a fighting stance.

I'd already won the fight the instant I made contact with his wrist. There was no chance of the guy maintaining his will to fight with pain bombarding his brain. No normal nervous system can ignore that degree of discomfort. I'd known that pain all too well following the injury that ended my baseball career.

What I hadn't considered immediately became apparent the moment I looked into the man's eyes. He was stoned out of his mind. His pupils were wide and fixed, and he wasn't backing down. There was nothing normal about his nervous system at that moment.

"If you want to hit somebody, hit me," I said, daring the man to advance.

"This ain't none of your business, man. That bitch—"

I didn't let him finish the absurd statement perched on the tip of his tongue. I stepped toward him with my right foot, pivoted on my left, and grabbed his broken wrist. Continuing toward him, I twisted his hand and arm across my body as I stepped forward with my left foot and drove him to the ground. I felt what was left of the bones in his wrist crumble under the pressure of my grip.

With a thud, he landed facedown on the mulch, and I thrust my left knee between his shoulder blades, securely pinning him to the ground.

Quickly checking my environment, I locked eyes with the young woman who'd climbed back to her feet and was watching in awe at the scene unfolding in front of her.

"Get out of here," I said sternly.

She didn't flinch. "Kill that son of a bitch. He's a pedophile!"

Anyone who would intentionally hurt a little kid, especially by exploiting their innocence, didn't deserve to live. But as Clark was so fond of reminding me, we were not in the punishment business. Sometimes, though, regardless of the business we're in, right is right, and the innocent deserve retribution.

Penny had been creeping ever closer. She was still holding the cell phone like a shield in front of her, but she wasn't dialing yet.

Turning back to the coked-up lowlife beneath my knee, I pressed a little harder on his spine. "Is that true, Zoro? Before you came out here waving your knife around and threatening that woman, were you messing with little kids?"

With a mouthful of mulch, he mumbled something that rhymed with *duck-cue*, and I took that as an acknowledgment of guilt. I lifted my knee from his back, grabbed a handful of his hair, and yanked him to his feet. In one fluid motion, I spun him around and introduced his face to the rough-cut lumber of the rugged fence. His lips and nose opened up, and blood trickled down the splintered wood slats.

With my right knee in the back of his left thigh, and my elbow planted solidly beneath his skull, I pinned his body to the fence.

I turned to the woman. "What's your name?"

"Mary," she said through clenched teeth. "Sister Mary Robicheaux."

"Make the call," I said to Penny, motioning toward the cellphone with my chin. "Tell them there's an unconscious man behind the Columbia who attacked and tried to kill a young woman."

"But he's not unconscious."

I spun the man around, clasped his broken wrist in my left hand, and forced it across his chest and over his left shoulder. Then I delivered a punishing knee strike to his crotch, causing blood and spittle to spray from his mouth. I finished with a battery of punches right out of Clark's Krav Maga classes, leaving the man slumped against the fence, broken, beaten, and most thoroughly unconscious.

Penny was dialing.

"Sister," I said. "Are you all right?"

"Yes, I'm okay. Thank you. I don't know what would've happened if you hadn't come along."

"I'm glad you're okay. The police will be here soon, and this'll all be over. Why did you say this man is a pedophile?"

The woman looked down with disgust at the man's limp form. She was pretty in the way that strong, confident women are when they know they're on the right side of an issue—not arrogant, but determined and self-assured. The fear I'd initially seen on her face had been replaced with a look of satisfied vengeance.

"I'm a teacher at Saint Francis, and that animal. . . ." Her eyes glistened.

"It's okay now, Sister Robicheaux. Look, there's the police now."

A black-and-white St. Augustine Police cruiser pulled up, and two of the biggest humans I'd ever seen poured out.

"What's going on here?" the larger of the two cops asked while placing his hat on his clean-shaven head.

I read the nameplate attached to the flap of the right breast pocket on his starched, pristine uniform: K. O'Malley.

I'll bet the K stands for Kevin, I thought. *That's a good Irish Catholic name for a defensive lineman turned police officer.*

"I'm Sister Mary Robicheaux, and that man attacked me with that knife." She pointed toward the switchblade sticking in the ground near the unconscious lump of a man.

"Are you okay, Sister?" the policeman asked with sincere concern in his tone.

"Yes, officer. I'm fine, thanks to this man."

The woman hugged me as if I had saved her life. I didn't think I'd done anything special. I couldn't imagine anyone not intervening. It just seemed like the right thing to do.

O'Malley looked at me and then back at the attacker.

"I just happened along and couldn't let him hurt Sister Robicheaux. When he pulled the knife, I had to step in."

I produced the set of Secret Service credentials given to me after I completed my training at The Ranch. Covert operatives aren't supposed to show up in police reports and local newspaper articles, and I had been instructed to avoid these situations.

"I'm on vacation and just heading to dinner," I told the officer. "I'd rather not get involved deeper in this thing if that's okay with you. I'm sure you understand. Escaping the job is hard enough as it is."

O'Malley folded my credentials and handed them back to me. "Yeah, I know how it is. Enjoy your dinner, Mr. Unnamed Good Samaritan. I think we can handle it from here."

I nodded in appreciation to O'Malley, returned Sister Robicheaux's hug, and took Penny's hand. We continued toward the Columbia. I didn't look back, but Penny couldn't help herself.

She put her arm around my waist and stealthily slipped her fingertips into my back pocket, retrieving the credentials I'd shown O'Malley. I tried to stop her, but she was quick and leapt away backward as she opened the small leather wallet.

"So that's it," she said, staring into the wallet. "You're a fed." She folded the wallet and tossed it back to me.

"Not exactly." I still wasn't ready to come clean.

"Yeah, not exactly is right," she said. "Feds can't afford boats like yours, but at least now I know you're really one of the good guys."

I returned the credentials to my pocket and held the door for her. "Chivalry is alive and well, my lady."

I asked to be seated in Liz's section, and the hostess led us upstairs to a small table in the corner. Liz had been our waitress the night I'd been abducted by Colonel Tornovich's goons. She'd been a bright, bubbly personality with just enough spunk to make her interesting and entertaining. She was my favorite waitress in my favorite restaurant in all of Florida.

"Hey, I remember you!" said Liz as she came bouncing up to the table with a brilliant, sincere smile on her face.

"Hey yourself. How've you been?" I asked.

"Good. Just running food and pouring drinks. It's good to see you again. Who's your friend?"

Before I could make introductions, Penny said, "Hey there. I'm Penny. But I'm not his friend. I'm actually his parole officer, and this is his mandatory monthly report."

Liz shook Penny's hand then looked at me. "I like this one. You've got your hands full, big boy."

"I most certainly do," I admitted. "How about a pitcher of sangria, if you haven't lost your touch."

"Ha! Did Beethoven forget how to play the piano? Of course I haven't lost my touch. I'll be right back."

While Liz was gone, Penny pored over the menu, making oohing sounds my brain related to things *not* on the list.

"Everything sounds amazing," she said. "How do you ever decide?"

"I don't. I just eat whatever Liz brings out, and I've never been disappointed."

She folded the menu closed, slid it to the edge of the table, and took my hand. We locked eyes, and the corners of her mouth turned down in a thoughtful frown. "That was amazing what you did out there."

I offered an abbreviated smile.

"You probably saved that woman's life, you know."

"No," I scoffed. "He wasn't going to kill her. He was trying to scare her. If he'd wanted to kill her, he wouldn't have done it in public. I think she probably started it."

"What?" Penny's eyebrows rose in disbelief. "You think the nun picked a fight with that guy?"

"Yeah, I think she probably did. I think she believes he's been messing with a kid, or kids, in her class, and she was fed up with it. So, I think she dressed in street clothes and confronted him. I don't know. That's just what I think, but I'm not very smart."

Penny fixed her eyes on the multicolored glass lampshade above our heads and sighed. "You know, I think you might be right. What do you think will happen to him?"

I took a long swallow of water. "I don't know. If he is a pedophile, he'll be going to jail for a long time, and I've heard those kinds of people don't do well in jail. I think even convicts hate pedophiles."

"I've heard that, too." She looked over my shoulder and smiled.

Liz returned with a tray holding a pitcher, fruit, two bottles, and two big glasses. She went to work squeezing and muddling, pouring and stirring, and giggling all the while. It was fun watching her work. She poured a glass and placed it carefully in front of Penny, then lifted the tray and began walking away.

"Hey," I called after her. "What about me?"

"Oh, did you want some? I didn't think it was okay for you to drink in front of your parole officer. But if she says it's okay, then I guess I could pour one for you."

Penny's face hardened into a look of consternation. "Oh no, it's not acceptable for a parolee to drink in front of his parole officer, but I think you should pour another one as a backup for me . . . and leave the pitcher. I'll make sure he behaves."

The two shared a good laugh at my expense, and Liz placed a glass of the ruby red sangria on the table in front of me.

"What are we eating, guys?"

Penny spoke up. "We'll eat whatever you bring us."

"Excellent choice," she said. "I'll be back soon. In the meantime, you behave, mister." She pointed a scolding finger at me.

"Not a chance," I quipped.

"So, seriously," Penny continued. "You really are a good guy, you know that?"

I didn't know what to say.

"Whatever else you are—even if you never tell me the whole truth about it—there's a good heart in that chest of yours, Chase Fulton."

"I want to tell you," I whispered. "It's just that—"

She pressed her finger to my lips. "Not here. Not now. Let's just enjoy our sangria and whatever Liz brings out for dinner. Okay?"

I bit her finger, and she playfully tugged at my bottom teeth, then pulled her finger from my mouth.

"As you wish," I said.

She stuck out her bottom lip. "Don't you mean, as you wish, Princess Buttercup'?"

I wrinkled my brow and stared at her.

"Don't tell me you've never seen *The Princess Bride*."

"I have no idea what that is," I admitted.

She pulled a straw from an ignored water glass and initiated what I assumed was supposed to be a sword fight.

"My name is Inigo Montoya. You killed my father. Prepare to die!"

I shrugged, and she frowned in exasperation.

"We're renting it tonight," she said. "It's the greatest movie of all time."

"I haven't watched many movies in the past few years. I've been a little busy."

Liz materialized beside the table with a huge tray balanced over her shoulder. A waiter slid a set of folding legs beneath the tray as Liz carefully lowered it into place. The small dishes looked irresistible. Liz described each item, as plate-by-plate she unburdened the tray and filled our table with the Spanish feast.

After eating for what felt like hours, we were incapable of deciding which dish was the most amazing. Sangria continued to appear, and Liz came and went as if she could read our minds.

We paid the check, thanked and hugged our marvelous waitress, and headed down the stairs, wondering if it was possible to salsa with that much food in our stomachs.

Penny joked that the paintings of the family who'd owned and operated the restaurant for so many years looked like Spanish royalty. Anyone who'd tasted their cooking knew the family was most definitely royalty.

Although the foyer of the Columbia was large enough to comfortably handle the crowd awaiting their seats, when the weather was good, most patrons preferred sitting in the ornate courtyard just beyond the beautiful wooden double doors. I'd always loved the transition from the colorfully tiled interior to the lush, elegant courtyard, but what I discovered as the heavy doors closed behind us was something I didn't expect.

6

That's Not What I Do

Sitting with her hands folded neatly in her lap and a somber look of anticipation on her face was Sister Mary Robicheaux in full nun regalia. When she saw us exit the Columbia, she leapt to her feet and shuffled toward us, holding her habit a few inches higher than it was designed to lay.

I'd been attacked by all manner of men in countless situations, but I'd never experienced the anxiety of being rushed by a nun. I opted to stand my ground and see what happened next.

She grabbed both of my hands, stared into my face, and then pulled me in for a long, sincere hug. I didn't resist, and I returned the hug.

She took a step backward. "Thank you for what you did this afternoon. That man is the devil's errand boy. You don't want to know the things he's done. I know I shouldn't have followed him and confronted him like I did, but he's evil—the darkest of all evil. The kind of man who thrives on hurting children; beautiful, innocent, little children."

I took the nun's hands in mine. "Slow down, Sister. Let's talk someplace else, okay?"

She caught sight of the crowd of tourists who were standing, staring, and listening intently to every word she'd said. Her face blushed red, and she seemed to shrink inside her habit.

"Oh, my. I'm . . . I . . . of course, we should go someplace else. I'm so sorry."

In an effort to distract her from the onlookers, I stepped closer and placed my hand gently on her shoulder. "It's okay," I said.

We walked toward the Plaza de la Constitución, an open, park-like area with monuments, cannons, and even a few quiet, almost-private spots to sit and talk. We found an unoccupied bench and took a seat. Sister Robicheaux sat between Penny and me and nervously scanned the area for curious ears.

"Like I was saying," she began, "what you did this afternoon was amazing, and I can't thank you enough."

I held her hand. "No thanks are necessary. I'm just glad you're all right."

"I'm fine," she said. "But it's not me that you or anyone else should worry about. It's those innocent children. As I told you before, that man is the worst of all evils. He preys on defenseless children and. . . ."

I watched her swallow hard in a vain attempt to quell her rage.

"It's okay," I said. "It's over now, and you and those children are safe."

"I told you. It isn't me who's in danger. That man is going to be out of jail tomorrow, and he'll be right back at the playground or the beach—anywhere he can find a vulnerable child. He has to be stopped!"

"The police are involved now, and if he is what you say he is, he'll go to prison for a very long time."

"No!" she yelled, then calmed herself. "No, he won't go to prison. That's what I'm trying to tell you. He's been arrested before, and he always slips away, thanks to his greasy lawyer and his family connections. You have to do something to stop him."

"What? What do you expect me to do?"

"You're a cop or something. I saw the way Officer O'Malley looked at you after you handed him your badge, or whatever was in that wallet of yours. The look on his face was respect or admiration,

but you're obviously pure law—something bigger than the local police. You have to do something."

"Look, Sister. You have the wrong impression of who and what I
am. I'm not a cop at all. I'm—"

"What Chase is trying to say, Sister, is that he works for the government, but he's not in law enforcement. This is a matter for the
local police, and you should let them handle it."

I hadn't expected Penny to come to my rescue. It had given me
time to prepare what I'd say next.

"She's right, Sister. That's not what I do. I can't help you."

"Oh, bullshit," she said as if it were the first time she'd ever used
that word. "Don't tell me you can't help me. At least tell me the
truth and say you *won't* help me. But don't tell me you *can't.*"

Her accusation hit me like a bullet to the chest. *What's the benefit of possessing the skill set I've developed if I can't use it for something
as noble and truly good as protecting innocent little children from a
predator?*

I cleared my throat, glanced at Penny, and then locked eyes with
the nun. "Here's the truth. I want to help you, but I have other responsibilities that cannot be shirked. Tell me how I can get in touch
with you, and I promise I'll talk with you tomorrow afternoon, but
there's nothing I can do before then. Do you understand?"

"God bless you, Chase. That is your name, isn't it?"

"Yes, Sister. I'm Chase Fulton. Here's my cell number." I passed
her a small square of paper. "Call me tomorrow afternoon when
you have time, and we'll talk about what can be done. Okay?"

"Thank you, Chase. And you, too, miss."

"I'm Penny." She stood and shook Sister Robicheaux's hand.

"God bless you. God bless you both." Without another sound,
Sister Robicheaux disappeared westward out of the park.

She left me wondering what had just happened and what I'd
agreed to do.

"That was weird," Penny said.

"What do you think she wants me to do?"

"I think she wants you to kill that man. After all, that's what you do, isn't it?"

"No! That's not what I do," I protested, but my words were hollow, and I suddenly remembered my vow to never lie to her. "I mean, what I do is complicated. And that woman is a nun, for God's sake."

"Exactly," she said. "For God's sake is right. She's trying to protect the children she loves from an animal, and then you show up, a knight in shining armor on a white steed, riding to her rescue. What do you expect her to think?"

I tried not to let Penny's words distract me from the impending reality of my job. "I have a meeting tomorrow morning with a guy who's sort of my boss. I have another assignment, and I have no idea what it is. I won't know until after the meeting, but whatever it is, it won't be something I can put off. And it won't be chasing a child molester."

Penny pressed her lips together, and her mouth formed a tight horizontal line. "I don't feel much like dancing tonight. Can we just go back to the boat?"

We crossed the Avenida Menendez and headed down the ramp to the marina. I was surprised to see lights on aboard *Aegis*; I hadn't left them on. That's when I noticed three figures relaxing, laughing, and drinking on the upper deck. Clark, Tony, and Skipper had discovered the boat was back at the marina and had made themselves at home.

"Clark, you remember Penny," I said, joining the party.

"Of course. Hey, Penny. It's nice to see you again." He leaned in for a hug.

"Penny," I said, "This is Tony and Skipper . . . eh, I mean Elizabeth. I've told you about her, and Tony is her boyfriend. He's a Coast Guard rescue swimmer."

Penny shook their hands. "I've heard a lot about you, Elizabeth. It's nice to finally meet you."

"It's nice to meet you, too," Skipper said, eying Penny up and down.

"And you, as well, Tony. A rescue swimmer. I'm impressed."

"Aw, it ain't no big deal, ma'am. I just yank folks outta the water who didn't have no business bein' in the water in the first place. It ain't near as glamorous as it sounds."

Tony's East Tennessee drawl worked for him. It made him sound humble and honest, which is precisely what he was.

We settled in, and Clark poured a round of drinks for everyone.

"So," I asked, "how are those flying lessons going?"

"Great," Skipper beamed. "It's amazing, and I love my airplane. I'm doing great, according to the best flight instructor in the world."

Clark blushed.

"*Your* airplane?" I asked.

"Well, I mean *your* airplane that you're letting me use."

"I'm just picking on you," I said. "As I told you before, it's as much yours as mine. I'm glad the lessons are going well. How many hours do you have so far?"

She sat up tall and threw her shoulders back. "Eight point seven."

"That's a lot of flying in a few days," I said. "Is she almost ready to solo?"

Clark shrugged. "We'll see how she does tomorrow, but so far, she hasn't shown any signs of wanting to wreck *her* airplane."

I smiled. "That sounds promising. Clark, are you happy with the plane?"

"It's a good airplane. You made a good decision."

"That's good to hear. I'm looking forward to flying it some, myself."

"So, how was the sail down the coast?" Tony asked.

Penny answered before I could speak. "It was great! But it wasn't as exciting as the evening we just had."

Everyone perked up. Exciting evenings were of great interest to the people I considered to be my family.

"Don't make us guess," said Skipper. "What made your evening so exciting?"

"Chase got in a fistfight."

"Dear God." Clark slapped himself on the forehead. "Please tell me you didn't lose another fight."

I'd developed a track record of losing fights before Clark had spent weeks teaching me Krav Maga, the Israeli hand-to-hand fighting style practiced by the Israel Defense Forces, and Mossad, the Israeli intelligence service.

"Oh, no. He didn't lose." Penny had a hint of pride in her voice. "He broke the guy's arm and knocked him out for messing with a nun."

The group belted out, "Messing with a nun?"

"I didn't know she was a nun at the time. We just walked up on a confrontation between a man and a woman, and I didn't like the way he was pushing her around. He pulled a knife, and I stepped in. It was no big deal."

"No big deal, my ass," said Penny. "The nun found us after dinner. She claims the guy is a child molester or something, and she wants Chase to take him out."

Clark's eyes grew wide. "What did you tell this nun, Chase?" Clark's tone made it clear he didn't like anything about the situation.

"I told her that's not what I do, and that I'd talk with her tomorrow after meeting with Dominic."

"And what are you going to tell her tomorrow?" Clark asked.

"I don't know," I admitted.

"I'll tell you what you're *not* going to tell her. I don't care if she's Mother freakin' Teresa. You're not going on some vigilante trek for justice. That's not what you do. That's not what *we* do."

7

Ground Zero

Clark was a good friend and had taught me skills that would keep me alive on more occasions than I'd ever be able to count. But he was mistaken when he assumed that he had the standing to arbitrarily dictate who I would and would not help.

Sister Mary Robicheaux may not have been Mother freakin' Teresa, but she was passionate about stopping a predator from hurting children. Refusing to help her was not in my future, regardless of Clark's dictatorial forbidding. The all-consuming thought of how I could help her had kept me awake most of the night. That was, however, a can that would temporarily be kicked down the road.

I sat on the upper deck of my catamaran, alternately watching the sun rise over St. Augustine Beach in one direction, and watching my handler, Dominic Fontana, walk with a determined and confident gait down the ramp and onto the dock from the other direction. He checked his watch twice in less than thirty seconds. He was nervous. I'd never seen him nervous. Whatever mission he had been burdened with delivering was going to be far more than typical.

"Good morning, Dominic. Come on up."

He squinted at the bright morning sun and shielded his eyes with a leather binder he held firmly in his left hand. Dominic typically wore a shoulder holster under his left arm, so he rarely carried anything in his right hand. Tradecraft becomes ingrained in the behavior, mindset, and actions of operators, and those old habits die hard. Dominic wasn't wearing a shoulder holster that particular morning, but that fact hadn't prevented him from keeping his right hand fully available. It was a practiced, long-developed instinct.

"Oh, hey. Good morning, Chase. I'll be right up. Is Clark here?"

"Yeah, and there's coffee in the galley."

He stepped aboard and soon appeared at the top of the ladder with his binder tucked under his arm and his coffee mug held firmly in his left hand.

We shook hands, and he took a seat. Dominic was one of the smoothest, most relaxed people I'd ever known. He never appeared to be in a hurry or worried about anything. The Dominic Fontana who sat in front of me didn't match the man I knew as my handler.

As if he thought someone were watching him, he looked around, nervously shifting his position, and crossing and uncrossing his legs.

"Relax, Dominic. Are you all right?"

He wiped his upper lip with the back of his hand after swallowing a mouthful of coffee.

"Yeah, I'm okay, Chase. It's just this mission. I don't know. It's not what I expected would come down the pipe for you. I'm not sure if it's a good idea."

The man had my attention. I placed my cup on the table beside me and leaned forward. "Let's see it."

He stared at his leather binder. "You can say no, Chase. You don't have to accept everything that comes down. You can always say no."

"Let me see, Dominic." I reached for the binder, and he reluctantly released it.

I leaned back and crossed my legs as the thick, partially redacted file came to rest on my lap. I was shocked to see it written almost entirely in Spanish.

"Since when do we get redacted files?" I asked, holding up a page that had more lines blacked out than visible.

"I'll have the clean version soon, but for now, that's all we have." He rechecked his watch, then glanced anxiously over the Bridge of Lions across the Matanzas River.

"Is Clark here?"

I slid the sheet back into the file. "Yeah, he'll be up in a few minutes. Does this involve him?"

"That's what I want to talk to you about." Dominic stared through the deck, presumably to ascertain whether Clark was on his way up. He cleared his throat and pointed to the file. "This one's in Panama, back where. . . ."

"Where my parents and sister were murdered," I said, letting him off the hook.

"Yeah, exactly." Some of the tension in his face relaxed. "It's the Chinese this time." He paused.

"I'm listening."

"Look, Chase. We don't know who killed your family—"

"Somebody knows," I said.

"Yes, somebody knows everything, but that's not what this is about. This has nothing to do with your family's murder. This is about money and power."

"Everything's about money and power, Dominic. Tell me what you want me to do."

He nervously cleared his throat again, reached out, and flipped to the final pages of the file.

"We believe they're going to sink a ship." He poked his long, bony finger at a high-resolution satellite photo that showed a container ship passing beneath a bridge.

I studied the picture, but I was lost. "Okay, it's a bridge over a river or canal with a cargo ship."

"It's not just any bridge," he said. "It's the Puente Centenario over the Panama Canal."

"At Paraíso," I whispered.

"Yes, at Paraíso," he said, watching me carefully.

I bit at the corner of my lip and tried to suppress the cacophony of agonizing emotion rising in my throat. "That's where. . . ." I couldn't force the words past my tongue.

Dominic took the file from my hand. "Yes, that's where your family passed away."

"Murdered!" I growled.

"I beg your pardon?"

I scowled. "Murdered. That's where my family was murdered. They didn't pass away. They were slaughtered, and it happened right there." I pointed at the picture. "That's ground zero, as far as I'm concerned."

Dominic closed the file. "I won't lie to you, Chase. That's why this assignment is yours if you want it. There's no other operator on the planet with as much connection to this place as you. That's a double-edged sword for us, though."

He paused, but I didn't flinch.

"On the one hand," he said, "you may focus that bile you're tasting in your throat right now and turn it into the fuel to complete this assignment with perfection. The other side of the sword is the one that scares the hell out of me."

I nodded as I pictured what could go wrong if I hit the ground in Paradise and turned into the trembling, terrified boy I was the last time I was in Panama.

"What's the assignment?"

"Why don't you have another cup of coffee? Once you're fully read-in, it's your mission, and there's no backing out. Right now is your last opportunity to say no."

I stared coldly into his eyes. "What's the mission, Dominic?"

He pulled a brown envelope from the file and tore open the wax seal. Several eight-by-ten aerials slid from the envelope. I thumbed through the stack. They were pictures of ships of every size, from thirty-foot cruisers to Panamax cargo ships of enormous proportions.

"Let's start with a little background on the Panama Canal," he said. "There are three sets of locks at each end of the canal that raise fourteen thousand ships a year, eighty-five feet above sea level, up into Lake Gatun, and then back down to sea level on the other side. You can imagine what an impact closing the canal could have on the world economy. They're building new locks and dredging, but for now, the largest vessel permitted through the canal is nine hundred fifty feet long and a hundred and six feet wide. Of course, the draft can be no greater than thirty-nine and a half feet in the tropical fresh water of Lake Gatun. That'll all change when the new locks are finished . . . if that ever happens."

I tried to focus on his briefing and quell my hatred for the last place I'd ever seen my family.

He continued as if he were briefing a Cub Scout troop on an upcoming camping trip. His mastery of communication techniques was epic.

"Currently, the largest ship to routinely transit the canal is a Chinese freighter called the AAS *Pearl*. It's owned and operated by Advanced Asian Shipping, and it's far more than it appears to be on the surface."

He lifted his mug and swallowed the last of his coffee. I had questions, but I chose to continue listening.

"The *Pearl* is definitely a cargo ship, and a big one, but that's not all she is. She's also an exceptionally advanced intelligence-gathering platform. The Chinese Ministry of State Security likes to believe their little listening ship is the world's biggest secret and that nobody knows except them. We'll let them keep believing that for now, but we've been using that ship as a dumping ground for disinformation for years. We feed them so much bullshit, it's a wonder there isn't a cloud of methane gas floating around that boat everywhere it goes."

I raised my eyebrows in impatience, and he got the message.

"Okay, so here's what we believe is going to happen. They're going to flood their ballasts in either the Miraflores or Pedro Miguel Locks, and then sit her on the bottom. Because of her size, there will be very little room for salvage divers to inspect and repair the alleged damage. That will effectively close the lock and shut down the southern end of the canal."

"Why would they do that?"

Dominic squinted. "We don't know for sure, but we have some guesses. My theory is that there's a lot more to it than just sticking a Chinese spy ship to the bottom of a lock."

"When?" My head spun with theories and questions.

"She left Valparaíso, Chile, yesterday morning." Dominic checked his watch again.

My mind immediately went to work drawing a map of western South America. "Valparaíso? What was a ship that size doing in Valparaíso?"

"We don't know, but satellite imagery doesn't show any changes in her cargo in Chile," he said.

With my mental cartography project still churning, I said, "It's about three thousand miles from Valparaíso to Panama City, right?"

"Yeah, that's right," he said. "It's just over three thousand miles."

"Can she make twenty knots?" I asked.

"She makes almost twenty-four in good weather, and currently, there are no storms off the western coast of South America."

My brain stopped drawing maps and turned into a calculator. "So, she'll be in the canal in four days."

"Probably." He closed one eye and went to work doing the math.

"Okay," I said. "So they're going to sink a spy ship in a lock and close the canal. The only reasonable explanation is that they want to listen and watch as we react to a catastrophic closure of the canal. They want to know what we'll do and how quickly we'll do it."

Dominic smiled. "Bingo. They're going to gauge response for a future mission."

"It's pretty ingenious," I admitted before swallowing the last sip of coffee. "More coffee?"

"Don't you want to know what we want you to do?"

"I think I already know what you want. I'm an assassin. You want me to figure out who's going to sink the ship and stop him."

Dominic chuckled. "Well, no, not exactly. Let's get some more coffee, and I'll help you pack for Panama."

Clark met us in the galley. He had just brewed a fresh pot and was yawning himself awake.

"Good morning, sleeping beauty. It's about time you joined the land of the living." Dominic reached for his son's hand, then pulled him in for a fatherly hug.

Clark wiped the sleep from his eyes. "Hey, Dad. I didn't know you were coming so early. How are you?"

"I'm great, but it's not early. It's nearly seven o'clock. I thought you Green Beret–types slept twelve minutes per day or some ridiculous such thing."

I laughed. "That's what I thought, too, Dominic, but this particular Green Beret seems to need at least twelve hours a night."

Clark ignored us and enjoyed his first cup of coffee.

"Chase and I were just discussing a little operation in Central America. He's in, and if he wants you there, we can certainly authorize that. He'll fill you in later, but for now, if you'll excuse us, we have a few more things to discuss."

"Sure," said Clark, squinting and still yawning.

I suspect Clark had the same measure of curiosity as most people. One of the many things that surprised me about him was his ability to suppress the insatiable need to know. I suppose he knew I'd fill him in, just as Dominic had said, but it had to be tough pretending to be so nonchalant.

Back on the upper deck, Dominic returned to his briefer persona. "We're not ruling out the necessity of you doing what you do best in Panama, but everyone hopes you won't actually have to pull a trigger. This is more of a babysitting assignment than anything else. We're sending in a ninja of sorts—someone who's a little bit of a challenge to control. We need you to get him on board that freighter. Then, after he collects the information we need, it'll be up to you to get him back off that ship and into the hands of the analysts before he gets away."

I eyed Dominic over the rim of my cup. "Gets away?"

He smiled. "Yeah, the asset you'll be escorting isn't what you'd call predictable. His name is Diablo de Agua, and he's, well, let's say a bit of a wild card."

"I'm not following," I confessed.

"Diablo de Agua is hard to explain. There's quite a bit wrong with him, but he's incredibly useful when the situation calls for a man with his particular skill set."

"Just what *is* his skill set?" I was fully engaged.

"As I mentioned before, he's a bit of ninja. He's small and lightning fast. He doesn't like to fight. Instead, he prefers to escape, but that doesn't mean he can't fight. He's lethal and has no capacity for remorse. If forced to do so, he'd walk through another human being as if they were nothing more than a doorway. He moves undetected and remembers absolutely everything he sees and hears. He just has a little trouble functioning in normal society."

"So, he's a psychopath?"

"Oh, no. He's no psychopath. He's simply capable of ignoring what would terrify and haunt the rest of us."

"That's pretty much the definition of psychopathy, Dominic."

"Okay, then, Dr. Fulton. Diagnose him as you see fit, but your job is to get him in, get him out, and hang on to him long enough for someone to debrief him."

I thought about what he'd said, but it all sounded way too easy. "What's the catch?"

"There's no catch," he protested, unwilling to make eye contact.

"So, we're just going to let the Chinese sink a ship in the Panama Canal?"

"It's their ship," he said. "Who are we to stop them from sinking their own ship? Besides, there's that whole Neutrality Treaty that says we can't interfere in the affairs of the nation of Panama."

"I took history, too, Dominic. The Neutrality Treaty says we can do what is necessary to defend the Panama Canal if we believe it's under attack, and we can also do whatever is necessary to reopen the canal if it becomes closed by some hostile action."

"You're right, but what we *can* do and what we *will* do are often two very different things, my little history scholar."

"Indeed," I surrendered.

"Okay, so I'm going to pick up this water devil of yours and deposit him on board a Chinese freighter in the Panama Canal, and then gather him back up after he escapes from the sunken Chinese freighter. Then, I'm supposed to deliver him in a nice, neat little package to some analyst who can debrief him. And that's all?"

Dominic laughed. "Have you ever known anything to be that simple?"

"Here it comes." I shook my head. "I've been waiting for this particular shoe to drop."

"While you're waiting for Diablo de Agua, you're going to inspect the Bridge of the Americas and the Centennial Bridge for signs of potential sabotage. That's where Clark comes in. I suspect you could use his help. It's not like those are little footbridges. This isn't *Three Billy Goats Gruff.*"

I shrugged. "Okay, let's get Clark up here. He needs a full briefing. It looks like we're headed to Panama."

8
Treetop Flyin'

I'd promised not to lie to her, but I certainly couldn't tell her the truth. I crawled back into bed beside Penny and brushed the hair from her face. She inhaled deeply and reached for my hand.

"You've come to tell me goodbye, haven't you?"

"No," I said. "Not goodbye. I've come to tell you all the truth I can, and to also tell you that I hope you'll still be here when I get back."

"Where are you going?"

"Central America," I said, confident in my honesty.

"Are you going to have to kill anyone?"

"Probably," I admitted, "but if I do, I promise they'll be bad guys."

"Promise me you'll come back," she whispered.

"I promise."

"Then I promise to be here when you do." She pressed her lips to mine.

When we parted, I said, "Listen. Skipper has been living in a B and B, but I think it would be a good idea if she moved back aboard the boat. Are you okay with that?"

She smiled. "Of course I'm okay with that, silly. She was here before me, and it's not like she's competition. She's like your sister."

I laughed. "You're not seriously worried about competition, are you?"

She looked deathly serious. "You're a hot commodity. Just ask Earl."

"You're funny. I'm going to talk with Skipper. I'll see you in a couple of weeks."

She held my face in her hands and whispered, "Please be careful, Chase. You still owe me a couple kids."

"And a black lab," I said, kissing her again.

Skipper wasn't happy about being left behind, but she wasn't ready for the field yet, and she definitely wasn't prepared for an assignment like Panama. She was, however, happy to be moving back aboard *Aegis*.

* * *

We were wheels-up out of Naval Air Station Jacksonville before lunch, and living *pura vida* before supper. The Ticos of Costa Rica use the phrase *pura vida* to mean everything from *hello* to *kiss my ass*. The direct translation is *pure life* or *simple life*, but it seems to be the phrase they use when they can't think of anything else to say.

The citizens of Puerto Jimenez never cast a second glance at the Gulfstream jet with American markings. To them, it didn't matter who we were, where we were from, or who we were there to kill. To them, it was all *pura vida*, baby.

Puerto Jimenez is situated on Pavon Bay on the southern Pacific side of Costa Rica. It's one of the most picturesque stretches of ocean, beach, and rainforest in all of Central America. Perhaps my Costa Rican Spanish wasn't as good as I believed it to be. I thought *Pavon* meant peacock, but I didn't see nor hear any sign of the proud, feathered loudmouths in the short time we were there. What I did hear had no tail feathers but was just as unique as the peafowl.

"Well, looky here. I'll be damned if the agency ain't sent Pretty Boy Floyd and Baby Face Nelson down here to my jungle to stir up some shit."

He wore part of a Polynesian shirt that hadn't been washed—maybe ever—brown cargo pants, green jungle boots, and a hat that would've made a great doormat to someplace no one ever wanted to go. His skin was like leather stretched across a timber frame then baked for an hour too long. What hair I could see was wild and solid white. It protruded from beneath his rag of a hat and curled upward toward the sun as if it were trying to escape the madness of its roots. Aviator glasses and a cigar that would've made a great walking cane completed the man's wild look.

"I hear you two are looking for a ride to Panama City or thereabouts." The words fell out of his mouth as if the only thing holding them in was the alcohol on his breath.

Clark looked at me and shook his head. The Gulfstream that had delivered us only moments before was already fueled and taxiing out for takeoff. We each had a rucksack and two rolling Pelican cases full of equipment. The man eyed our gear as if he were thinking about relieving us of it and turning it into a few quick dollars to support his bad habits—and it certainly looked like he had no shortage of those.

"If you'll excuse us," I said, "we've got a lot to do."

He stepped within an inch of Clark, peering over his shoulder and eyeing our gear.

Clark unshouldered his ruck, and in one smooth motion, placed his palm on the man's chest. "Back up, asshole."

With blinding speed, the old man thrust Clark's arm up and over his head, and he swept his legs. Clark hit the ground with a thud, landing facedown with his right arm twisted and pinned behind his back by the old man's left knee. The muzzle of a Colt .45 Government came to rest against the back of Clark's head, precisely where his spine became his brainstem.

I reacted just as I'd been trained. I took a step backward with my right foot and reached for my weapon with the full intention of sticking a bullet in the man's right ear, but I didn't draw. Before my hand had found the grip of my pistol, I found myself staring down the barrel of a second Colt .45 aimed at my nose.

The old drunk had pinned Clark to the ground and drawn a pair of pistols before either of us could react quickly enough to stop him.

Just as quickly as the man had subdued us, he leapt to his feet, holstered his .45s, and grabbed a pair of our Pelican cases. "Come on, let's go. We've got a long night ahead of us. Oh, and you two should stop underestimating how dangerous this jungle is. It's the things you least expect that'll get you killed down here."

Clark climbed to his feet and dusted himself off. "Look, old man. If you try to pull that shit again. . . ."

The man never changed expressions. "If I pull that shit again, it'll be to save your life or mine, so quit the idle threats and get in the helicopter."

Clark's left eye narrowed and he took in a long, deep breath through his nose, trying not to explode. I'd seen Clark explode, and it almost never ended well for those on the receiving end.

Unsure of what else to do, we followed our new friend across the airport tarmac and into a tin-covered hangar that looked like it belonged in an aftermath scene.

"Stow your gear on the chopper and strap it down. It's going to be a bumpy ride."

The man disappeared through a sheet hanging over a doorway, and he left me and Clark standing there—me amused, and Clark still pissed.

"It's never dull," I said as I started loading the helicopter.

"You're right about that, Pretty Boy Floyd."

We strapped our gear to the floor of the UH-1. Bell Helicopters named it the Iroquois, but the rest of the world knew it as a Huey. We started a preflight inspection and found no fewer than twenty bullet holes in the fuselage of the old bird. It appeared she'd seen more than her share of action. I suspected the old guy behind the curtain was no different and probably had a few bullet holes of his own.

The thirty-foot-tall metal doors on the front of the hangar rattled and creaked in protest as Leo shoved them to their stops at the ends of the worn steel tracks. The old man returned, but the transformation he'd undergone behind the curtain was remarkable. His torn floral print shirt had been replaced by a green flight suit, and where the floppy ragtag hat had been, now sat a black cowboy hat with the First Cavalry Division emblem gleaming on the front.

"I should've known," chuckled Clark. "He's an Air Cav cowboy."

"That's right, Baby Face." He fingered the brim of his hat. "And these Stetsons are a lot sexier than those silly-ass green berets."

He twisted the handle on the pilot's door and climbed inside. Donning a headset, he went to work flipping switches and turning knobs on the forty-year-old chopper. Finally, the rotors began to turn, slowly at first, and then fast enough to turn every freestanding object in the hangar into an airborne squirrel, darting and twisting as if it had no idea where to go next.

The man yelled over the roar of the engine and rotor blades. "Well, don't just stand there. Get in."

We leapt inside, shielding our eyes from the flying debris.

"Is he really going to fly this thing out of the hangar?" Clark yelled.

I slid the door closed behind me. "Looks like it!"

We strapped ourselves into a pair of webbing seats and grabbed headsets from hooks on the forward bulkhead.

"Hang on back there. I've never tried this before," came the tinny voice through the headset.

Clark shook his head and crossed himself.

"I didn't know you were Catholic," I said.

"I am today."

The Huey's skids left the hangar floor, and we hovered toward the doors. The air inside the hangar was a tornado of dust, debris, and garbage, and I had no idea how Air Cav could see through the brown cloud.

Finally, sunlight filled the cabin, and we began to pick up speed. The airport disappeared beneath us, and we headed out across Pavon Bay.

When my heart finally settled back into a normal rhythm, I spoke into the microphone of my headset. "You're insane."

The pilot glanced over his shoulder. "Thank you. Now one of you get up here and fly. I've got work to do."

Clark unbuckled his harness and crawled into the left side of the cockpit.

"Do you know what you're doing?" asked the pilot.

Clark inspected the controls and instrumentation, then placed his feet on the pedals and his hands on the cyclic and collective. "How hard can it be if an old cavalry troop can do it?"

The pilot gave Clark the finger and crawled out of the cockpit. As he passed my seat, he stuck out his hand. "I'm Leo, by the way. It's nice to meet you. Now come help me get the gun set up."

I shook his hand, tossed off my headset, and disconnected my harness. Leo and I hung an M-60 machine gun on a bracket by the door and a can of thirty-caliber ammo beneath the weapon.

"Are you expecting trouble?" I asked, looking over the machine gun.

"Nope, but if we find some, we'll damn sure be ready for it."

He slid open the door and locked it at its stops. He then clipped a nylon strap to his waist and rotated the gun out of the open door. Before I knew what was happening, he'd poured a stream of rounds into the jungle canopy below, yelling, "Yeah, baby!"

Grinning, he turned to me. "You ever shot an M-60, kid?"

I shook my head. He yanked the strap from his waist and fastened it around mine.

"Go ahead. Have some fun. There ain't nothin' down there to hit but monkeys, parrots, and jaguars, and we ain't got enough bullets to put a dent in any of those population groups."

I slid into the open doorway, pulled the huge rifle to my shoulder, and squeezed off a five-second burst. The power in the gun was undeniable, and a ribbon of bullets laced its way through the jungle canopy below.

He leaned in close to my ear and yelled. "Just remember, we're doing a hundred knots across the ground, so if you have to shoot something, shoot where it will be, not where it is. This ain't no sniper rifle. This here's a spray-and-pray kinda play-pretty. Just don't melt the barrel, and try not to fall out."

With that, Leo left me alone with his play-pretty as we skimmed over the jungle canopy, barely above the treetops. Clark seemed to be just as at home at the controls of a helicopter as he was in anything with wings.

I pulled another headset from a hook above the door and slid it on. Leo was regaling Clark with stories of his glory days in Vietnam. I watched the jungle pass beneath us and listened silently.

"Yeah, it was a hell of a day. The whole damned valley was on fire. I'd been a pilot for less than eight weeks, and I'd been in the country for four whole days. We were hauling bodies and soon-to-be bodies out as fast as they could load 'em up. I was hanging out the window with my .45 in one hand and yelling at the G.I.s to hurry up, when this piece of shit Huey we were in started spinning like a top about six inches off the ground. The first thing that went through my head was that we'd lost the tail rotor. We were about to prang into the tree line and hopefully get a ride out of there with a crew that still had a helicopter with all the important pieces on it."

I thought about my father and the horrors he must've seen in that war. From what I'd learned about him from Padre in Charleston, my father was a warrior of the highest order. I wondered if Leo ever met my father.

Leo continued. "So, I was squirming my head and shoulders back into the helicopter, and we were still spinning like a . . . hell, like something that spins a lot. Anyway, that's when it occurred to me that we were spinning the wrong way. If we'd lost the tail rotor, we'd be spinning to the right, but we were spinning left, backing up, and climbing. The CW4 in the right seat was old. I mean, really old, like thirty-two or something. I knew if anybody on Earth could get the airplane under control, it would be him, but that didn't stop me from grabbing the controls. The cyclic was in my lap, the collective was full up, and the left pedal was pinned to the floor. The airplane was doing exactly what old Chief What's-His-Name was telling it to do, but I couldn't figure out why he'd be telling it to do that. I was dizzy, confused, and intrigued, but all three of those turned into shit-my-pants scared the instant I saw my pilot . . . or what was left of my pilot. His body was still sitting there in the right seat, but his head was gone. I don't know who or what shot him, but I knew somebody was going to have to fly that helicopter."

I wondered how many thousands of stories just like that one and worse were floating around in the heads of the veterans of that war. War has to be the worst thing that humans do. I guess the worst scars of war are the ones no one ever sees—the ones left indelibly on the minds of those who lived the horrors and survived. Perhaps their bodies survived, but a part of all of them died with every pull of the trigger, and with every brother they watched fall. I knew Clark had to bear more scars than he'd ever show me, but I hoped he knew I'd listen if he needed to talk. But maybe that's not what soldiers do. Maybe they prefer to fight the demons alone rather than risk letting them loose and seeing what the demons might do to the people they love.

While I was playing backseat psychotherapist, the Huey banked hard right and started diving into the jungle canopy. I braced myself against the M-60 and leaned back, trying to take Leo's advice and not fall out of the helicopter.

Before I could think to ask what we were doing, a cloud of red-brown dust engulfed us, and we settled to the ground, landing like a butterfly in the only clearing for fifty miles.

The engine fell silent, and the rotors spun to a stop overhead. Leo hopped from the Huey and headed for a bamboo hut a hundred feet away. Clark and I crawled from the chopper and followed. When we reached the bamboo hut, we discovered Leo counting out American hundred-dollar bills into the hand of a wrinkled old man behind a bamboo table. Everything in the place was made of bamboo, except the floor was jungle dirt with Persian rugs scattered around.

Without a word, Leo strolled out of the hut, picking up two bottles of liquor from a shelf near the door. I watched the old clerk, or whatever he was, disappear out the back, and I soon heard an engine roar. The oldest, most decrepit fuel truck I'd ever seen lumbered its way toward the Huey.

"I needed fuel." Leo held up his two bottles of clear liquor. "And the chopper needed gas."

"What is this place?" I asked as I swatted mosquitoes and half a dozen other flying things I couldn't identify.

"This, Pretty Boy, is Tienda de Bambú. It's your basic one-stop-shop in the rainforest for whatever you need, from tequila to jet fuel, and almost anything in between."

The Bamboo Store in the middle of the jungle. And they have jet fuel. Amazing.

The fuel truck, such as it was, completed its task of gassing up the Huey, and then lumbered its way out of sight. We climbed back aboard.

The turbine whistled itself up to an eventual roar, and the blades started turning.

"Are we going to be needing this gun?" I reattached the lanyard to my waist.

Leo looked over his shoulder. "I hope not, but let's not put it away just yet."

I started to spit out something witty when a flash of movement caught my eye from the back of the chopper where our gear was strapped down.

Perched like a jungle cat atop one of our Pelican cases was a small, sinewy, dark-haired man. I immediately drew my pistol and leveled it between his black eyes.

I expected to see his hands go up in surrender, but he smiled, exposing a metal ring and pin clenched between his teeth. My eyes moved to his left hand, where he held a pinless, standard-issue hand grenade between his thumb and forefinger. With the slightest pressure required, he held the spoon in place. I knew if I pulled the trigger, I'd spend the next ten seconds hoping to find that loose grenade rolling around the floor of the chopper before it went off. We had undeniably reached an impasse.

"Uh, guys, we've got a visitor back here."

Clark and Leo turned to look back, and Leo laughed.

"Oh, yeah. I probably should've told you about him. Pretty Boy, meet Diablo de Agua."

I holstered my pistol and made a mental note to shoot Leo if I ever got the chance.

Diablo pulled the pin from his mouth, slid it back into its slot, and dropped the grenade into a satchel at his waist.

Diablo never looked directly into my eyes. Instead, he kept his focus on my pistol, even after I'd returned it to my holster.

His eyes darted about as if he were surveying me for additional weapons. Finally, he rose from his crouch atop my Pelican case and moved silently to the door. His legs weren't long enough to reach the skids, so he sat with his feet dangling outside the helicopter in midair.

Leo was flying, but Clark stared backward out of the cockpit, not taking his eyes off the man Leo had called *Diablo de Agua*. He finally glanced at me and then back at the bizarre, little man. I shrugged, and Clark shook his head and chuckled.

We rose from the clearing and watched the Tienda De Bambú disappear behind us. Unlike the water devil, my legs reached the skids, so I sat beside him and offered a headset. He glanced at the green David Clark headset but never reached for it. I went to put it on his head for him, but I backed off, not knowing what he might do if I actually touched him.

"I'm Chase," I yelled over the roar of the engine and rotor.

For the first time, he made eye contact with me, but he wore a blank expression of disinterest and gave no response.

We flew on for another hour as Diablo carefully surveyed the jungle canopy below. His eyes were like those of a cat; they darted toward any movement in the trees. I half expected him to leap from the chopper when something caught his attention. He would lean forward to get a better look, but he never jumped. And he never said a word.

We landed in a clearing barely larger than our helicopter on an island due south of Panama City. Just before the skids touched down, Diablo leapt from the chopper and promptly dissolved into the forest.

"Where are we?"

"Come on, Pretty Boy. Don't you know your Central American geography?" Leo laughed as if he were the keeper of all knowledge. In that group, he was exactly that when it came to the land and the islands.

"I'm afraid you have me at a disadvantage. I didn't pay a lot of attention to where we were going. I was too busy worrying about that little freak and what he was going to do. That's one weird little dude," I said as I scanned the tree line in a vain attempt to locate him.

"Ha! He's harmless, as long as he's on your side. But you're right. He's a little odd. Did he talk to you?"

"No, he didn't talk to me. He didn't say a word. He just threatened me with a grenade and then jumped out and vanished as soon as we got close to the ground."

Leo saw me staring into the trees. "Forget about spotting him, son. He's part of the rainforest now. You'll only see him if he wants you to see him. I've known him for the better part of a decade, and he's never said more than a dozen words to me. He's strange, but there's nobody better at what he does."

In his typical style, Clark stood, and I knew he was silently taking mental notes.

I asked what we were both thinking. "What does he do?"

Leo spat and then wiped at his mustache. "Well, he gets into places no one else can, commits everything inside the place to memory, and then escapes without ever being seen. It's the damnedest thing."

"What good does it do for him to commit anything to memory if he won't tell anyone what he's seen?"

"Oh, he'll tell one person," Leo said.

I waited, but he clearly wasn't going to volunteer the name. Impatiently, I asked, "Who?"

"Ginger."

"Who's Ginger?"

"Ginger is an analyst who used to work at Langley. Now she works for us." Leo looked at his watch and then at the sun. "Let's get some netting over the chopper before it gets dark."

Camouflage netting was something Clark understood well. He pulled the two heavy bags from the back of the helicopter and rolled out the mesh. We tied the blades to the skids, and I climbed on top of the airframe. In no time, our Huey was virtually invisible from above.

"Bona," said Leo.

"What's Bona?"

"That's where we are," he said. "We're on the island of Bona. There's nobody else here. It's just an uninhabited rock in the Pacific with more trees than most. We'll spend the night here while Diablo decides how he wants us to get him on that ship, and then we'll do whatever he thinks is best."

"So, that little freak is in charge of this mission?"

"No, Pretty Boy. You are. This is your circus, and you're the ring-master. I'm just the driver, and that 'little freak' out there is your main attraction. Now, I think it's time you met Ginger."

We climbed into the chopper and Leo pulled out a large, black case. He pulled a satellite dish from the case and arranged it facing almost straight up. He plugged a laptop computer into the satellite dish, pressed the power button, and waited.

The computer screen came to life, and Leo went to work typing lines of instructions. The screen soon filled with the face of a god-dess. Ginger was probably around thirty years old, with the greenest eyes I'd ever seen, and locks of flowing red hair, over which she visibly had no control.

"Hey, Leo. Where's my little cabana boy?"

"Hello, Ginger. Meet Pretty Boy and Baby Face."

Clark and I leaned in to face the screen, neither of us having any idea if the gorgeous redhead could actually see us.

"Pretty Boy and Baby Face . . . really?" she said.

"They probably have names," Leo said, "but who cares?"

"It's nice to meet you guys. I'm Ginger. In case Leo hasn't told you—and he's probably not told you much of anything—I'll be your analyst for this mission. I'll debrief that sexy little devil when it's all over, and we'll decide what to do from there. Sound good?"

"Sure. It sounds good to me," I said. "But I have some questions."

Ginger smiled. "I'm sure you do, but answering your questions isn't what I do. Your boat will be off Isla San Jose in thirty-six hours. Tell that beautiful little man to keep himself alive, and don't you dare let anything happen to him."

The screen went black, and Ginger was gone.

I'd never worked with an analyst before, so I had a lot to learn about what she would and wouldn't do for us. I had a pretty good idea that the list of things she wouldn't do for Diablo was quite short.

Trying to think tactically, I said, "Let's plan for two-hour watches. That'll give each of us four hours of sleep."

Leo laughed uproariously. "You boys can stand watch if you want, but there won't be so much as a mosquito getting anywhere near this chopper as long as Diablo's out there. If he don't kill it, he'll scare it away no matter how big or bad it is. I'm gettin' eight hours of quality sleep, and you two can do whatever the hell you want as long as you don't keep me awake."

So much for my tactical thinking.

Clark finally spoke. "Don't feel bad, Chase. I have no idea what's going on, either. I would've set a watch, too."

"Thank God. I was beginning to think I'd entered the twilight zone."

"No, I don't think this is the twilight zone. I think it may be more like the temperate zone, but either way, I'm in favor of a good night's sleep. You heard the woman. Our boat's going to be here in thirty-six hours. I suspect things are going to get pretty exciting soon."

We settled in for our first night in the Panamanian jungle.

9

Bulls on the Hill

Dawn broke over the Panamanian coastline, and the smell of a fire lured me from my sleep. I'd spent the night on the floor of the helicopter on top of a sleeping bag and beneath a mosquito net. Leo had been wrong about Diablo protecting us from the mosquitoes, and the net hadn't worked. Tiny bug bites dotted my skin, but such is life in the tropics.

As it turned out, the fire was the product of Diablo de Agua. He was cooking fish over the coals of a small fire near the edge of the clearing. He was barefoot, shirtless, and turning the fish over the fire with his bare hands.

Clark, Leo, and I crawled from the Huey simultaneously, and Diablo actually smiled as he saw us approaching. We all made a visit to the tree line for a morning necessity, and then one by one, we made our way back to el fuego del Diablo. I'd always expected the devil's fire to be bigger, and I thought the same about the devil himself.

When I took a seat, Diablo pulled a nice-sized fish from the coals and handed it to me with a brief nod of his head. I took the fish and bounced it on my fingertips. It was too hot to hold, and Diablo laughed as he watched me fumble the fish. It either finally cooled, or I lost sensation in my fingers, and I ate every ounce of meat from the bones.

Clark and Leo joined us, and they each had a nearly identical experience with a fish that was too hot to touch.

Leo finally got his scalding-hot fish under control. "Do you have any feelings at all, you little freak?"

Diablo smiled and placed his hand over his heart.

The psychologist in me had a field day with that one, but I didn't think I'd be getting Diablo de Agua to open up to me or anyone else anytime soon.

He offered another fish to each of us, and we all cautiously accepted. I broke a small twig into two pieces to receive my fish. Clark opted for a flat rock as a plate, and Leo slid a flight glove onto his left hand. Again, Diablo laughed.

With breakfast behind us and the sun turning the air into an oven, we retreated to the shade of the camo netting over the Huey.

I'd been planning through the night, and the time had come to put my plan into action. "Ginger said our ship was thirty-six hours out last night. That's less than twenty-four hours remaining. Tomorrow morning, the AAS *Pearl* will enter the canal at Panama City. We believe they're going to sink her in either the first or second set of locks, essentially shutting down the canal. They plan to gauge our reaction to the event. Knowing how we'll respond, and especially how long it'll take for us to react to a catastrophic event in the canal, is an incredibly valuable piece of intelligence. Langley thinks the Chinese are planning a major attack on the canal in the next few months. Knowing what sort of response to expect gives them an invaluable tool for planning such an attack. If we don't respond for eight, or even ten hours, that is an eternity when chaos is afoot."

Leo cleared his throat. "So, you guys are supposed to stop the Chinese from sinking their own ship? Is that why you're here?"

"No, not at all," I said. "We're going to let them do all the sinking they want, and Diablo here is going to be aboard that ship watching and listening to every move they make."

I looked at the ninja. "I assume you know Mandarin and Cantonese?"

He locked eyes with me. At first, his brow was wrinkled and his mouth formed a small frown, then a look of recognition came over his face, and his eyes widened. A broad smile appeared, followed by what I took as a look of mischief. What a mysterious character he was.

Leo had seen the look as well, but he didn't hesitate. "How do you plan to get that little devil on board that ship?"

Remembering Diablo's legendary ability to get into places he didn't belong, I turned to him. "Do you have any ideas?"

Once again, he stared at me with a look of recognition, but he didn't speak.

"Look, a mission like this is hard enough when communication is good. It's impossible if you don't talk. I need your input."

"*Bote de piloto.*"

I was relieved to hear him actually speak, but his idea was no good.

"Unfortunately," I said in Spanish, "putting you aboard the pilot boat won't do any good. Both the ship's captain, Chen Jianguo, and his second-in-command hold a Panama Canal Pilot's rating, so as long as either man is on the bridge, there's no requirement to have a canal pilot aboard."

Diablo hung his head. I assumed the gesture meant he was unhappy that his idea wouldn't work, but I was wrong. He lifted his head, glanced at Leo, and then at the Huey.

"*Saltare.*"

I thought about his suggestion and remembered my first mission when I'd jumped from a helicopter onto a container ship bound for Havana. The fall wasn't bad, but it was under different circumstances. I was leaping aboard a friendly ship making eight knots in relatively calm seas in the northern Caribbean. Diablo was talking about hopping from a Huey onto a Chinese freighter steaming at twenty-three knots through the Pacific. If we got caught, it would be an act of piracy at best. At worst, it would be a gunfight above one of the world's largest freighters. I didn't like either of those possible outcomes.

I'd read volumes about the psychology of command. *The Art of War* by the Chinese General Sun Tzu was one of my favorites. A recurring theme through that great tactician's bible is that all war is based on deception. If I could make Captain Chen believe I was weak and in dire need of his aid, I could pluck the hairs from his beard while he believed I was handing him gold coins.

"*Bueno. Vas a saltar,*" I said.

"What do you mean, 'he'll jump'?" said Leo.

"I mean, he'll jump, and you'll convince Captain Chen that you're lost and scared and weak. Just like Sun Tzu said. When you're strong, appear weak. We're going to beat him with his ancestor's own words."

"You're insane," he said.

"Indeed, I am, but I'm also in charge. Now figure out how to talk your little friend there into teaching you enough Mandarin to talk your way out of getting shot while hovering over the deck of that ship."

I motioned for Clark to join me, and we headed off toward the tree line.

"He's right, you know. You are insane."

"I know," I admitted, "but sanity and ops like this don't go together. We have to get Diablo on the deck of that boat and then pick him back up after this is all over."

"Fine," he said, "but what are we going to do once we drop the crazy little dude on that ship?"

"We're going to steal a boat and go for a swim."

Clark shook his head. "I can't wait to hear this one."

"Langley thinks the Chinese may be planning to blow either the Bridge of the Americas or the Centennial Bridge after they sink the freighter."

"Why?" Clark's mouth was agape as he waited for my explanation.

"Imagine what that would do to the canal. It would shut it down for weeks at best, and most likely months. In addition to that, it would also make the sinking look more like an act of terrorism than an intentional act of self-sabotage. It's brilliant."

"And insane," he huffed.

"When was the last time the Chinese did anything that wasn't insane?"

"You have a point," he admitted, "but that's over-the-top, even for the Chinese."

"I agree, but that doesn't mean they're not going to do it."

He shrugged. "So, if we find out they're going to blow one of the bridges, what then? Do we stop them, report them, or just watch?"

"I don't think watching is an option, and who would we report it to? I think our only option is to try and stop them. What do you think?"

He grinned. "I think I'm glad you're in charge."

"Thanks."

"By the way," he said, "my Mandarin sucks, but my Cantonese is pretty good. If you're planning what I think you're planning, I'm pretty sure I can convincingly pull off the role of a scared, lost Huey pilot to whoever's on the bridge of the Pearl. They won't see the little devil falling from the sky. But we're going to have to do it under cover of darkness. We'll never pull it off in the daylight."

"Perfect."

Finally, something was going right.

"Now, all we need is a boat," I said. "I think we need to go shopping."

Clark put on that mischievous, crooked smile. "I'll ask Daddy for the keys."

We found Leo and Diablo huddled under a tree, practicing distress calls in a language that resembled a form of unknown Asian.

Clark laughed. "Don't worry, Leo. I'll take care of the character acting if you'll get us as close to that freighter as possible so our little devil can hop aboard. Deal?"

"Now, that I can do," said Leo, obviously relieved he didn't actually need to learn a new language in twelve hours.

"Speaking of flying, how do you feel about a little recon mission? We need to find a boat that we can"—Clark made quotation marks in the air—"borrow."

"That sounds like a lot more fun than learning Chinese from a mute. Let's go." Leo stood on shaky legs and stretched, his knees popping like firecrackers. "It's hell gettin' old, boys. I don't recommend it."

"I'd say it beats the alternative," I quipped.

Leo pursed his lips. "I suppose you've got a point there."

We pulled the camo netting from the Huey and climbed aboard. We were soon climbing out of the clearing on Bona and heading north toward the southern end of the canal.

"We're thinking a workboat from the fuel depot on Taboguilla might be the best option," said Clark.

"Sure," Leo said. "Whatever you guys think is best. But there's a marina and anchorage with about a thousand boats at Flamenco Island. I think that might be worth a look."

Clark glanced at me, then back at Leo. "Hey, this is your neighborhood, Mr. Rogers. Flamenco sounds good. Let's have a look."

Leo adjusted the directional gyro to agree with the magnetic compass, and lowered the nose, picking up a few more knots of airspeed. "We'll fly over Taboguilla on the way so you can have a look, but I think you may like the selection a little further north even better."

We flew over the fuel depot and saw two freighters and a half dozen small working boats tied to the docks. The location was good, but I didn't know how seriously they took their security. I certainly didn't need to get caught stealing a boat in Panama. I snapped a mental picture of Taboguilla and planned to compare it to Flamenco.

Leo pointed out the Flamenco Island Lighthouse and Fort Grant as we approached from the south.

"Look at all those nice, beautiful boats anchored out there with nobody watching over them," he said.

"They're ripe for the picking," I admitted, "but how do we know which ones are unoccupied?"

"Anchor lights," he said as if I was supposed to know what he meant. My look of confusion must have encouraged him to continue. "If the anchor lights are on during the day, that means there's most likely nobody aboard to turn them off and on, so the boat's probably empty."

"Brilliant." I tried to pick out anchor lights in the bright morning sun, but it wasn't easy.

"I know you boys don't want to leave your fingerprints on this little shit show of yours, but you can always rent or buy a boat. There's no chance of ending up in a Panamanian jail cell that way."

Clark turned to me. "Why didn't *you* think of that since you're in charge and all?"

Leo chuckled. "Let me tell you a little story. There was this young bull standing beside an old bull on top of a hill, looking over a meadow full of cows grazing on the green grass. The young bull said to the old bull, 'Hey, let's run down there and have us one of those fine-looking cows.' The old bull looked down at the bright-eyed, excited young bull, and said, 'I've got a better idea. Let's just walk down there and have all of them.'"

I was getting smarter, but I still had a lot to learn. Perhaps I'd be an old bull someday.

10

A Bridge to Hell

It should've come as no surprise that Leo, our resident old bull, knew a guy.

"There's a guy up in Gamboa I know who'd be glad to sell you a boat if you've got the cash. He likes American dollars. Have you got any of those?"

Leo seemed to ignore the helicopter when he flew. It was almost as if the Huey was an integral part of him, and that they had some unwritten but unbreakable agreement that each would instinctively take care of the other.

"We have a few," I said, "but where's Gamboa?"

"It's about fifteen miles up the ditch on the eastern shore. He's not a company man, but he's a friend of the cause. If he knows you're with me, he'll trust you enough to sell you a boat without too many questions."

"How about no questions?" I asked. "I don't want either of our names bouncing around down here after we're gone."

"Ha, so you don't want anybody to know Pretty Boy and Baby Face were in Central America, huh?"

"No, it'd be better if we were ghosts."

"Anonymity ain't cheap in the jungle, but it can be bought if you have enough of them American greenbacks."

"I have the controls!" Clark declared from the left seat.

Leo lifted his hands in an obvious surrender of the aircraft, and we started a high-speed dive to the left.

With his hands full of Huey controls, Clark pointed with his chin. "Look at those two boats side-by-side just south of the ferry terminal at Snake Point."

I was impressed. Clark knew his Panamanian geography and a little Spanish. *Punta Culebra* made up the southwestern tip of Naos Island and housed the terminal for the ferry to Tobago Island.

Just south of the point, a pair of open-deck workboats were making fifteen or twenty knots and running close enough together, that from our altitude, they looked like one boat.

"They took on some cargo near the ferry terminal," Clark said. "Before they got it tarped, I thought I saw explosives markings on the crates."

"How the hell did you see that from all the way up here?" Leo scoffed.

"Baby Face has young eyes," Clark quipped.

As we drew closer, Leo said, "Those look like salvage tenders. They haul gear and personnel for the salvage crews around here. I can't think of any reason why they'd be hauling explosives, though."

Two crewmen from the southernmost boat stared skyward, obviously wondering why a helicopter was diving on them. Clark must have noticed them, as well. He broke hard right and came to a hover just west of Fort Grant.

"Let's give them time to swallow the bait, and then we'll see where they go."

Clark's ploy worked. The two crewmen turned and nonchalantly made their way back into the pilothouse. To them, we must have appeared to be just another helicopter sightseeing tour. I didn't know anyone who used a Huey as a sightseeing chopper, but Central America doesn't necessarily play by the same rules as the rest of the world.

In a nearly motionless hover, Clark banked the chopper around to the right and started a gentle climb, appearing disinterested in the workboats.

We were anything but disinterested.

Leo had a pair of binoculars pressed to his eyes as we climbed to a thousand feet. That altitude gave us a nice vantage point to watch the boats without being too obvious.

Leo pulled the binoculars from his face and pointed toward the bridge. "It looks like they're headed up the canal toward Balboa."

Clark maneuvered the chopper to remain well clear of the international airport to the west and still be as inconspicuous as possible. We flew up the east side of the canal, trying to keep the boats in sight.

As they passed beneath the Bridge of the Americas, they split up. One headed to the beach just north of the bridge, and the other continued northward toward the first set of locks.

"Which one had the explosives?"

Obviously trying to guess correctly, Clark flew ever closer to the bridge. "The one headed for the beach took on the crates, but I think they loaded some of them onto the other boat, as well. They both have tarps on deck now," he said.

I took the binoculars from Leo and focused on the boat headed for the beach. There was something on deck covered by a green tarp, and the other boat carried a similar load. It was quickly becoming impossible to watch both.

"Put me on the beach!" I said.

"What?" came the stereo reply from the cockpit.

"Put me on the beach near that ferry terminal. It can't be more than half a mile to the bridge from there. I can make that in under three minutes. Get me down there."

Clark dumped the collective and dived for the beach. Sixty seconds later, I was at a full sprint, running north along the shoreline. I took cover behind one of the huge sets of concrete pilings supporting the Bridge of the Americas.

I laid eyes on the bridge and felt a lump form in my throat. The last time I'd seen it, I was a teenager, and my father, mother, and little sister had just been murdered less than twenty-five miles to the northeast. That had been eleven years before. Someone I hadn't known woke me up, threw a blanket over my head, and forced me

into the back seat of a Volvo station wagon. At the time, I had believed my parents were missionaries, helping at an orphanage on the
outskirts of Panama City. The man who'd pulled me from our bungalow and hustled me into the Volvo sat beside me and spoke
twenty-two words I'd never forget.

"Listen to me, Chase. Guerillas have killed your parents and sister, and we're going to get you out of here."

Inside my fourteen-year-old mind, I imagined gorillas—great
apes—attacking and killing my family. I couldn't understand. When
the sun came up, I was sitting in a window seat above the wing of
an airplane climbing out of the international airport that was, at the
time, Howard Air Force Base. I watched the rising sun gleaming off
the superstructure of the bridge and wondered when I'd see my
family again. The reality and finality of my situation hadn't hit me.
Perhaps it never would. I wondered where I was going and how
long it would take to get there. My catcher's mitt was still in the
bungalow, along with my best pair of cleats. Somewhere between
Panama and America, it occurred to me that my mitt and cleats
weren't the only things I'd never see again. They were gone. Dead.
All of them. My entire family.

I was alone on an airplane, and I had no idea what would happen next.

When we had landed, I didn't recognize the airport. I'd flown in
and out of Atlanta's Hartsfield airport a couple dozen times with my
parents, but wherever I was, it definitely wasn't Atlanta. The plane
came to a stop, and the other passengers stood and began making
their way toward the door. I couldn't move. I didn't know what to do.

*What's outside the door of the airplane? What is the world going to
look like without my family in it? Where am I supposed to go?*

I wanted to believe my family would be waiting at the bottom of
the stairs when I walked off the plane. I imagined my sister in her
bright yellow dress, pirouetting on the tarmac, and complaining
about having to wait for me. She wouldn't be there. She'd never be
there.

When the plane was finally empty, I stood on trembling knees and tried to gather the courage to walk through the door. Unlike the rest of the passengers, I had no bags, no books, nothing. There was nothing left. Everything I had, including the bodies of family, was still in Panama.

I held the handrail as if it would somehow protect me from the rest of the world as I treaded painful steps down the airstairs toward the tarmac, every step feeling like a dagger through the soles of my feet. The world was a blur; nothing was familiar. I believed that was how the world would look for the rest of my life.

I couldn't focus. Sounds were muffled roars to my ears. Every figure in front of me blended into another. Nothing had an identity of its own. Everything melted and moved like molten lava. As my palm left the handrail, I collapsed to my knees and vomited on the gray carpet at the bottom of the airstairs. It felt like I was watching myself from a great height. I wanted to wipe my face and stand up, but I couldn't make my body move. No matter how much I tried, I was powerless to do anything other than kneel on that terrible gray rug and tremble beside what had been the contents of my stomach. I knew it was wrong. I knew I had to get up. But there was nothing I could do.

Finally, a gentle hand landed on my shoulder, and a woman knelt beside me.

"You're going to be all right, Chase. Let's get you inside."

It sounded as if she were talking through a long tunnel. I turned to face the woman, and she had no eyes, no mouth. She was touching me, encouraging me to stand and come with her, but her face was like a puzzle that had been put together incorrectly. I blinked and stared at her until I could barely make out her features. When I could finally see her, she wore an expression of utter sadness. I wanted to help her. I wanted to know why she was so sad, but I couldn't help myself. How was I supposed to help anyone else?

"Where am I?"

"You're safe, Chase."

"Where?" I repeated.

"You're at Shaw Air Force Base in South Carolina, and you're safe."

"My family—"

The woman stopped me. "Let's get you inside."

"I need my mitt."

The woman's look of sadness turned to confusion.

"My baseball glove . . . I need my mitt."

"Come on inside, Chase."

I turned back toward the plane and waited for my mother and father to descend the stairs. They were coming. They had to be just behind me.

My father appeared in the door of the plane and started down the stairs. I reached for him, and he froze. He was wearing an Air Force flight suit. My father wasn't a pilot. I watched as his eyes beseeched the woman beside me to get me off the tarmac. Then my mother appeared in the doorway and bounced down the stairs, but she was also wearing a flight suit, and her long, dark hair was short and light. I turned to the woman beside me and then back to my parents, and I realized they weren't my parents at all. They were the flight crew. I'd merely wanted them to be my parents. I wanted to vanish. All of those people had no idea what was happening, and I was the center of attention. I just wanted to be gone. I didn't want to be somewhere else. I wanted to disappear.

The lady pulled more forcefully. "We can't stay out here on the flight line, Chase. We have to go inside."

The mirrored windows reflected my mother and father walking behind us in their flight suits and my sister leading me into the building. It was all so clear.

It must have been days, or maybe decades later—I couldn't fathom the passing of time—when I awoke in a hospital room, completely alone. Sounds were crisp and clear. Things were no longer melting and running together. I was wearing sweats and a T-shirt I didn't recognize as mine, and I couldn't identify the room, but for the first time since the flight, I was coherent.

"Good morning, Chase," said a young woman in nurse's scrubs. "How are you feeling?"

"I feel good. How are you?"

She froze, stared at me, and finally smiled. She reached for my wrist and stared at her watch as she counted my pulse.

"Are you hungry?"

I nodded.

"Good. I'll be right back," she said.

She kept her word and returned promptly with a tray of eggs, bacon, an orange, a biscuit, and a carton of milk. I was starving, and I devoured the meal as if I hadn't eaten in weeks. Perhaps I hadn't.

"Slow down," she cautioned. "You don't want to make yourself sick. There's plenty more, and I'll bring you all you want. You don't have to be in a hurry."

I finished, hoping she was serious about bringing more. She was. I ate two more helpings of everything just before a man in a suit and tie walked into my room and sat on the edge of my bed.

"Good morning, Chase. I'm Dr. Fairchild. How are you feeling?"

"I feel good. I was hungry."

"That's good," he said. "Do you know what day it is?"

"Yes, sir. It's Thursday, December fifteenth."

"Chase, it's Monday, December nineteenth. You've had a challenging few days. Do you feel like talking about it?"

I bowed my head and swallowed the lump in my throat. "What am I supposed to do? Where am I going to live? How am I going to finish school?"

The doctor licked his lips then drew in a long breath. "Okay, if that's where you'd like to start, I can answer those questions. In fact, those are the easy ones."

"Right now, those are the only questions I have, Dr. Fairchild. Well, I have one more. What sort of doctor are you?"

"I'm actually two different kinds. I'm a psychologist and psychiatrist. It's my job to help you deal with what's happened, and to make sure you have the tools you need to get through this."

"How do you get through anything when your whole family has been murdered? Huh? How? How do you do that? Is it even possible?"

He smiled, and I hadn't expected that.

"I knew you had more questions, and we'll get to all of them, especially the ones you don't know you have yet."

"Is this some kind of game? Because I'm not in the mood for games. You come in here telling me I don't know what day it is and that you're here to help me deal with the fact that everybody I love is dead. That's not a game to me, Doctor."

"You're right, Chase. None of this is a game. It's all very serious and will be the most difficult thing you'll ever experience, but I can make it easier. I can help you understand and cope with the emotions you're feeling. The anger, the loss, and the depression."

He paused, presumably waiting for my response, but I had none.

"Okay, then. Let's start by answering the first questions that popped out of your mouth. You want to know what you're supposed to do. The answer is long and far from simple, but in short, you're supposed to grieve. You're supposed to miss your family, and you're supposed to experience the pain of loss. That is perfectly natural. Everyone does it differently, and that's fine. There's no wrong or right way to grieve. You're supposed to just let it happen. You'll most likely have outbursts. You'll lash out at the people, like me, who are trying to help you. We're going to be understanding and tolerant, and eventually, you'll begin to feel less angry, and you'll realize that you're still alive. You'll come to realize that if you could talk with your family, they would tell you to live your life and make the most of every day. Eventually, you'll realize these things, but for now, it's okay to grieve the way your mind chooses. As long as you're not hurting yourself or others, we're not going to stand in your way. We're here to support you."

I felt overwhelmed. I didn't have the wherewithal to sort out the emotions I was feeling. I couldn't tell the difference between the pain caused by the anger and the pain caused by the loss. I was experiencing every negative emotion, all at the same time. I had just enough sense left in my crumbling psyche to understand and accept that I needed Dr. Fairchild's help.

"So, you want to know where you're going to live. Fortunately, that's not a concern. Your parents were wonderful people who loved you more than you'll ever know. They made certain you would be well cared for should the unthinkable occur, and they made specific preparations for both your housing and education."

"Well," I blurted out, "this certainly qualifies as unthinkable."

"Yes, Chase, it certainly does. Arrangements have been made for you to enroll in the Central Georgia Military Academy. It's a preparatory school for boys. It's one of the finest prep schools in the country. Not only will you be provided a wonderful education, you'll also live on campus and have access to everything you'll need."

"Do they have a baseball team?"

Dr. Fairchild laughed. "Yes, as a matter of fact, they do. One of the best baseball teams in the state. Do you play ball?"

"Yes, sir. I'm a catcher. It's the only thing in the world I'm good at."

"Then I'm certain there will be a place on the team for you," he said. The lines around his eyes and mouth dissolved, and he relaxed his shoulders.

"You know what, doc? I'm sorry. That was crazy selfish. I'm supposed to be grieving, not thinking about playing ball. I shouldn't have said that. I'm sorry."

"Chase, remember, we all grieve in our own ways. Baseball is obviously important to you. When we suffer great losses, our minds cling to the things that make us feel better. For some people, it's alcohol or drugs. For others, it's music, art, or yoga. It doesn't matter what it is as long as it isn't hurting you or those around you. There's absolutely nothing wrong with thinking about playing baseball. But I have to tell you, it speaks volumes about your character that you apologized for thinking about baseball when you believe you should be thinking about your family. You're a fine young man, and you're going to be a great man very soon. I'll certainly do everything in my power to support you, and the same is true for all of my staff. We're here for you, Chase. We're all here for you."

I spent Christmas in Dr. Fairchild's hospital or asylum or whatever it was. When school reconvened in January, I found myself in a bizarre new world.

I was primarily homeschooled because my family traveled so much. Sometimes I'd attend regular schools, but never for long. The structure of the military school was rigid, but I grew to enjoy the routine, and I developed the same expectation of high standards from myself that the school expected of me and every other cadet. I excelled in the classroom, but I was at my best on the baseball field.

The coach had been a major league catcher for six years. There may have been no one on Earth better suited to teach me to catch. "I was a natural-born catcher," he said, "but even naturals need coaching."

Thanks to Dr. Fairchild, I left the hospital well-equipped to adjust to life at the Central Georgia Military Academy. Thanks to the teachers at CGMA, I learned how to study, digest, and retain information. From them, I learned how to learn. And thanks to Coach Bryce Garner, I learned to command the baseball field from behind home plate. I graduated from the academy with a 4.0 and a full athletic scholarship to play ball at the University of Georgia. That's where I met the man who would change my life forever—Dr. Robert "Rocket" Richter, the greatest psychology professor on Earth.

After my promising baseball career came crumbling down around me when I suffered a debilitating injury to my right hand during the College World Series, I'd felt the same emptiness and loneliness that I'd felt after the death of my family. Dr. Richter had been instrumental in recruiting me into the world of covert operations.

Without him, I wouldn't have been crouching behind a ten-thousand-ton concrete column holding up the Bridge of the Americas in Panama. Without him, I wouldn't have been watching three men unload bricks of plastic explosive from a wooden crate.

The Huey's blades slapped against the sky, and I looked up to see Clark and Leo heading south out of the mouth of the canal. I'd seen enough to know the men on the boat weren't heading to a salvage job with their explosives; they were going to create salvage work for some unfortunate souls. And I planned to stop them.

11
Fallen Devil

It's impossible to do anything in a Huey and not be seen, but Clark and Leo plucked me off the beach efficiently and covertly in that lumbering beast of an aircraft. I found my way to my seat and donned my headset.

Clark wasted no time probing me for intel. "What did you learn?"

"It's plastic explosive, and they're unpacking the crates and loading the bricks into airtight plastic bags. I counted at least three hundred pounds, but there's probably more."

"Did anybody see you?" asked Leo.

"Well, I'm sure someone did, but the guys on the boat were too worried about the explosives to look for me. They didn't even seem to notice the chopper when you came back across the bridge."

"That's good," he said. "Other than paranoia, there's no reason they'd suspect anyone to be watching them."

"Where did the other boat go?" I asked.

"They went up the creek at Corozal and tied up in the trees. It looked like they were unpacking the explosives as well, but I couldn't tell if they were bagging them." Clark was talking with his hands, demonstrating how the creek angled northeast off the canal at the little town of Corozal.

"Why would they put plastic explosives in plastic bags?" I asked, hoping Clark or Leo knew more about the explosives than I did.

"I don't know," came the answer in unison.

"All right," I said. "Let's get out of here and check in with Ginger. We need to know where the Pearl is. I know a little devil who's just itching to get aboard that thing."

Without a word, Leo turned the chopper back to the south and started picking up speed. We were soon back on Bona. I climbed out of the Huey and noticed Diablo once again had something cooking over a small fire at the edge of the clearing. Upon closer inspection, I saw it was a turtle and two snakes, and though I needed the calories, nothing about it appealed to me. The more I thought about trying to stomach that meal, the better the MREs sounded.

I should've been more open-minded about the turtle and snakes. Dinner was far better than I'd feared. It didn't taste like chicken, but it wasn't bad.

"I think we should check in with Ginger," I said.

Diablo's eyes lit up. So far, I'd heard the man say less than a dozen words, and I'd only seen three expressions from him: grinning, somber, and glee at the mention of Ginger. He rarely focused on any one object for more than a few seconds, but every time he glanced at me, he stared as if he knew me from somewhere but couldn't quite remember my name. I found the look unnerving, but I wrote it off as another peculiarity of a particularly strange little guy.

Ginger's face filled the screen of the laptop computer. She called Leo, Clark, and me by name, but when she came to Diablo, she winked and smiled a devilish little smirk, displaying her gorgeous dimples. "You're the only reason I hope to get kidnapped someday, Diablo. I just know you'd come rescue me."

He blushed.

I wonder if women know how much power they have over us weak men.

"Okay, enough *Love Connection*. Where's our ship?" Leo demanded.

"I thought you'd be calling about that very thing. She's nine hours south-southwest of Isla Del Ray and making just under twenty-three knots."

"Perfect," I said, not realizing I'd actually said it out loud.

Everyone turned to me as if I'd been given the floor.

"Sorry," I mumbled. "I didn't mean to interrupt. I was just thinking about the timing."

"It's okay," said Ginger. "I was thinking the same. Have you come up with a plan to get my little Latin god on that ship safely?"

Diablo smiled and continued staring at the screen.

"Yeah, we'll put him on board tonight," Leo said. "I figure they'll be in the first set of locks at daybreak."

"What else do you need from me?" asked Ginger.

"Are there any other ships in close proximity to the *Pearl*?" I asked.

"I thought you might want to know that little tidbit of information," she said. "There are no ships anywhere near the *Pearl*; however, there's a cruise ship steaming from the west that looks like she'll arrive at the south end of the canal at about the same time as the *Pearl*. She's a Holland America ship, and at the moment, they are a DAT at the southern entrance to the canal."

"What's a DAT?" I asked.

"Dead ass tie," said Ginger. "They'll get there at the same time if neither changes course or speed."

I laughed. "Thanks, Ginger."

Leo closed the connection. "We'd better get moving."

We pulled down the camo netting, Diablo covered all evidence of the fire, and then we were airborne.

With the island of San Jose forty miles away, we made the flight in twenty-five minutes at barely above the tops of the waves.

"They've got pretty good radar up at International. I'd rather not have anybody wondering who we are." Leo tried to explain the wavetop flying, but I think it was just an excuse to show off.

There was a dirt runway cut into the east side of San Jose, and Leo put the Huey down at the northwest end in a blinding cloud of red dust and sand. When the cloud settled, Leo said, "Come on. Help me with the gas."

Leo had the most interesting fuel stops of any pilot I'd ever met. We rolled five fifty-five-gallon barrels of jet fuel out of the jungle.

Leo attached a hand pump to the top of one of the barrels and con-nected the hose to the tank on the Huey. After cranking until I thought my arm was going to fall off, we topped off the Huey and stashed the barrels back in the tree line.

Diablo was lying on his side, sound asleep on the floor of the Huey.

"Does he always do that?" I asked

"That'll probably be the last sleep he gets for the next few days."

I wondered what went on inside Diablo's head. *Is he as wild as he appears to be? Is he insane? Am I?*

We ate MREs, meals ready to eat, from thick, plastic bags, and thought about what the night would bring. The sun disappeared behind the trees, and the jungle environment of the island came to life with the sounds of animals that dared not make a sound in the light of day.

The demands that were about to be placed on our shoulders were greater than most men would ever bear, but we'd gladly shoul-der the burden for the millions of Americans who unknowingly hid behind the protection we provided. They'd never know us, but we'd never stop beating back the wolves at the gates. Those wolves would never stop coming, and I prayed we'd never quit beating them back.

"Get some sleep," said Leo. "Diablo will wake us up when it's time to go."

I rolled out my sleeping bag to provide at least some measure of padding. I didn't understand how Diablo could sleep on the hard, aluminum floor of the Huey. I draped mosquito netting over myself to avoid falling victim to the swarms of insects that owned the night in the rainforest.

To say that I slept would not be accurate. It was more like a rest-less, slow-motion wrestling match with my sleeping bag. Perhaps I caught a few minutes of sleep, but certainly not enough. Diablo left the chopper and faced the northern sky. The cup of the Big Dipper was falling below the horizon, indicating that it was almost mid-night at eight degrees north of the equator. Diablo's clock was far more dependable than my watch.

I folded my mosquito netting and rolled my sleeping bag into a tight ball while Diablo woke Clark, then Leo, who'd been snoring for hours. Clark stretched his arms over his head and yawned broadly. Diablo knelt beside Leo and whispered something, and then they turned to look at me. I didn't like whatever was happening.

Leo climbed down from the Huey after completing his preflight inspection. "Are you boys ready to go play hide the devil with the Chi-coms?"

Diablo was wearing a pair of black cargo pants and a long-sleeved, skin-tight black shirt, looking like the ninja he was described as being. He took up his position as far back in the chopper as possible, while Clark and Leo climbed into the cockpit. I took my seat just behind the cockpit and pulled on my headset. The old chopper whistled to life, and the rotor blades turned slowly, but soon they were nearly invisible in their racing arc above the fuselage. The cloud of dust had settled, and we were soon clear of the rocky coastline of the island.

Leo pulled a pair of night vision goggles down over his eyes and flew the old chopper along the tops of the waves at nearly two miles per minute.

"You ready to talk some Chinese bullshit, there, Baby Face?"

Clark cocked his eye at Leo, who looked like a mustached bug beneath the night vision goggles. "You just worry about finding that ship, and I'll worry about talking us in and back out, old man."

"Old man?" Leo scoffed. "I'll show you that an old man can kick your young ass if you don't start showing me some respect."

"Sure you will," laughed Clark. "As long as you don't break a hip."

The lights of the coast were invisible soon after takeoff. It was easy to believe we were the only humans on Earth, but as Diablo sat motionless, silent, and perched on a Pelican case, I doubted he was actually human.

Diablo wasn't the only silent one aboard. As if an unseen force had consumed the chopper, no one spoke a word as we scoured the horizon, searching for the AAS *Pearl*.

How hard can it be to spot one of the largest freighters to ever sail through the Panama Canal?

Finally, the lights of the gargantuan freighter came into sight, and Leo playfully punched Clark's shoulder. "Well, look what I found, Baby Face. It's time you turn on that Chinese charm and earn your keep."

Diablo was tying a small dry bag around his waist and peering through the windscreen toward the *Pearl*. He pulled on a pair of thin black gloves and crawled toward the door of the chopper. He moved like a cat, his every movement perfectly intentional, and the look on his face was one of utter concentration.

The nose of the Huey rose, and the bulk of the massive freighter loomed in front of us. As we climbed toward the superstructure of the ship, I saw a terrifying view of the windscreen full of cargo containers. Leo flipped the switch, sending voltage to the powerful searchlight mounted beneath the nose of the chopper.

Clark yelled, "*Bāng women! Women mílùle! Todì shì no tiáo lù?*" into the handheld, marine VHF radio.

My Mandarin is terrible, and what I know of Cantonese would fit in a thimble, but I was pretty sure that roughly translated to, "Help us! We are lost! Which way is land?"

Leo tried to look like a lost, frightened pilot and shined the searchlight directly into the bridge of the freighter.

The ship's radio operator said, "*Guān dēng! Dōng!*"

Even in my limited understanding, I knew that meant something like "Turn off that damned light and fly east."

Leo kept the bridge illuminated and yelled over his shoulder, "*Vaya con Dios, Diablo!*"

Diablo grabbed my arms and looked at me. He said, "*Olvidate de las esclusas. Protege el puente. Archie estaría muy orgulloso de ti.*" Then he lunged through the open door and plummeted into the night.

I dived for the door and watched him fall toward the containers and onto the deck of the mighty freighter. I remembered my descent from a helicopter onto the deck of a similar but smaller ship northeast of Havana. The impact of landing on the container had sent waves of pain through my legs and into my back. My fall had been ten feet, but Diablo had just fallen at least twice that distance and landed like a pouncing cougar. His motion never stopped as he continued forward, rolling over the edge of the container and scampering down the side like a spider. He disappeared into the chasm of darkness between the containers.

I felt the Huey bank left and pick up speed. Leo kept the light trained on the bridge as we clumsily flew away toward the east. Once clear of the mountains of containers on the deck, we dived for the surface of the ocean and continued accelerating until the freighter was nothing more than a flickering dot on the western horizon.

Diablo's words finally hit me. I was so surprised to hear him speak in complete sentences that I hadn't let his words sink into my head.

He'd said, "Forget about the locks. Protect the bridge." That was simple enough, but the last thing he said was, "Archie would be proud of you."

My father, James Alan Fulton, had been such a fan of the Archie cartoons that everyone who knew him well called him Archie. Diablo had just told me that my father would be proud of me.

A shiver of emotion ran through my spine as I tried to piece together how Diablo could've possibly known my father. And more importantly, was it possible that he knew the truth about what happened to my family?

Does he have the answers I've been seeking for over a decade? How will I be able to pin him down and get him to tell me what he knows? Will I ever see him again?

12
Negotiating 101 in Panama

The hour-long flight back to Bona felt like it took all night. I couldn't stop thinking about what Diablo had said, but I was going to have to find a way to push that to the back of my mind. There was far too much to do over the coming forty-eight hours to be focused on something a madman said just before he jumped from a helicopter and onto the deck of a freighter.

The clearing where we'd landed on Bona was a challenging landing site in the daylight with no wind, and the night delivered a whole new set of challenges. Leo had night vision goggles, but it was still windy, and there was no visible moon. Apparently, he was up for the challenge. He set the Huey down as gently as if it were a calm summer day.

"Not bad," offered Clark.

Leo chuckled. "You do anything long enough, and you're bound to get good at it or die."

We tied the blades and waited for the engine to cool before hauling the camo netting up and over the chopper again. Our cook was aboard a Chinese freighter somewhere at sea, and we were famished. It was MREs again, but I would've preferred another snake.

Clark had anticipation in his eyes. "So, what do we do now, boss?"

"We finish our shopping trip," I said.

Clark cocked his head as if he wasn't following.

"We never finished our boat shopping trip. We got interrupted by a couple boatloads of plastic explosives."

"Oh, yeah. You're right. Leo said he knew a guy if we had the cash."

Leo yawned. "We'll go see him as soon as the sun comes up. I'm going to get some sleep 'til then. Since our perimeter guard is learning his way around a Chinese ship, I guess it'll be up to you two to make sure nobody sneaks up on us."

"Well," said Clark, "since you're in charge, I guess I'll stand watch. Besides, I don't need as much sleep as you soft civilians do."

"You'll get no argument from me," I said. "It's good to be king."

Either no one cared that we were there, or Clark held the bandits at bay. No unexpected visitors surprised us overnight.

As the sun began heating the morning jungle air, we lifted off and headed north. I was surprised when we landed at the Panama Pacifico International Airport and actually bought fuel from a real fuel truck. I'd begun to believe Leo had an endless supply of jet fuel stashed all over the Central American jungle.

"Your Spanish is pretty good, right, Pretty Boy?" Leo raised eyebrows at me.

"Yeah, I'd say it's a little better than pretty good."

"Good. In that case, I need you to listen up when we get to where we're going. Let me know if anybody says something like, 'Shoot the old guy with the helicopter,' or 'That's him. Get him.'"

I laughed. "Okay, I can do that. But where are we going?"

"To get you a boat, kid. Try to keep up."

We lifted off from Panama Pacifico and headed north again, but we were back on the ground in less than two minutes. Leo shut down the Huey and cautiously stepped to the ground.

Clark's eyes were wide, and he was obviously thinking the same thing I was. "What is this place, Leo?"

Leo looked around nervously. "This is Naval Base Vasco Nuñez de Balboa. This is where we'll find my friend with your boat . . . if we don't get shot first."

"What do you mean, if we don't get shot first? Is this guy your friend or not?" I demanded.

"Yeah, Pablo's my friend, but I have a bit of a history with the Panamanian Navy. I'm not their favorite hombre. As long as we can get to Pablo before we come across anyone else who knows me, we'll probably be fine."

"Probably?" Clark and I echoed.

Before we'd made it twenty steps away from the chopper, two Panamanian sailors pulled up in what looked like part of an old Datsun truck with no glass and no bed. A pair of wooden pallets were strapped to the frame behind the cab. I listened closely, hoping nothing like "Shoot the old guy" came out of their mouths.

"*Buenos días, señor,*" one of the sailors offered in a friendly, unthreatening tone. Around their waists were green web belts with holstered sidearms. A pair of rifles rested on the seat of the truck.

"We need to see Pablo, *el hombre del barco,*" Leo said without offering any greeting. I thought that was bad form, but I was a long way from home and in someone else's backyard.

"*Sí, sí. Ven con nosotros,*" said the driver.

Leo glanced at me.

"They want to take us to Pablo," I said, pointing toward the wooden pallets.

We climbed aboard and headed east toward the canal. We rounded an old, dilapidated building with rusty siding and only part of a roof.

"*Pablo esta ahi,*" said the driver.

"Pablo's in there," I said.

I thanked the driver and slipped him an American ten-dollar bill. He smiled and drove away, leaving a cloud of white smoke behind him.

We rounded the corner of the decrepit building and found a shirtless man sanding the bottom of an old metal patrol boat lying upside down on the dirt floor.

"*Pablo! Mi amigo! Cómo estás?*"

Pablo's eyes lit up over his dust mask. He threw down his sander, wiped himself off, and ran toward Leo. The two embraced and had a little reunion.

Pablo's English was good; certainly much better than Leo's Spanish.

"Guys, this is Pablo, the boat guy. Pablo, meet Pretty Boy and Baby Face. They'd like to rent a boat from you, but they only have American dollars. You still take American dollars, don't you?"

Pablo's eyes lit up even more at the mention of good old American greenbacks.

"What sort of boat do you want, my friends?"

"Something relatively fast—maybe sixty or seventy kilometers per hour—and something we can use as a dive boat. We'll need to be able to climb back into the boat from the water without much problem."

"Sí, sí. I have just the boat for you, amigos. Follow me."

We walked out of the building and toward a fenced compound full of every variation of boat. Some were barely recognizable as boats, while others looked almost new.

"Are all of these for sale?" I asked as I scanned the compound.

"No, no. Just the one you want. You cannot have all."

I laughed at the misunderstanding brought about by the language barrier, but I supposed he was correct.

"Oh, I don't want them all. I just want that one." I pointed toward a rigid hull inflatable boat in the corner of the compound with "La Seguridad" stenciled on each side of the partially deflated tubes. Most of the time, appearances are accepted as fact, and needing to belong anywhere I wanted to be on the water, that was the cover I needed. No one would question a safety boat.

"Oh, very good choice, amigo. I will take off writing on boat for you. Is for you two thousand dollars U.S. because you are amigo for Leo."

"How much is it if I'm not Leo's amigo?"

"Is only one thousand then," Pablo said, then burst into a fit of laughter so hard he could barely stay on his feet.

Leo stuck out his bottom lip, demonstrating his best hurt-feelings look.

"Come, come, amigo. I am only kidding with you." Pablo patted Leo's shoulder.

"I'll tell you what we'll do," I said. "You leave the writing on the boat, and I'll buy the boat from you for three thousand dollars U.S., but if I bring it back to you within three days, you'll give me back a thousand dollars. How does that sound?"

Pablo closed one eye and looked toward the sky with the other. I could almost see the wheels turning.

"No, I think I do not like that idea, amigo. I think I only sell you the boat, and you do not bring back to me. Is for you to keep for two thousand dollars."

I mirrored Pablo's eye-closed, thoughtful posture, and I paused for dramatic effect. "Okay. Two thousand, and I keep the boat, but you've never met me, never heard of me, and you have no idea where the La Seguridad boat went."

I placed twenty hundred-dollar bills in Pablo's hand.

"What boat?" he said. "I don't know what you are talking about."

I smiled in appreciation of his understanding. I knew playing by the rules was not the way to get things done in Central America.

"You top it off and put it in the water, and we'll grab our gear," I instructed.

Pablo furrowed his brow. "Do you mean you want to buy petrol for *your* boat and for me to launch *your* boat for you, señor? That will be one hundred dollars to launch and one hundred dollars for petro . . . U.S. dollars, of course."

"Fifty for the launch and fifty for petrol."

"For one hundred you can have petrol or launch. Which do you want, señor?"

I handed Pablo two more bills and admired his negotiating skills. He smiled and went to work.

Clark and I requisitioned an old flatbed mule, a Korean War–era motorized cart used by the military to haul munitions and almost anything else that would fit on the bed. We unloaded our Pelican cases from the Huey and motored back toward our new boat.

Pablo had kept his word and hefted our boat, tubes now fully inflated, into the water and was filling the tanks with petrol. We loaded our gear aboard, and Pablo finished with the tanks. He sat down on the bank as if he were waiting for something else to happen.

I gave him an obvious look of curiosity, and he got the hint.

"I am waiting for you to start your boat. Everybody is happy customer."

It took several tries for the engine to fire, but when it did, it purred like a kitten. Well, like a large, powerful, angry kitten.

Clark keyed the mic on his handheld radio. "Leo, we'll meet you back at Bona after a little reconnaissance."

13

Don't Make Me Hurt You

Our boat was perfect. She hopped out of the water and onto plane in seconds and skimmed across the surface at over sixty knots. It was two thousand dollars well spent.

I decided we'd run up the creek at Corozal where Leo and Clark had seen the second workboat tie up with the load of explosives. I wanted to make sure it was still there and loaded with the cargo we'd expected. We quickly made the two-and-a-half-mile trip to the mouth of the creek.

I pulled back the throttle and slowed to just above idle speed, staying as quiet as possible. I'd much prefer arriving undetected than to garner the unwanted attention a high-speed boat in the creek would surely receive.

Clark pointed into a bend in the creek where a small slough cut off to the east. "There she is."

The workboat sat well-camouflaged beneath a canopy of overhanging trees. We idled by the boat, trying to appear uninterested. There seemed to be no one aboard. All of the hatches were secured, and there was no air conditioner that I could see. If anyone were closed up inside the boat, they'd be roasting in the Panamanian mid-morning heat. Even as resilient as the Panamanian people are, I couldn't imagine anyone choosing to be in that oven.

I continued up the creek until I found an inlet into the trees that was barely big enough to stick my boat in. I ran the fiberglass hull onto the rocky mud, and Clark quickly tied us to the trunk of a small tree. I pulled open the engine hatch, snatched the coil wire from the top of the engine, and pocketed it. I didn't need anyone making off with my new boat while I was out sniffing around for explosives.

We made our way through the thick brush and trees until we came to a spot where we could easily see the workboat. We watched in silence, hoping that if anyone were aboard, they'd move enough to cause the boat to sway, but it lay perfectly still in the calm, murky waters of the stagnant creek.

"If there's anybody on board, they're either asleep or dead," Clark whispered. "Either way, I think it's safe to board."

I nodded, and we made our way toward the boat, never taking our eyes off the deck. When we were less than two steps away, Clark whispered, "Shake or storm?"

Shaking the boat would mean giving up the element of surprise if there were, in fact, anyone aboard.

I said, "Storm."

We leapt to the deck and headed straight for the cabin door. The crate of explosives that we'd seen on deck the day before was gone, but we soon discovered another surprise I couldn't believe we'd both missed on the recon pass. The door into the pilothouse was secured with a hasp and padlock. If there was anyone inside, they were securely locked in from the outside.

"How did we not see that?" said Clark.

I shrugged and drew my pick set from the pocket of my cargo pants. I soon had the lock picked, and we were inside. There was no ventilation, and the boat smelled like a pigsty. There were four sets of foul-weather gear hanging from hooks on the forward bulkhead, and heavy rubber boots sat on the deck beneath each. Beyond the bulkhead were two neatly stacked sets of dive gear, including rebreathers and sophisticated dive computers. The gear and what lay just beside it were the only things in the pilothouse arranged in anything resembling order. To the left of the dive gear was a dilapidated wooden shelf with a stack of blasting caps and several coils of wire.

"Looks like they're planning to make a little noise," said Clark.

I pulled at a hatch in the deck of the cabin, hoping to find the plastic explosive. Before I could get the hatch fully open, I heard a sound that is unmistakable and impossible to ignore: the racking of a pump shotgun.

In angry Spanish, the voice behind the shotgun said, "Get on your knees and put your hands on top of your head. Now!"

Clark bore his eyes into mine. I knew he was asking himself the same question beating around in my infuriated brain. *Why didn't one of us post at the door for security?*

We had no choice but to obey. We hit our knees and laced our fingers together atop our heads. Mosquitoes swarmed through the open door and played at our noses, eyes, and ears. The urge to swat was almost irresistible.

The gunman pointed the barrel of the shotgun at Clark. "You, lie down. Facedown, with your hands on top of each other in front of you. Do it now!"

Clark obeyed, and the man powered the heel of his boot down on Clark's hands, causing him to yell out in pain. Then he stuck the shotgun barrel inches from my nose.

It was an American gun; a twelve-gauge Mossberg. I owned a nearly identical one, but I'd never seen it from that particular perspective. It's easy to be brave in principle, but it's a little tougher when you're looking down the barrel of a weapon that could instantly turn your head into Swiss cheese. Beads of sweat rolled down my face and the back of my neck. I swallowed hard and tried to keep breathing. I didn't know if the man intended to kill me, but based on how he'd chosen to subdue Clark, I believed he was well trained and potentially dangerous. I briefly considered grabbing the barrel and taking my chances in a wrestling match for the gun, but I was afraid I'd get Clark shot in the melee.

Before I could develop a plan to overpower the gunman, he tossed a pair of handcuffs onto the deck in front of me. "Put these on. Do it now!"

Shit. This guy isn't just well trained; he's a pro. We're in more trouble than I thought.

I lifted the cuffs from the deck and clasped them first onto my right wrist, and then my left. I took my time, careful to make no sudden moves that might make his trigger finger twitch. I was working out a plan, but it wasn't a good one.

The man raised the shotgun and hammered the butt into my shoulder in an obvious attempt to break my collarbone. I rolled my shoulder forward to deflect the blow, and I was knocked to the deck. Never removing his foot from Clark's hands, the man planted his knee on the back of my head, forcing my face against the ground. While I was pinned down with blood pouring from my nose, the man grasped the handcuffs, clinching them tighter until my hands tingled and paled.

It occurred to me that the man had just given me a vise—a pair of metal rings with a solid steel chain between them.

He placed the muzzle beneath my chin. "Get up slowly."

Perfect. He's playing right into my hand . . . cuffs.

I raised my right leg and put my foot on the deck. Placing my cuffed hands on my right knee for leverage, I stood as he'd ordered. As I started upward, I thrust my hands skyward and laced the chain of my cuffs just behind the slide while forcing the barrel of the shotgun up and over my right shoulder. With Clark on my left, there would be no way the gunman could hit him even if he did panic and squeeze the trigger. The positioning of the chain on my cuffs would prevent the gunman from racking the slide to chamber another round, but he'd have no choice but to take his foot from Clark's hands and dance with me.

I wrapped my hands around the receiver of the shotgun and forced the man backward, then waited for the inevitable echoing report of the gun. It would temporarily deafen me, but that was the least of my worries. I was far more concerned with the gunman getting away than getting off a shot. If he dropped the shotgun and ran, I wouldn't be able to get a shot off in time to stop him. I needed him to stay and fight.

Before the man could make his primordial fight-or-flight decision, Clark grabbed the heel of the man's right foot and yanked it
forward with incredible force. That threw the man off balance and
sent him falling backward. I continued pushing him, hoping he'd
release the shotgun as part of his natural reflex to catch himself. Instead, he clung to the weapon with all of his might. The force of his
weight falling backward pulled me with him as I gripped the gun
even tighter. I wasn't sure where the muzzle would fall when we finally hit the deck together, so I lunged, thrusting from the balls of
my feet to force the muzzle higher, and hopefully, over the gunman's
head. I didn't want the gun to go off, even if the shot flew harmlessly through the pilothouse door. A shotgun blast tends to draw a
lot of unwanted attention, even in Central America.

We crashed to the deck with a thundering collision of my weight
dropping solidly on top of the gunman. He let out a breathy grunt
and finally released his grip on the weapon. Clark jumped from the
deck and landed a knee squarely in the man's crotch. That little gift
sent more than a grunt through the man's throat. Before the echo of
the man's cry had left the cabin, Clark landed a chop to the side of
his neck, rendering him immediately unconscious.

I knelt beside the man's limp form and searched his pockets for
the handcuff key. I found it and quickly removed my cuffs, rubbing
my wrists and hoping to restore the circulation and feeling in my
hands.

Clark stepped over me, picked up the shotgun, and stepped
through the door. I watched him scan the tree line and then reenter
the cabin. "He's a single. I don't see anyone else out there."

"Good," I said, pulling the man's body toward a makeshift
wooden seat. I cuffed his right hand to a pipe on the starboard gunwale and slapped at his face, trying to wake him up.

Clark stood in the doorway, dividing his attention between the
exterior and the interior of the boat. He wasn't going to let another
surprise visitor show up unchallenged.

The man showed signs of waking up. To help ease him from his siesta, I found a bottle of water and threw it in his face. He gasped and spewed, then finally opened his eyes.

He focused on me and then on Clark holding the shotgun. The man shook his head in obvious self-disgust. Even though he'd been well trained, armed, and had the element of surprise, his expression showed he knew he'd chosen the wrong duo to face single-handedly.

I slapped his face twice more. "Look at me! Focus. You're going to answer some questions."

He responded in rapid-fire Spanish, saying he wasn't alone and that his team would be there any minute to rescue him and kill both of us.

I didn't sense conviction in his tone; I heard desperation and fear. If his team truly had been coming, he would've waited for them before attempting to overpower us and take back his boat. Maybe he wasn't quite the professional I'd pegged him to be. We'd soon find out.

I switched to Spanish. "What's your name?"

He spat in my face and thrashed against his restraints.

I smiled, wiped the spittle from my face, and threw an elbow to his left temple. His lights went out again.

"This guy's got a glass jaw," I said. "I don't know how we're going to keep him conscious."

Clark found green peppers beside a propane single-burner stove and bit the tip of one. He immediately spat the small piece of green pepper from his lips, and I watched a tear form in his eye.

"Oh, yeah. This'll do it." He handed me the pepper.

I forced it past the man's lips then slammed his mouth closed. He came sputtering and spitting back to life, tears streaming from both eyes.

"Stop passing out," I demanded.

He raised his left hand to his mouth and clawed at his lips in a vain attempt to cool the burn Clark's pepper had caused. I pulled another bottle of water from the crate behind me, opened it, and then held it in front of the man's face. He reached for it, and I quickly squeezed, crushing the plastic bottle and forcing over half of the contents straight up his nose. He reached for my throat, and I captured his thumb with my right hand. I twisted his wrist outward and down, pulling the muscles, tendons, and ligaments to their limits. The man opened his mouth to howl, and I threw a half-speed uppercut to his chin. I knew a real punch would send him back to the spirit world, and I needed him to stay with me and have a little chat. Blood flew from his chin and mouth, and his body surrendered. Although his mind may have possessed the desire to fight, his body had lost the ability.

"Now, let's try this again. What is your name?"

"Javier," came his weak response.

"Javier what?"

"Javier Ramirez."

"Is this your boat, Javier Ramirez?"

"No, it is not my boat. It is my boss's boat."

"Who is your boss?"

He closed his eyes and slowly shook his head side to side.

"I'm not a patient man, Javier. Don't make me hurt you. Tell me who you work for."

He pressed his lips together.

I grasped his index finger and yanked his hand up in front of his face.

"Do you like this finger, Javier?"

He closed his eyes again and whispered a Hail Mary.

"It's a little late for prayers, Javi. Who's your boss?"

He inhaled and stilled himself for the punishment I was about to unleash.

The psychology of interrogation is fascinating. It's okay to lie. It's okay to cheat. It's okay to scream or whisper, but it is never okay to appear weak. I'd threatened to break his finger, and I had to follow through. Anything less would only serve to embolden my captive and strengthen his resolve to resist.

I folded his left index finger across the back of his hand and felt it snap as the metacarpals succumbed to the force. He bellowed in pain, but I quickly shoved the water bottle into his mouth, muffling his scream.

I'd established that I wasn't going to tolerate his unwillingness to cooperate. Javier had just learned that I was a man of my word. If I threatened it, I would do it.

"Tell me who you work for."

He squeezed his eyes shut, spat out the plastic water bottle, and grunted. I yanked his broken finger forward, bringing it almost back in line with the remaining fingers. It felt like a sausage link in my grip.

"Okay, Javi. You win. I don't give a shit who you work for. Let's move on. Where are the explosives?"

Subconsciously, he cast his eyes toward the deck hatch behind me.

"Oh, is that right? They're down there, huh?"

I watched his Adam's apple rise and fall as he swallowed hard. He took a long, full breath, and nodded.

Clark flung open the hatch and shined a flashlight into the hold of the boat.

"Yep, there they are. Looks like three or four hundred pounds, nicely bagged and stacked."

I grabbed Javier's broken finger, pulling and shaking it as the swelling started to build. It was already turning black and had doubled in size.

"Would you look at that?" I said. "Do you know what swelling is, Javi?" I paused for dramatic effect. "Swelling is God's little splint. Don't worry. The pain will be over soon. Your brain will accept the trauma and block out the pain in *that* finger, but lucky for me, you have four more on that hand I can work on. Are you ready for number two?"

I wrapped my hand firmly around his pinky finger, and I moved in close. His breath stank of coffee, cigarettes, and jalapeno pepper.

"What are you going to do with those explosives, Javi?"

He must have found courage from somewhere deep within his soul, because the man turned to stone. His small, dark eyes stared straight ahead, and he didn't breathe.

I applied a few pounds of pressure to his pinky. His eyes bulged and his nostrils flared, but he still didn't speak.

"This is your last chance. Tell me what you were planning to do with those explosives."

He was silent, and I was once again forced to prove my resolve. I twisted the finger and folded it against the bottom of his hand. It snapped like a twig with remarkably little pressure. I wasn't prepared for it to break so easily. Instead of returning the finger to its original position, I forced his hand downward and pounded it against the gunwale. His eyes wilted and sweat cascaded down his face. I dropped his hand from my grasp and slapped at his face again.

"No, no, no, Javi. Don't you pass out again. We've still got work to do. Tell me what you were going to do with the explosives, and I'll stop breaking your fingers."

He shook his head like he was trying to shake off a bad headache.

"I don't know," he said.

"I don't believe you. Do you believe him, Clark?"

"Hell no. I don't believe him. Break a couple more then give him another chance to tell the truth."

I shoved his hand to his left knee, held it there, and picked up a heavy wrench from the deck. I quickly raised the wrench above my head. Javier's eyes rushed to the wrench and then back to his broken, swollen hand. The dark skin of his face turned gray.

He whimpered, "I . . . I . . ."

"You what?" I demanded.

Again, he turned to stone. I was impressed with his resolve, but I had no choice. The threat had been made, and I had to follow through. I hammered the wrench into the knuckles of his middle and ring finger, instantly crushing the bones and ripping open the flesh. He wailed as blood gushed from his hand.

I shoved the greasy, bloody wrench into his mouth to stop the bellowing. He bit down on the metal tool and whimpered like a child as I forced it against the corner of his mouth.

"You're not very good at this game, Javier. All you have to do is answer my questions, and I'll stop. You can go home to your family or your goats or whatever you have. Just answer my questions."

"You're a dead man," he breathed.

"I don't think you're in much of a position to be making threats, Javi. You had your chance to kill me, and you weren't man enough to pull the trigger. Now, I'm in charge. If you say one more word that isn't a direct answer to my questions, I'm going to do far worse than break your fingers. Do you understand?"

"What I understand is that you can do whatever you want to me, but you'll be dead before the sun goes down," he hissed.

I stood and planted my right knee in the bend of his elbow, trapping his arm against his thigh. I forcefully grabbed his hand. "One last chance, Javi. What were you planning to do with the explosives?"

He opened his mouth, bared his teeth, and lunged for my thigh. Before he could sink his teeth into my flesh, I twisted his bloody, broken hand through half a rotation, and felt the bones of his wrist surrender to the torque. He let out an animalistic groan, and his head fell limply to his chest.

"Damn it. He's out again." I released his arm and stood erect in the cabin. "I don't think he's going to talk."

Clark was still guarding the door. "They always talk," he said. "You just have to keep pushing. He'll break if you've got the stomach to push him far enough."

I drank a bottle of water and waited for Javier to return to the land of the living, though I knew that was the last place his brain wanted to be. He was much more content in the pain-free confines of the spirit world.

When he finally came to, Clark pressed the muzzle of the shotgun against Javier's top lip and leaned in. "Hey, Javier. I just want you to know that I want to kill you. I want to blow your worthless head all over this boat, but I'm not in charge. He is." Clark motioned toward me with his head. "I'm on your team, Javi. I want to end your pain, but my buddy here is crazy. He gets off on this kind of stuff. It's hard for me to watch, but I'm just hired muscle. I don't get to make decisions. Good luck."

Clark's Spanish was good enough to send a look of deepening dread into Javier's eyes, and he let the muzzle of the shotgun fall from the man's face and land in his crotch. The fear in Javier's eyes turned to terror, and he stopped breathing.

"Go ahead. Ask him again. I think his memory might be somewhere right around . . ."—Clark prodded at the man's groin with the shotgun—". . . here."

"Okay," I said. "One more try, Javi. What were you planning to do with the explosives?"

He thrust what was left of his left hand toward his crotch and yelled, "The locks! The locks. We were going to blow the locks!"

"When?" I whispered.

Clark pressed the muzzle deeper into the man's lap.

"When the big ship is in there," he panted.

"Good boy," I said. "Now, goodnight, Javi."

Clark drove the butt of the shotgun into the man's face, sending blood spraying in every direction, and his head fell backward like a ragdoll.

14
Down She Goes

"Is he dead?"

I felt for a pulse. "No, he's still alive, but he's going to wish he was dead. What should we do with him?"

Clark frowned. "We can't leave him here. When his buddies find him, they'll know we're watching, and we'll lose what little advantage we have now. We'll have to take him with us."

I looked down at his badly broken hand. "He's going to need a doctor."

"Yeah, he is, but we can't risk having him warn anyone that we're here. We'll splint it and keep him doped up on morphine until we can drop him in someone else's lap."

Returning to the task I'd begun before our now unconscious visitor arrived, I pulled open the deck hatch and shined a light into the hold. It was stacked with bricks of plastic explosive.

"We can't just leave this C4 in here. If they're thinking of blowing up the locks, we have to stop them."

Clark peered around my shoulder and into the hold. He let out a soft whistle. "That's a lot of C4, but our instructions were to observe, not initiate contact."

"We are well outside our mission parameters already," I said. "I can't, in good conscience, just let them blow up a lock. Sinking a ship in the lock is one thing, but are we really supposed to do nothing to stop them?"

"I don't know, but I don't like anything about it. The whole thing smells bad to me."

I checked our perimeter for anyone else approaching, but I saw no one.

"I need to tell you something that Diablo said to me before he jumped from the Huey."

Clark had been counting detonators but stopped what he was doing and faced me. "Okay, let's hear it."

"He told me to forget about the locks and protect the bridge."

Clark seemed to be considering what I'd said. He rummaged through a first aid kit and pulled out a package of smelling salts. He broke the vial and held it beneath the unconscious man's nose, and slapped him awake.

"Welcome back, asshole. Does your hand hurt?"

The man looked at his demolished hand and let out several whimpers.

Clark uncuffed his right hand and grabbed his thumb with a pair of pliers from the toolbox. The man shuttered in terror and tried to pull away.

"Listen to me very closely," Clark said. "You lied to us. You're not planning to blow up the locks. You're going after the bridge. Now you're going to pay dearly for that lie."

Clark planted his boot squarely in the man's chest, forcing him back against the gunwale, then squeezed and twisted his thumb with the pliers.

He screamed in terror. "No! No! I did not lie. We are supposed to blow the locks. The others are going for the bridge, but not us. Please! I'm telling the truth. Please stop."

Clark stopped twisting but continued applying pressure to the thumb, which was oozing blood from the torn flesh beneath the jaws of the pliers.

"How many teams are there?"

The man stared at the pliers and then spoke between each struggled inhale. "Two teams. Four men on each team. Please let me go.

I will go far away, and you will never see me again. Please. I need a doctor. Please don't kill me."

"Oh, no. That's not going to happen, Javi. If we let you go, you'll tell your team leader all about us. We can't have that. I've got a much better idea. Get on your feet. Now!"

He stumbled to his feet, knees trembling, and his face contorted in pain.

Clark dragged the man through the pilothouse and handcuffed his unbroken wrist to the wheel.

"Here's what's going to happen," said Clark. "You're going to drive this boat into the ocean, and we're going to sink it. I haven't decided yet if I'm going to uncuff you before we sink it. That depends on how well you behave."

The man's body was trembling, and he'd stopped sweating. His body was in the early stages of what would become severe shock.

"I think we'd better give him something to sit on. He's not going to stay on his feet much longer," I said, sliding a stool toward the helm.

Clark dug through the first aid kit and found a vial of morphine. He injected the man with a partial dose to ease some of the pain he was experiencing.

"I'll cast off and follow about three minutes behind," I said.

I left Clark and Javier aboard the workboat and leapt back to the bank. The crew had used a small Danforth anchor on a short section of rope to secure the workboat to the muddy bank. After working the anchor free, I laid it back aboard the metal deck. I tried to give it a shove away from the bank, but instead of moving the boat, my feet sank into the mud. The engines fired, and I watched the already murky water boil with mud as Clark backed the heavy boat from its hiding spot.

I was pleased to find my boat still where I'd left her. Javier's arrival had caused me to wonder how many more of his crew might be lurking about. After replacing the coil wire, the engine purred at the touch of the key, and I slowly backed out of the slough.

Traffic in the canal was picking up, and I was thankful to see dozens of boats of every description going about their business. The more boats there were to see, the less chance anyone would remember ours following a workboat out of the canal and into the Pacific.

We settled into a nice pace of about twenty knots as we headed under the Bridge of the Americas. I wondered if Javier was still conscious or if the morphine had sent him back to his favorite spot in dreamland.

After an hour at twenty knots, we were in a hundred twenty feet of water, just east of Bona. I brought the RHIB alongside the workboat, tied her loosely to the starboard hip, and hopped aboard.

Just as I'd suspected, Javier was sound asleep with blood still oozing from his battered, swollen left hand.

"He made it to the bridge, and then he melted," said Clark.

I didn't envy the next twenty-four hours of Javi's life, and especially the next fifteen minutes of it.

"Let's cut the hoses and get out of here."

Clark turned to the radar screen. "Fortunately, there's no one around, so we may be able to pull this off without any witnesses."

I pointed to our captive. "Except for him."

"Yeah, except for him," Clark sighed.

We moved Javier back to the rear of the pilothouse and re-cuffed his right hand to a pipe before we headed through the hatch into the engine room.

Just like the rest of the boat, the engine room was a mess. Oil and grease covered every surface, and the twin diesels were hardly recognizable; I couldn't believe they ran.

I found the three bilge pumps and cut the discharge hose from each, while Clark made sure all of the thru-hull seacocks were open.

"Okay, let's do this," I said.

Clark cut four hoses, and I sliced three. The bilge of the old workboat started filling up with seawater, and the bilge pumps got to work doing what they were designed to do. Though without their discharge hoses, they were swimming against the current and simply circulating filthy seawater within the boat. None of it was being pumped overboard. We headed back up the ladder to the pilothouse.

"I've got an idea." I rummaged through the first aid kit for another pack of smelling salts.

Once I found what I was looking for, I took a quick peek back toward the engine room, glad to see the water rising quicker than I'd anticipated. I wanted to get the old boat to the bottom as fast as possible without gathering any unwanted attention.

"Check the painter line. I want to make sure we've got a ride out of here when this thing falls out from under us," I said.

Clark loosened the painter and returned to the pilothouse. "It's good," he said.

The water continued to rise, and the main deck was soon awash with filthy seawater and what had been the contents of the bilge.

"I guess it's time to wake up our friend."

I broke the capsule of ammonia and waved it under Javier's nose. He shook his head and furrowed his brow as he tried to piece together the scene that was unfolding around him.

With his left hand, he pressed against the deck and tried to raise his head out of the water, then let out an agonizing cry as the pain rifled through his arm. Falling back to the deck, he thrashed about until Clark finally grabbed his collar and pulled him to a sitting position.

The water was almost knee deep to me and shoulder deep to Javi, who was sitting on the deck. His eyes were growing larger by the minute.

"Well, Javi, I guess you've lost what little usefulness you had to us. Oh, by the way, we're in about forty meters of water. Enjoy your dive."

With that, Clark and I turned to slosh our way out of the pilothouse.

Javier screamed and pleaded. "I'll tell you everything! Everything! Please, I'm begging you!"

My plan had worked. I'd established my willingness to be cruel, and there was no question in Javier's mind that I would stop at nothing to get the information I wanted. Sometimes it isn't easy getting a man's full attention, but I had Javi's.

"Oh," I began, "so, you do know more."

"Yes, yes! I know everything. Remove the handcuffs, please. I'll tell you everything!"

I patted my pockets. "Hmm, now where is that handcuff key?"

"Please, señor. Please!"

I pulled the key from my pocket as the water reached Javier's chin. He was on his knees on the deck, pulling hard against the handcuff around his right wrist.

I held the key inches from his face and whispered, "If you refuse to answer anything, or if you lie about anything, there will be no more warnings. Do you understand?"

He nodded in exaggerated, terrified motions. "Yes, yes. Just get me out of here!"

With the water continuing to rise in conjunction with Javier's degree of panic, I leaned toward his right hand and aimed the key for the tiny hole in the handcuff. At that instant, the workboat rolled violently to port, and I stumbled backward, catching myself against the chart table.

Sickened by what I had just felt happen in my left hand, I stared into my empty palm where the handcuff key had been an instant before. Javier's eyes widened in horror, and I fell to the deck, feeling for the tiny key among the piles of floating debris and garbage.

Javier started to pray, and Clark started to curse. The water was well past Javier's chin, and he was craning his neck to keep his nose above the surface. Clark leapt across me as I frantically continued to feel for the key. The gunwales of the deck disappeared beneath the waves, and I dived through the water, continuing my frantic search for the key. The salt water and debris made it useless for me to try opening my eyes, but I continued my search. The panic rose in my chest as I thought about what Javier was experiencing. I could stand up, get in my boat, and motor away, but he was destined for a watery, terror-filled dive to his death.

When I'd used every ounce of oxygen left in my lungs, I burst upward through the surface to see Clark standing over Javier with a fire axe raised high over his head. I shook the water from my face and tried to piece together the scene unfolding in front of me. Clark powered downward, slicing through the air and water with the heavy axe. Javier screamed a gurgling cry and turned away, forcing his head beneath the surface of the dirty water.

As the axe hit its mark, Clark dived beneath the surface and slid the handcuff from the pipe he'd just severed, then pulled Javier back to the surface with the handcuffs dangling from his right wrist. Javier was sobbing and still praying.

By the time we made it to our boat, all that was visible of the workboat were the lights and radar antenna. Clark shoved Javier aboard as the painter line came taut and began to pull at the bow of our boat. I drew Anya's knife from its scabbard on my belt and sliced the line before it could force the bow of the RHIB beneath the surface.

I didn't know why I'd brought her knife with me. After discovering it sticking out of Michael Anderson's back on Cumberland Island, I couldn't bring myself to let it go. Was I subconsciously clinging to Anya by refusing to ignore the single piece of material evidence that proved she was still alive? I stared at the glistening blade and black onyx handle against my greasy palm. I pictured the knife sinking through the depths and coming to rest in the sand beside the workboat on the bottom of the sea beneath me, but I couldn't open my hand. I couldn't let it go.

We climbed aboard, caught our breath, and wiped the salt water from our faces.

"Well, that got interesting," said Clark.

Javier was lying on the deck. His chest was heaving, and whispered prayers were still escaping his trembling lips.

He stared up at me. "Who are you?"

I spat a piece of debris from the corner of my mouth. "Believe it or not, we're the good guys."

15
Domino Theory

We brought the RHIB up on plane and headed for the protected inlet and beach on the northwest side of Bona. The seas were two to three feet, but our boat continued to impress. It cut through the waves and made over forty knots. It wasn't a comfortable ride, but I was thankful for Pablo's contribution to our mission.

We made the beach at high tide and made a call to Leo.

"We've got a gift for you. Can you meet us at the cove on the northwest shore?"

"A gift? What do you mean, a gift?"

"Just get here ASAP," I said, and ended the call.

The Huey was soon hovering over the beach and blowing sand everywhere. I don't know how he did it, but Leo put the chopper on the ground between two stands of trees with less than two feet of clearance on either side. I could make a helicopter fly in the direction I wanted, and I could put it on the ground as long as there wasn't a tree or telephone pole in sight, but I'd never have skills like Leo.

By the time he had the chopper shut down, Clark had Javier's hand and arm splinted and bandaged, and another healthy dose of morphine waiting to be administered.

In front of the injured man, I knelt in the sand with a twenty-pound anchor and short length of line in my hands. I tied the anchor to his left ankle. "Okay, Javi. I'm going to ask you some more questions, and you have two options. Number one, you can answer my questions quickly and honestly. If you do, that helicopter is your ride out of here. You'll be taken someplace safe where a doctor will take care of your arm. Option number two is that you hesitate the least little bit or give me an answer I believe to be anything short of the absolute truth, and you and my anchor go for a swim. Do you understand?"

"Sí, yes, I understand."

"Who do you work for?"

"His name is Domino. That's all I know. He owns the boats, and he pays me in cash. I do what he says, and I don't ask questions."

"Very good, Javier. Now we're getting somewhere. Who does Domino work for?"

"I don't know," he said, his eyes full of timid fear.

"Okay, Javi. I believe you. What is Domino going to do when he discovers you and his boat are missing?"

He immediately cast his eyes to the ground. "He will believe I have stolen his boat and deserted him. He will find me, and he will kill me."

"Look at me, Javier. I'm the man you need to worry about killing you right now. Which bridge?"

Confusion whirled in his labored eyes.

I lifted the anchor and held it above his bandaged hand. "Don't mess with me, Javier. Which bridge is Domino planning to blow?"

"America."

"The Bridge of the Americas, and not the Puente Centenario?" I tapped his hand with the shank of the anchor.

"Yes, yes, Bridge of the Americas. They are planting the other explosives under the Bridge of the Americas. Why would we want to blow the Puente Centenario? There's nothing in the water there."

His confusion gave me some measure of reassurance. If I believed him, we only had one bridge to protect.

"Where's the other boat?"

"I think they are at the ferry dock, but I don't know for sure."

I turned to Clark. "Is there anything else?"

He shook his head and stuck the syringe of morphine in Javier's thigh.

"Get him out of here, and get him some help, Leo."

I untied the anchor from Javier's ankle, and Clark pulled him to his feet and put him aboard the Huey. Leo took off and soon disappeared to the north.

The Pacific tide had turned and begun to fall, and my new boat would soon be high and dry if we didn't get it off the beach.

I tossed my threatening anchor back into the RHIB, and Clark and I shoved the boat into the surf and climbed aboard. We motored around the north side of Bona and turned to the east. As we passed Taboga Island, the traffic jam of vessels waiting their turn to enter the canal came into sight. There must have been six dozen ships resting at anchor.

Clark slapped my shoulder and pointed to the southeast. I followed his finger into the distance, and we saw the AAS *Pearl* looming on the horizon. Even at that distance, the *Pearl* dwarfed the rest of the freighters in the area. She was a behemoth.

"How do you think our little devil's doing on that beast?"

I laughed. "I suspect no one on that ship even knows he's there yet."

"You may be right," Clark yelled over the roar of the engine. "I hope he's okay."

I pulled the throttle back and turned to Clark. "I need to tell you something else."

Clark held on as we slowed, and the boat settled into the water from being up on plane. "What is it?"

"Remember when I told you Diablo told me to forget about the locks and protect the bridge?"

"Yeah, I remember," he said.

"Well, that's not all he said."

Clark cocked his head and narrowed his eyes. It was obvious he thought I'd kept some piece of mission-critical information from him.

"He also said, 'Archie would be proud of you.'"

"Yeah? Who's Archie?"

"Archie is my dad, Clark."

He bit at his lip and sat on the Hypalon tube beside the helm. "Damn, man. Do you think he knew your dad?"

I shrugged. "I don't know. How old do you think he is?"

"Who knows?" said Clark. "I'm sure he's older than he looks, but he's in too good of shape to be much older than me. He moves like he's twenty-one. Stuff starts to hurt around thirty-five. When did . . ." He paused, obviously unsure how to finish the question.

"They were killed in December of eighty-nine," I said.

He cast his eyes skyward, doing the math. "That was almost twelve years ago. Diablo could've been around back then, but I don't know."

"Why do you think he'd say that to me?"

"I'm not sure," he said, "but you don't need that in your head right now. We've got a lot of work to do."

"I know. I just thought I should tell you."

He nodded. "I'm glad you did. Now, get your head in the game and let's see if we can keep that big bridge in the air."

I pushed the throttle to the stops, and the boat jumped out of the water and again settled into her pace atop the waves. I was tempted to turn out to sea to have a closer look at the enormous freighter, but I had to stay focused. I turned to the north and headed the boat across the Bahia de Panama and the southern end of the canal, but I couldn't stop looking over my shoulder at the *Pearl*.

Clark went to work setting up our dive gear while I headed for the ferry terminal, hoping to see the other explosives-laden workboat. I'd known the Panama Canal was busy, but I never imagined freighters would be lined up by the dozens waiting their turn. It was an impressive sight. I wondered if the *Pearl* would also wait in line, or if because of her size, she had some superior status within the system that granted her preferential treatment.

My stomach rumbled, and I thought about Diablo. Even though he was little more than half my size, he still had to eat. I wondered if he'd sniffed out a stowaway rat or two on the *Pearl* and made a meal of them. When all of this was over, I had every intention of getting the truth out of him. I had to know if he had known my father. I had to have some answers about what happened that night in December of eighty-nine. I deserved some answers . . . if there were any to be had.

The ferry terminal came into view, and I noticed the anchorage around it was bustling with cruisers and commercial boats. It was going to be a challenge to find the workboat, even if she was in the area.

"All right. The gear's all set up. We're ready to go," Clark said as he joined me at the helm.

I pointed to an exposed sandbar just southeast of the ferry terminal. "Look. There's a few boats tucked in behind that sandbar. That could be our guys."

Clark pulled a pair of binoculars from his kit and scanned the area. "There are eight boats back there, and three of them look like they could be Domino's crew. I say we come in from the southeast and do a drive-by."

I kept the boat at full throttle and headed for the south end of the sandbar. The water was shallow, but we drew less than twelve inches when up on plane, and only about two feet when she was at rest. If the workboats could get in and out of there, we definitely could.

The sandbar and shallows appeared to be half a mile long. The speed and flexibility of our boat would gobble up that distance in less than forty seconds. We rounded the southern tip of the bar and turned northwest, paralleling the beach. The sandbar acted as a barrier island and broke waves before they reached the beach, making the water behind the bar as smooth as glass.

Clark lay on the bow with the binoculars pressed to his face. I squinted against the wind and sun and kept moving north. As we approached the three suspect boats, I slowed to idle speed and crept by, making no wake. With "La Seguridad," the Spanish equivalent of *Safety*, stenciled in bold white letters on our tubes, almost no one would question us poking around—except perhaps the local police.

134 · CAP DANIELS

I'd been surprised how few official boats there seemed to be in the area.

The first vessel that came into view wasn't a boat. It was a ship. It was over two hundred feet long and carried an unidentifiable collection of equipment. There were two submersible ROVs and a minisub in cradles on the deck and a helipad on the bow. The ship had a quasi-military look about it and displayed an American flag atop the Panamanian courtesy flag. Painted across the stern in bright white letters against the haze gray paint of the hull was *R.V. Lori Danielle*.

She wasn't our target, so we moved on. The first two workboats were loaded with construction material—blocks, lumber, and paint —but the deck of the third was empty, just like Javier's boat had been.

Clark glanced back at me from his position on the bow and nodded toward the empty deck of the third boat. I nodded once in silent acknowledgment and continued idling ever closer.

The door to the pilothouse was tied open with a greasy length of line, and puffs of white steam wafted through the door. Clark drew his pistol, tucked it between his leg and the tube of the boat, and motioned for me to get closer.

If this was the second explosives boat, the white steam represented an unexpected wrinkle in their plan. A broken-down boat could be a lucky break for the good guys.

A shirtless, dark-skinned man with a filthy rag in one hand and a wrench in the other, came stomping through the pilothouse door. He was cursing and wiping sweat from his brow.

I'd allowed us to drift a little closer to the boat than I'd planned, and the man looked up in surprise when he saw us so close to his stern. He didn't reach for a gun or appear nervous. He just kept wiping his head with the rag.

In Spanish, I said, "Good morning. Do you need some help?"

The man shook his head. "No, I need a new wife! Mine poured diesel fuel instead of oil into the engine, and now I'm going to kill her."

"I'm afraid we can't help you with that, but good luck," I said as we drifted by.

"Yeah, good luck. Ha! She's the one who needs the good luck." He headed back into the steam-filled pilothouse.

Clark laughed. "See, that's why I never got married. I don't need diesel fuel in my oil."

"Something tells me that's not our guy," I said.

"Yeah, I think you're on to something there."

We continued north toward the ferry terminal, but no more boats matched the one we'd sent to the bottom. The anchorage north of the terminal was littered with cruisers of every description. There was even a sailing catamaran that looked remarkably like *Aegis*. I had to get a closer look at that one. We motored through the anchorage at just above idle speed to avoid casting a wake and disturbing the cruisers.

The catamaran was brilliant white and rigged nearly identically to *Aegis*. I admired her strong lines and stability in the water. She wasn't moving an inch while some of the other smaller boats in the anchorage bobbed and swayed on their moorings.

Boats are unlike any other material object on Earth. They have a presence about them that is tough to describe, but the cat was a sleeping lioness, resting peacefully until it was time for her to prowl. If that one sailed anything like *Aegis*, she could prowl with the best of them. Seeing her gave me a small feeling of homesickness. I had a job to do, and I would fulfill my responsibilities, but I thought about Penny and Skipper back in St. Augustine. I missed them both, and the feeling surprised me. Missing Skipper made perfect sense. She'd been like a little sister to me for years, and having her back in my life was one of the greatest experiences I'd ever known. But Penny was a different story. I couldn't quite put my finger on why I was missing her. She'd become a recent fixture in my life, but our relationship was unique. We were both strong, independent personalities, but for some reason, we seemed to need each other.

I wasn't sure I'd ever be ready for a wife and a typical life, though there was nothing typical about Penny. She and I had agreed that we'd simply enjoy spending time together without expectations and without actually defining our relationship.

I glanced back into the cockpit of the catamaran, half expecting to see Penny and Skipper sitting on deck, having cocktails, and laughing over stories about me. They were thousands of miles away, but for some reason, they'd popped into my head when I should've been laser-focused on the task at hand.

I'd see them soon enough . . . I hoped.

16

He Lied

Clark pulled me from my daydream. "They're not here," he said.

I turned to take another look at the *Pearl* as she continued her approach toward the Bridge of the Americas and the first set of locks in the southern end of the Panama Canal.

"Do you know if she'll go straight in, or will she have to wait like the others?" I said.

Clark was my senior by seven years, so for some reason, I thought he knew more about how the world worked than I did.

"How should I know?" he said. "You're the smart one. I'm just here to keep you alive."

"I thought I was the pretty one and you were the smart one."

"Yeah, you just keep thinking that, and let me know how that works out for you, college boy."

Clark had joined the army straight out of high school instead of heading off to college like I did. He liked to remind me that he was killing bad guys while I was playing baseball and chasing co-eds. He had a point, but he'd done his share of co-ed chasing himself, even if he hadn't spent much time in the classroom.

"I think our timer starts ticking the instant she goes into the first lock," I said. "The explosives intended for the lock are swimming with the fishes, so like Diablo said, we have to protect that bridge."

Clark nodded in silent agreement.

We motored out of the anchorage and saw a pair of Panamanian National Maritime Service vessels racing south from beneath the bridge. The boats were larger, more intimidating versions of ours, and had mounted machine guns on their foredecks, and large, glass-enclosed pilothouses. I hoped they weren't coming to intercept the pair of American operatives masquerading as safety officials on the Bahia de Panama.

The boats ran in a staggered formation with the lead boat ahead of the second one, and the trailing boat offset just outside the wake of the leader. They had to be making fifty knots or more. Running from them would be a futile effort, so I turned bow-on to what would've been their wake if they continued southward. I didn't want to do anything that looked suspicious to the men on those boats.

The officers manning the machine guns on the foredeck were wearing helmets, goggles, and flak vests. As they flew past us, the gunner on the trailing vessel turned to face us. I wasn't sure I liked the attention, but I was soon relieved when he raised one hand from the gun and waved. I returned the salute and pressed the throttle forward to maneuver across the three-foot wake headed our way.

Clark looked back over his shoulder. "That was close."

"Yep, it sure was," I said. "Hang on. We're going to get rattled around a little."

Clark pressed his foot against the front of the center console and wedged himself against the tube as the first wake met our bow. I'd brought the boat up to twenty knots before the wake arrived, and we pierced through it with no problems. I decided to have a little fun with the second wake and pushed the throttle to its stop. We quickly accelerated through forty knots and met the second wake with energy to burn. We left the surface of the water and sailed through the air. The boat never faltered, twisted, or misbehaved. She slid back into the water like a knife and retained every knot of speed she'd carried into the jump. I wanted to figure out a way to get the boat back to the States with me. I was starting to fall in love.

With speed still building, I turned us north and headed for the bridge. When I'd watched the crew bagging the bricks of plastic explosive, they'd been near the eastern end of the bridge, so I decided to start our search there. We anchored in twenty feet of water north of the eastern piling.

The Bridge of the Americas is a beautiful bridge spanning the Panama Canal and connecting South America to North America. It has two major pilings situated a quarter mile apart on either side of the canal. The span clearance is just over two hundred feet at high tide. Explosives placed in large quantities and detonated on or near either of the pilings would be enough to, at best, render the bridge unsafe for traffic, or at worst, send the bridge crumbling into the canal. The number of explosives we'd discovered on the workboats was more than enough to do precisely that. The second boat was nowhere to be seen, so the explosives had most likely already been set. It was up to Clark and me to find them, disarm them, and get away. Each step relied on the previous one. First, we had to find them.

To the south, two patrol boats were taking positions on either side of the *Pearl*. Since her captain was a licensed Panama Canal Pilot, there would be no pilot boat—only the armed escorts. Clearly, she wasn't going to be waiting in line. I couldn't see the Miraflores Locks from our position, but I imagined the Pacific gates were open, awaiting the arrival of the *Pearl*.

We donned our dive gear, including a pair of LARS-V rebreathers, and rolled over the side. The water was murky with visibility of no more than three or four feet. Finding the explosives in good visibility would've been a challenge, but finding them in water that looked like mud was going to be almost impossible.

Clark and I met beneath the boat and descended together. When we hit the muddy bottom, we decided to split up and search separately. It would cut the search time in half and double the amount of ground we could cover. Although I couldn't see him in the murk, he swam away to the southwest, and I started my search.

I was looking and feeling for any disturbance in the seafloor. If a team of divers had planted explosives, there would be some evidence of them disturbing the bottom. The longer I searched, the more frustrating my task became. The visibility was reduced to near zero as I swam to the west into deeper water. Using my torch made it worse. Like shining high-beam headlights into fog or snow, it turned the water in front of me into a wall of reflections of particulates. I stowed my useless torch and kept feeling my way through the mud.

My hand struck something that felt like a tree trunk—cylindrical and hard. I felt along the object and followed it toward the center of the canal. It never changed shape or size in the fifty feet I traced it. I wasn't sure what I'd discovered, but it definitely wasn't plastic explosives or a detonator cord. I turned to follow it back toward the piling, running my gloved hand along the smooth surface. When I reached the footing of the bridge pile, it occurred to me that the object must have been one of the many underwater cables spanning the canal, carrying telephone, data, and electricity between North and South America. I discovered four more of the massive cables before something slammed into the top of my head. My full-face mask was knocked off and it immediately filled with salt water.

As I was trying to figure out what hit me, a pair of strong hands grabbed my shoulders. I was about to be in the fight of my life, and I was at a terrible disadvantage. I had a flooded, dislodged facemask and a stream of bubbles pouring skyward in front of my face. I was blind, without air, and badly disoriented.

I tried to retreat to reseal and clear my mask, but I couldn't escape the other diver's grip. Realizing that I was about to inhale two lungs full of water, I reached for the knife on my belt. If I was going to find out what awaits assassins on the other side, I wasn't going alone. This guy was coming with me even if I had to—as Anya would say—*gut him like pig* with her knife.

The aggressor removed his right hand from my left arm and situated my mask back on my face. I pulled the bottom of my mask away from my chin, and the water evacuated immediately, leaving me with a clear mask and all the air I needed.

Why would he hit me and then save my life?

"Are you okay, college boy? I didn't see you. It's like swimming in a sewer down here."

"I almost introduced my dive knife to your liver," I said, relieved to hear Clark's voice.

"A little jumpy, are we?"

"No, I just wasn't expecting you to swim into my skull. Did you find anything?"

"A pistol, a fishing rod, and two pairs of sunglasses. How about you?"

"I found a bunch of big cables, but nothing explosive," I said. "Let's head back to the boat, if we can find it, and check out the other side."

"I'll race you to the top, bubble boy."

Racing to the top had been a long-standing joke between Clark and me. I had an irrational fear of getting decompression sickness, commonly called "the bends." It's a condition that occurs when nitrogen gas suspended in divers' body tissue expands rapidly from surfacing too quickly. It's like shaking up a carbonated drink and unscrewing the lid. The nitrogen gas comes out of solution and forms bubbles, just like the carbon dioxide in the carbonation. It causes all sorts of nasty symptoms and can be fatal.

Clark had been diving for twenty years and never worried about getting bent, but it was almost always in the back of my mind each time I was underwater. The accepted standard is to ascend at one foot per second, but I liked to double that safety margin to two seconds per foot. I was in no hurry to race to the surface with Clark or anyone else.

I surfaced after Clark, who was already in the boat. "What took you so long?" he asked, pulling me back aboard.

"I was just enjoying the scenery on the way up." I pulled off my mask but left the rest of my gear in place, knowing I'd be back in the water as soon as we crossed the canal.

Clark pulled up the anchor. "Maybe the viz will be better on the other side."

"It can't be any worse," I said as I headed the boat to the west.

Clark pointed up the canal. "Look," he yelled over the engine noise. "The *Pearl* will be in the locks soon."

He was right. The *Pearl* was a couple miles north of the bridge, and the southern gates of the first lock were less than a mile off her bow. The Miraflores Locks are a two-stage set of locks that would raise the ship fifty-four feet, and if she didn't sink, she'd continue into Lake Miraflores toward the Pedro Miguel Locks and end up at Lake Gatun. But I was pretty sure the *Pearl* wouldn't be seeing Lake Gatun anytime soon.

"Do you think they'll sink her in the first stage or the second?" I yelled back.

"I think I'd sink her on the high side. That'd make a bigger mess and make it a lot harder to clean up, but that's a two-sided lock, isn't it?"

"Yeah, they're parallel," I said.

"Then sinking a boat on one side won't close the locks, will it?"

"It will now. The western side has been shut down for maintenance for six weeks, with another twelve weeks scheduled. The eastern side is the only operational lock right now."

"Hmm, that's convenient," Clark huffed.

The western side of the canal was significantly deeper than the eastern edge. We tried to anchor in forty feet of water, but without enough rope to get the anchor to bite, we had to move closer to the shoreline and increase our swim distance. Finally, we anchored in a spot still far enough away to keep anyone from swimming out and taking advantage of our abandoned boat.

We double-checked our gear, I pocketed the boat key, and overboard we went. I was pleased the visibility was much better, and I could actually see my fins. Clark gave the signal, and we were on our way to the bottom. Although there wasn't much natural light at depth, the actual visibility had increased to ten feet or more. I could finally use my torch without being blinded in the fog.

We decided to conduct an arm's-length grid instead of risking another head-on collision. Clark swam on my left at an arm's distance away, and we scanned the bottom around the foundations of the bridge pilings. After eighty minutes underwater, we'd searched every inch of the foundations and a swath of the bottom near the foundations. Not only were there no explosives, there was no sign that anyone had been on the bottom. Except for the cables that were plainly visible, we didn't find anything.

Back on the boat, we pulled off our dive gear and sat on the tubes while drinking bottled water. Dehydration can cause decompression sickness, and I wasn't taking any chances.

"So, what do you think?" I asked.

"I don't know, man. There's nothing down there."

I replayed Javier's interrogation in my head, trying to determine if I'd been duped. "Do you think Javier was lying about which bridge they were going to blow?"

"I don't think so. He seemed surprised that we'd even ask him about the Centennial Bridge."

"That's the impression I got as well, but there's nothing here," I said.

Clark's eyes widened and he stared through me. "What did you just say?"

I stared back. "I said there's nothing here."

"That's exactly what Javier said about the Centennial Bridge. He said, 'Why would we want to blow the Puente Centenario? There's nothing in the water there.' Or at least that's what I think he said. My Spanish isn't as good as yours."

"The cables!" I yelled. "They're going to blow the—"

An echoing roar rolled down the mouth of the canal like thunder in a canyon.

My heart stopped. "That little son of a bitch. He did lie to us. They just blew the locks."

17

A Snap

Clark yanked the anchor from the mud and hauled it aboard. At the touch of the key, the engine fired, and we were headed up the canal. It was three miles to the Miraflores Locks, but I could already see the smoke rising. The scene unfolding in front of us was mayhem of the highest order. I'd never seen anything like it.

I tried to make sense of what I was seeing, but it was utter chaos. Alarms bellowed, and people ran in every direction. Panic had consumed the scene. Water cascaded over the remains of the lower gates of the lock in a huge waterfall. The stern of the *Pearl* was resting at an unimaginable angle. The top of her rudder was exposed, and she listed to port. Her hull was pinned against the walls of the lock. Her keel had come to rest on the bottom of the shallow lock with her bow jutting skyward and her stern weeping helplessly down toward the Pacific sea level. The main deck was still well above water, but the towering stacks of containers were beginning to list and succumb to gravity's angry insistence. To see the massive freighter in such a perilous condition was impossible to comprehend.

"It looks like they sank the Pearl between the intermediate gates and blew the downstream gates to stick her to the bottom."

Without looking back at me, Clark said, "I think you're right, but that wasn't enough noise for four hundred pounds of C4. I don't think they're finished."

The torrent in front of us churned with rolling waves of surging water as if it were alive. The creek where we'd discovered Javier's boat was billowing with a white foamy wall of water rushing southward. Someone had opened the bypass dam in a desperate attempt to alleviate some of the pressure from the badly damaged locks and the enormous ship stranded within them.

I couldn't fathom the recovery operation that would be required to resolve the disaster.

Clark finally turned away from the horrific scene. "What will happen if they blow the upstream gates?"

I couldn't come up with a good answer. "I don't know, but I think it might wash the *Pearl* back out into the canal."

"Not if she's on the bottom," he said.

I don't know what I thought was going to happen when they sank the *Pearl* in the locks, but the reality of the event was far worse than anything I could've ever imagined.

Clark stood in the bow, shaking his head. "We've got to get out of here."

He couldn't have been more correct. It was time for us to run. I pushed the throttle forward, brought the boat about, and headed south away from the chaos. With the incredible volume of water rushing through the bypass channel, I expected the canal to be turbulent, but the further south we went, the calmer the water became.

A massive second explosion rang through the air. I swung the boat around. The western side of the lock that had been down for maintenance was pouring smoke, dust, and plumes of brown water into the sky. They'd blown the intermediate gates on that side, rendering the reopening of the parallel lock completely out of the question.

There was nothing we could do except continue south. Returning to the locks would only put us in more danger. By the time we'd almost reached the bridge, in stark contrast to the turmoil upstream, the surface of the water looked like glass.

The serenity gave me the opportunity to concentrate and piece together a plan. "I think we have to get back in the water. If those cables are rigged to blow, they're probably rigged in a daisy chain instead of all the C4 being in one place. That's how I'd do it."

"I think you're probably right," Clark said. "We have to go at it from both ends and meet in the middle."

"Exactly. I'll put you in the water on the west side, and then I'll run across and anchor on the east in the shallows. Will our coms work that far apart?"

Our full-face masks had electronic communications built in so we could talk to each other underwater, but I'd never tried using them a thousand feet apart.

"I don't know," he said. "But I guess we'll find out."

By the time we reached the western bridge piling, Clark was already in his dive gear and poised to go overboard. I slowed the RHIB to ten knots, and he rolled backward, vanishing beneath the murky surface.

I shoved the throttle forward and turned toward the east bank. Emergency response vehicles raced northward from Panama City, and a fleet of boats headed for the Miraflores Locks. I wondered if any of the men aboard those boats knew what unthinkable disaster lay before them and what they would do once they arrived on scene.

I set the anchor and pulled on my gear. Seconds later, I was back in the nearly silent world of zero visibility. I followed the foundation of the bridge piling and descended through the soup. I found one of the tree-trunk-size cables and followed it into the depths of the canal.

I left the key in the boat. What was I thinking?

There was no time to go back for it. I'd just have to hope no one wanted my boat more than I did.

I swam toward the center of the canal, allowing my gloved right hand to slide along the smooth surface of the cable. With near-zero visibility, my sense of feel had replaced my sight. I pressed my dive computer to my mask and watched the depth display reach sixty-two feet just as my right hand struck something solid.

I stopped kicking and felt the object carefully. It was the size of a shoebox, had a pair of thin wires coming from one end, and was affixed to the cable with a mechanical band. I couldn't see it well enough to know if it was a device that was supposed to be part of the cable system or if it was an explosive charge. I pressed my mask as close to the object as possible and discovered it to be relatively clean with no marine growth of any kind. It was fresh, and it was a block of C4.

Clark's voice crackled through my comms. "Are you in the water yet?"

"Yeah, I'm wet, and I've found a device. It appears to be a block of C4, maybe three or four pounds, with a pair of wires leading on down the cable."

"I've found two of those already," he said in a tinny, electronic voice."

"Did you disarm them?"

"Yeah, I just pulled the blasting caps out and left the charges on the cable. I've not cut anything yet. How about you?"

"I'm doing the same," I said. "I don't want to cut anything until we know how it's all wired."

Clark asked, "How many of these cables are there?"

His question froze me in my tracks. I had no idea how many there were. If we couldn't find a way to ensure that we'd searched every cable, there would be no way to know if our mission was complete.

"That's the million-dollar question," I said. "How many do you think there are?"

"I count six."

I quickly did the math. Six cable runs of over a thousand feet each. I pressed my dive computer back to my face. Seventy-seven feet.

While I was trying to determine how long we could stay on the bottom, Clark asked another question that stopped my heart. "Uh, Chase, when do you think they plan to set these off?"

Suddenly, my bottom-time calculations no longer mattered. Not knowing when the explosion would come meant we had to disarm everything we could find as quickly as possible.

"If I were running the op, I'd blow them now to disrupt as much commo and electric as I could."

"Trying to think like a maniacal Chinese tactician is not something my brain can do, but I can't imagine them waiting much longer."

I swam as quickly as I could while still keeping my hand on the cable. I found three more charges and removed the detonators from each. When the visibility started to improve, the work became easier, but it was still nerve-racking. If the charges were on a timer and we didn't get them all disarmed before the time ran out, they'd blow, and there would be nothing we could do to stop them. If they were on a remote and someone was waiting to set them off when some event on some timeline occurred, we were equally screwed. All we could do was continue disarming the charges as quickly as we could find them.

Exhaustion set in after two and a half hours in the water. I could hear the fatigue in Clark's voice and feel it in my spine. Even if we gave up the search for more explosives, we couldn't head directly to the surface. Because of the amount of time we'd spent at depth, our bodies were loaded up with nitrogen, and we were in for a long decompression stop to let it off-gas from our bodies. I wasn't interested in my bloodstream turning into a fizzy fountain.

"How you doing, Clark?"

"I'm hurting. How about you?"

I drew in a long breath. "I'm okay. Just a little tired. I think there's just one more cable. Where are you?"

"Uh, I'm on the murky side at forty feet."

I pressed my computer to my face. "I'm just below you at fifty-five. I'm coming to you. Hold your position. We'll finish together."

"Roger."

My fatigue, coupled with the non-existent visibility, made finding Clark more difficult than I'd expected. I finally brushed against him ten minutes later. We moved to the final cable and began to fin for the depths. We discovered two more charges and removed the detonators just as we'd done with the previous twenty-seven devices we'd found. The visibility was slightly better at the bottom, and I could see Clark's face for the first time. We both sighed behind our masks, wondering how much longer we could keep this up. I was thirsty, hungry, and exhausted, and his drooping eyes showed he felt the same way. In silent acknowledgment of each other's condition, we continued on.

With the slightly improved visibility and the aid of our torches, we discovered a device near the cable at the center of the canal. We'd found the mother ship.

According to my computer, we were in seventy-eight feet of water.

"It's times like these when I wish I'd gone to EOD school," Clark mumbled.

Explosive Ordnance Disposal is a highly specialized craft developed over thousands of hours of study and years of experience. Neither Clark nor I were formally trained in the craft. What little I knew had come from books, and Clark's experience had been mostly as an observer in actual combat situations. We were out of our element, over our heads, and quite literally, under pressure.

"What do you suppose that is?"

"I don't know," I said, "but I'd guess it's the brains of this spider-web of death."

"I think you're right. It looks like we're going to have to—" An alarm on his dive computer went off. He pulled the instrument toward his face and shook his head. "No wonder I feel like crap. My scrubber is failing. I've got high CO_2 levels."

We each carried a high-pressure, steel, seventy-five cubic foot bail-out bottle with thirty-two percent nitrox. I helped Clark connect his tank to his mask and switch from the closed-circuit re-breather to breathing from the bottle.

"Let's plan to meet at twenty-five feet just north of the east piling," I said. "We'll let the computers work a deco plan from there."

Clark had no choice but to surface, grab a couple of nitrox tanks, and head back into the water to decompress and off-gas the nitrogen in his body. The minute or two he'd be out of the water wasn't good for him, but there were no other options.

"Are you sure you're going to be okay with this thing?" he asked.

"I have no idea, but what choice do we have? I'll pull the rest of the detonators from the charges on this cable, and then I'll spend a little time making sure this thing, whatever this is, doesn't make anything go boom. I'll meet you at twenty-five feet in twenty minutes or so, and we'll plan the decompression."

He flashed the okay signal and began his long, slow ascent through the soup and toward the surface.

I counted my fin kicks as I swam westward to ensure I could find my way back to the device after I'd pulled the detonators from the C4. I wished I had carried my GPS for that part, but the cumbersome buoy that had to be floated every time I needed a precise location fix was more trouble than it was worth for that kind of work

I found two more blocks of C4, disarmed them, and turned back for the center of the canal. I heard ships and smaller boats moving overhead, but I couldn't see them. It was an eerie sound in the lonely and dark depths of the canal.

Counting my kick cycles worked nicely and delivered me back to the precise spot I'd left. Wires left the box in directions that didn't make any sense. If our assumption about blowing the cables was correct, all of the wiring should've been headed toward the charges on the cables, but at least a dozen wires led south toward the Pacific Ocean.

I swam and traced the wires, having no idea what I'd find at the other end. I counted two hundred seventy-nine kick cycles, almost three hundred yards, and saw the massive trunk line running east and west across the floor of the canal. I assumed it contained electricity. C4 charges lined the metallic casing. There must've been thirty pounds of plastic explosive—enough to bring down the Empire State Building, and certainly enough to sever the trunk line.

I could try disarming the charges, or I could swim back to the hub and try disabling the circuit from there. Like Clark's, my scrubber had to have been only minutes from failure, so time was not on my side. I turned and kicked to the north. I'd take my chances with the circuit.

The second my hand made contact with the controller, my dive computer started screaming.

Damn it. I need more time.

I found the low-pressure hose from my bail-out bottle and connected it to my regulator. I'd have about thirty minutes of nitrox before I'd be sucking on an empty steel tank.

The surface of the box in front of me was perfectly smooth with no buttons, knobs, or dials of any kind. I had to get inside. I pulled Anya's knife from its sheath, thankful I hadn't sent it to the bottom with Javier's boat, and I went to work prying on every corner and seam of the box. Finally, a crack the width of my thumb opened up, and I pulled with all my strength until I'd peeled the box open enough to get my hands inside. The torch mounted to the side of my facemask shined into the box, illuminating a maze of wires, tubes, and circuitry that made no sense to me. An electrical circuit underwater was enough to baffle me.

How can any of it work in this environment?

Everything was taking twice the time it should have. I checked my pressure gauge: fifteen hundred pounds. I decided I'd work on the circuits until I had a thousand pounds, and then I'd cut the wires leading to the trunk line and head for Clark. I was running out of ideas, options, and air all at the same time.

I've spent a great many hours of my life having no idea what I was doing, but I'd never before found myself eighty feet underwater, three hundred yards from thirty pounds of C4, with a box full of circuitry I didn't understand in my lap. I checked my pressure gauge again: eleven-fifty. I tried to slow my heart rate and breathing, but it wasn't happening.

I stuck my face in the box, hoping I'd see something that looked familiar, something I could disengage or deactivate, something to make me believe I was actually making progress.

Pressure check: one thousand fifty pounds.

Think, Chase, think. It's a circuit. It has a power source, and . . . that's it!

I frantically searched for anything I believed could be a power source—a battery, a capacitor, a hamster on a wheel. I pried a component from the box and exposed a compartment holding a battery. It had two posts with watertight connections and a wire leading from each—one red, one black.

I double-checked the wires exiting the box and leading to the explosives, and I considered cutting them. However, I feared there might've been something built into the circuitry that would send a signal through the remaining wires, detonating the plastic explosive. Surviving an explosion so near to that much C4 was doubtful.

Pressure check: nine-fifty.

My time was up. I had to either cut one of the wires from the battery or cut the wiring to the detonators. I thought it might be a good time to talk to God. If I screwed this up, I'd soon be having my first face-to-face with Him.

"Please don't let me kill myself."

I cut the red wire leading from the battery. Nothing. Well, nothing except the little accident that necessitated a clean pair of shorts. But there was no click, no snap, and most importantly, no explosion. Perhaps I'd made the correct decision. In the interest of keeping a stray spike of rogue voltage from finding its way to the detonators, I cut the external wires, too. I gathered the bundle of wires and placed my foot on them against the muddy seafloor. I slid the blade of the onyx-handled knife beneath the wires and pulled. Cutting them wasn't as easy as I'd expected, and they put up quite a fight, but Anya's knife and I were winning.

That's when I heard it.

Sound travels about four times faster underwater than it does through the air. That creates a unique set of problems when trying to determine the origin of sound at depth. I heard a snap, like a twig breaking underfoot. It wasn't a sound I'd ever heard in all the hours I'd spent underwater. It was impossible to determine where it had originated or how far away it was.

A concussion pummeled through my chest and head, and I watched the world around me dissolve into perfect, empty darkness. No sound. No light. Nothing. Just vast, utter desolation.

18

My Coffin

I found myself in a terrifying freefall, and I clung to everything I could touch—anything I perceived as stable—but the falling continued. The darkness into which I was propelled gave way to a brilliant white field of nothing, as if I were flying through a blizzard of snow. I thought I heard muffled voices from a great distance. Sickness consumed my gut, and I tried to vomit, but nothing would come. Every sensation I was experiencing was foreign to me. In a dizzying plummet, I was spinning and falling into some bottomless pit—maybe into Hell. My vision was lost in the endless chasm of brilliant white, and my perception of the world had lost all foundation. Nothing made sense. Everything hurt, and I was alone, imprisoned in my horror, pain, and confusion.

The endless falling had to stop. Surely there had to be a bottom. The spinning was maddening. The tighter I clung to everything in my grasp, the faster I spun, and the farther I fell. I clamped my eyelids shut so tightly I could feel the muscles in my jaws cramp and spasm in protest. No matter how firmly I closed my eyes, the incessant white light blinded me more and more.

Am I dead? Is this what happens when the soul departs the flesh? Is there no judgment? No pearly gate? No streets of gold? No flames? No angels? No demons? Is there nothing but the white, burning light, and the relentless, spiraling, terrifying descent? Are there no sounds but the hollow echoes from beyond the light? Is there nothing more?

And then there was more, or perhaps, less. Tiny shafts of colored light pierced the white. There was pressure in my ears, but the distant sounds were gone. I lay in perfect silence and watched the shafts of color become beams, and finally, fields of green and blue. I reached out to grasp at the colors, but my hands met a wall—a solid, endless, invisible wall. I was encased in a coffin that I couldn't see, but that I could feel. The sensation of falling stopped but was replaced by a ringing tone in my head that wouldn't go away. It was deafening and maddening, but I was eternally thankful I was no longer falling.

My vision continued to improve, but the more I could see, the more terrifying and confusing my condition became. Encased in a glass coffin, the ringing still screamed in my ears, and every muscle of my body ached as if I'd been run over by a truck. I slowly returned from my horrific journey to wherever I'd been, but I was still lost, still confused, and still imprisoned.

Distorted objects formed into blocky silhouettes. Shapes that may have been people moved around, busy at some invisible task. I tried calling out to them, but the sound of my voice only echoed inside my coffin, and no one looked my way. Perhaps the shapes were only spirits without the capacity to hear, see, or help me.

Unable to make sense of the world beyond my confinement, I closed my eyes and tried to piece together what had happened.

Through the incessant ringing in my ears, I heard a voice, tinny and hollow.

"How are you feeling?"

"What?" I mumbled.

"I said, how are you feeling?"

"It hurts," I managed to say.

"I'm sure it does, but it's good to see you awake. Can you tell me your name?"

I blinked my eyes and tried to focus. There appeared to be a man, or perhaps a spirit, standing just beyond the walls of my coffin.

Could he be the voice I'm hearing?

"Can you tell me your name?" the voice said again.

"Can you tell me yours?" I said.

He laughed. "I'm Dr. Shadrack."

"Is this the fiery furnace, Shadrack?"

He laughed again. "Are you Jewish?"

"No, no, I'm not Jewish. I'm Protestant. Does that matter here?"

I still had no idea where I was, but I vividly remembered the story from the Book of Daniel about Shadrack, Meshach, and Abednego in the fiery furnace.

"I'm sure you have a lot of questions, my young Protestant friend, but for now, just relax and try to rest."

"Wait," I demanded. "Where am I? What is this place?"

"You're in a recompression chamber aboard the research vessel *Lori Danielle*. You have a nasty case of the bends, but we're going to take care of that. You have a few more hours before we can start bringing you up, but I'll be back to check on you from time to time. Get some rest."

The bends? How did I get bent? I've not been in the water.

So many incomprehensible things had happened in the last four years of my life. Me lying on my back in a recompression chamber on a research vessel I'd never heard of, with every cell of my body trying to explode, was just one more episode I'd have to file away in the "How'd this happen?" drawer.

I tried not to think about being trapped in a glass tube, but that's easier said than done. Fred—the psychiatrist at The Ranch where I was transformed from a former baseball player into an assassin—had taught me some meditation techniques, and I put them to good use. I was able to remain calm and relaxed, and I soon drifted off to sleep.

"I made to you promise, Chasechka."

"Anya?" I tried to force my eyes open.

"For you, it is to rest while I keep promise."

"What promise? What are you talking about, Anya?"

Her tone and Russian-accented English were unmistakable. I could pick out her voice from a thousand others. It was her. I couldn't see her, but I could feel her next to me, and I could almost smell her long, blonde hair. I was certain of almost nothing else, but it was her. I'd longed to hear that voice again—to listen to her say my name and to feel her in my arms. I'd loved her once, but she'd been nothing more than an actress. She played a role, pretending to love me, inch by inch working her way into my life so she could report my every move back to the Kremlin, back to her SVR masters, back to Russian intelligence. I'd watched her take a bullet to the back and fall to her death, but since that horrible day, I'd seen hopeful glimpses of her still being very much alive and lethal. She'd been the deadliest assassin I could have ever imagined—far more dangerous than me, and far more cunning and competent.

"I made to you promise on beach in Key West island to tell you everything I know about your family."

Chills ran the length of my spine, and every hair on my body stood erect. She *had* made that promise. She'd vowed to tell me everything she knew as soon as our mission to rescue Skipper was complete. Anya had played an invaluable role in that mission, saving both my and Skipper's lives before losing her own. I believed I'd never hear her voice again, and that I'd never learn what she knew about my family.

"Tell me," I demanded. "Tell me what you know!"

"You must relax, my Chase. I will tell you everything I know, but you will not ask questions. For you, it is only to listen to my voice. Yes?"

I nodded and bit at my bottom lip in anxious anticipation of what I was about to hear.

"There's a plastic squeeze bottle beneath your left hand if you get thirsty."

That isn't Anya's voice.

"What?"

I blinked and tried to focus, but my vision was still too dull to discern more than blurry, irregular shapes.

"If you get thirsty," said Dr. Shadrack, "there's a bottle of water beneath your left hand. You've been in the chamber for just over two hours, and you still have a long time to go. Drink all you'd like.

You have a catheter in place, so you don't have to worry about going to the restroom. How are you feeling?"

I leaned toward the clear glass of the chamber. "Did you see a beautiful, blonde Russian woman out there?"

He laughed, "No, I'm afraid I didn't. But I'll certainly keep my eyes open for one, and if she shows up, I call dibs."

I lay back, found the water bottle he'd described, and took a long drink. The water was warm and bitter, but I was thirsty.

I tried Fred's meditation exercises again. I wanted—I needed—Anya to come back. Through grogginess and confusion, scenes of being underwater flashed into my mind, and I was uncertain of everything in those dark, brief flashes of memory.

I'd been given drugs to help me rest, and it was difficult to hold my eyes open. The brief flashbacks continued.

Clark! Clark was in the water with me.

I beat on the glass of the recompression chamber. "Clark! Where's my partner, Clark Johnson? He was with me in the water."

I vaguely saw a figure growing nearer, and Dr. Shadrack's voice filled the chamber once again. "Mr. Johnson is in our other recompression chamber, just over there."

I imagined him pointing, but of course, I couldn't see what he was doing.

"Is he all right?" I breathed.

"He's going to be fine. He wasn't as close to the explosion as you. He's suffering from decompression sickness, but he isn't wounded."

"What explosion?" I asked.

"Just get some rest and drink your water. I'll be back to check on you in a bit."

"I want to talk to Clark," I said, trying to sound authoritative.

The figure outside the chamber stopped moving away and appeared motionless.

"Okay," he finally said. "I think we can do that, but the connection is going to be shaky. I'll have to hold the handsets together."

I could see him shuffling around, and then Clark's electronic, hollow voice filled my chamber.

"How you doin', college boy?"

"I feel like I've been stepped on by an elephant a few dozen times, and somebody's inside my head banging on a gong, but other than that, I'm doing okay. How about you?"

"I guess you were right about the bends," he said. "I should've been more careful, but somebody had to get you some help, and I was the only volunteer in the neighborhood."

I tried to piece the shards of my memory back together. "What happened, Clark?"

"What do you mean what happened?" he said.

"I don't remember anything. I have no idea what's going on. Can you put it together for me?"

He cleared his throat. "That Dr. Shadrack looks like quite the jackass. Wouldn't you agree?"

"I can't see him," I said. "My vision is pretty screwed up."

"That's okay," said Clark. "I was just testing to see if he could hear me before I briefed you on how we got here."

"Did he react?" I asked.

"Nope. He just stood there looking bored. So, here's what happened. The Chinese sank a freighter in the Miraflores Locks and blew the gates, so you and I were defusing a quarter ton of C4 attached to the underwater cables beneath the Bridge of the Americas. That's when you set off an underwater fireworks show. You breached out of the water like a dolphin at SeaWorld. I scooped you up, threw you in the RHIB, and ran for the ship we saw in the anchorage carrying the American flag. Why did you leave the key in the boat, by the way? You never do that?"

"What?" I mumbled again.

"Never mind about the key. Anyway, I figured they'd have a doctor aboard the research vessel, or at least know how to get you to one. By the time we got on board, I was getting pretty sick, and you still weren't conscious. They patched you up and threw us both in a chamber. Now you're pretty well caught up."

Flashes of the scenes Clark had described danced in my head but wouldn't come together to form complete memories.

"Did you say the Bridge of the Americas . . . in Panama?"

"Yeah, we're in Central America, Chase. Are you okay?"

I listened to the rustling of the plastic-covered pillow beneath my head and reached for my water bottle. I shot another long stream of bitter, warm water into my mouth and forced myself to swallow. I heard the click of the handset returned to its cradle on the outside of my coffin. Another forced swallow of water emptied my bottle, so I threw it as hard and far as I could. Based on the sound of the plastic bouncing off the glass, that was about six feet.

How could I have been in an explosion in the Panama Canal and not remember it?

Memories poured through my mind of my time in the Nebraska Medical Center after I'd broken my hand in the final game of the ninety-six College World Series. I initially hadn't remembered that accident, either. Perhaps I was re-experiencing that same phenomenon.

My eyelids grew heavy, and my breathing became rhythmic and deep. Sleep absorbed me once again.

"I did not know them, of course. I was child when they were killed, but I read file on both of them."

I whispered, "What was in the file, Anya? You have to tell me."

"Is record of training and military service. Your father was in navy and mother was not. Both were educated at university. Your father was . . . I do not know English word. *Nabirat'*."

"Recruited," I said.

"Your father was recruited in hospital after injury in war. He met your mother at university, and she volunteered for service to country with him."

"Yeah," I said. "I know all of that. Tell me who killed them."

"I do not know who killed them, but it had to be done. There were rules then. Rules of KGB and your CIA. Agents did not kill other agents. Professional courtesy is what your President Reagan called rule. Your father ignored rule. He killed nine Russian officers."

"My father didn't work for the CIA, so he wasn't bound by those ridiculous rules."

"You do not understand, Chasechka. Rules were not only for CIA. Rules were for everyone in intelligence community. So, that is why many people wanted your father to be captured or killed. Your mother was also very dangerous woman, Chase. She was like me. This for you is hard to understand, but is true."

I couldn't picture my mother hurting a fly. She was the most loving and nurturing person I'd ever known. She'd certainly been nothing like Anya Burinkova, the SVR assassin.

Anya continued. "File does not say who killed them, but there are photographs of their bodies. File also does not have interrogator's notes. That means there were no questions. They were killed quickly."

I tried to hold back tears. "How?"

"They were shot. I am sorry, but you will never know who killed them. You must stop chasing their killers. That is a chase that will never end until you are also dead, and I do not want that, my Chasechka. *YA lyublyu tebya.*"

Dr. Shadrack's voice once again filled the chamber. "We're going to start bringing you up now. How do you feel?"

"What?" I shook my head and tried to understand what he was saying.

"We're going to bring you up slowly now. You've been at depth for almost three hours. How do you feel?"

"I'm hungry."

"There's an air lock above your head. There's another bottle of water and some astronaut food in there."

"Astronaut food?"

"Yes, it's the same kinds of meals NASA sends into space for the astronauts. The conditions inside the chamber make normal food look a little unappetizing."

"I can't see anyway," I said, "so it doesn't matter."

Without being able to see the latch on the air lock, it was a clumsy task, but I removed the water bottle and the sealed package of astronaut food.

"Can you tell me your name now?" the doctor asked.

"Yeah. I'm Chase Fulton."

"Excellent." He sounded relieved. "Now, how about the date? Do you know what day it is?"

I thought for a moment. "No, I don't know the date, but in my defense, I didn't know the date before I ended up in here. It's sometime in early September."

"That's close enough," he said. "It's Monday, the tenth of September."

"Thanks," I offered. "This astronaut food is terrible. What's it supposed to be?"

"I have no idea," he said. "I don't eat it."

"And this water," I said. "Either my taste buds are screwed up, or this water tastes like shit."

He chuckled. "Your taste buds are fine, I'm sure. The water contains vitamin supplements and pain medication to help you relax."

That explains the sleeping, I thought, *but it doesn't explain Anya.*

19

Aye, Captain

The next two hours of my life were spent gradually ascending from the dive I'd taken in the recompression chamber. My ears popped a few thousand times, and my vision had improved, but I still couldn't make out details outside of the glass.

By the time Dr. Shadrack opened the hatch and slid me out of the chamber, I'd spent all the time I'd ever wanted inside that coffin.

The doctor pressed a stethoscope against my chest. "Take a big, deep breath, and slowly let it out."

I did as he'd ordered and then squinted as he shined a light into each of my eyes.

"How are you feeling, young man?"

"Not great," I admitted. "I'm pretty sore. What happened to me?"

He chuckled. "Well, we aren't sure, but you look like you've been washed and sent through the spin cycle a time or two. You're going to live, but you may have your doubts about that over the next few days."

"Can I sit up?" I asked, squirming on the gurney.

"Sure you can." He raised the head of the bed, but I could feel him hovering closely by my side.

"How's the vertigo?"

"It's better," I told him, "but my ears are ringing like a church bell."

"That's called tinnitus," he said. "When you got blown to the surface, the nitrogen in your body came out of solution and formed a few billion bubbles. At least one of those bubbles ended up in the blood vessels that feed the eighth cranial nerve behind your ear. That nerve does a lot of things. It's responsible for sending balance and spatial orientation information from the inner ear to the brain. That's why you probably felt like you were spinning and falling. The fact those symptoms have ceased, or have at least reduced, indicates that the recompression therapy has restored the blood flow to that nerve."

"Why are my ears ringing?"

"That's another symptom of damage to that eighth cranial nerve. In time, the ringing will decrease, and hopefully diminish altogether."

"How about my vision? Why can't I see?"

He cleared his throat. "I'm afraid that one is a little more complex. Blindness is sometimes associated with barotrauma, but not necessarily with the particular nerve we're talking about. It's also an excellent sign that you're now seeing shapes and colors. With continued recompression therapy, I think it's reasonable to expect that your vision will return—possibly even to normal."

I tried to focus on several objects moving around the room in front of me. "I need to talk to Clark."

"He's down in the crew mess having some dinner. Do you feel like eating?"

"Yeah. I'm hungry," I said, "but please tell me you have something better than that astronaut food."

"I think we can put something together for you. We're going to reconnect you to some monitors, and I'll send someone down to let Mr. Johnson know you're out of the chamber."

By the time I was attached to a machine that beeped every time my heart beat, I heard Clark pull up a chair.

"How you doin', bubbles?"

"Bubbles? Really? That's what you're going with? Bubbles?"

Clark laughed at his own joke. "It seemed appropriate, somehow."

"I don't know how I'm doing. I feel like I've been used as a punching bag for a few hours, and my vision is all screwed up. Are you okay?"

"Yeah. I'm all right. I got bent pretty bad. I was still on the surface when you set off the C4. When I saw you surface, I knew I had to get you out of the water and find a doctor. I thought this boat was probably our best shot at finding a crew who could speak English and get us the help we needed."

"It looks like you made the right decision. What is this boat?"

I could see Clark's outline moving in front of me. I assumed he was looking around to see who was listening. "It's a real research vessel, but it's also an agency asset when they're not studying bugs on the ocean floor—or whatever they do. The captain knows who we are and what we're doing here, but I don't think anyone else on board knows. I had a talk with him through the glass while I was in the chamber. I get the impression he knows a lot more than he's saying."

"Has anyone done a BDA?" I asked.

I needed the battle-damage assessment. My memory was returning, and I was still responsible for the operation. There were a lot of unanswered questions, and I had a lot of loose ends dangling in the water.

"No," he said. "So far, all we have are some satellite images and radio chatter. It's pandemonium out there."

"What about our boat?"

"It's aboard. The bosun hoisted it out of the water and stowed it on deck. I went to check on our gear after I came out of the chamber. It's secured in a couple lockers."

I rubbed at my eyes. "How's your vision?"

"My vision is fine," Clark said. "My only issue is that I didn't deco on the way up. You're the one who looked like he was shot out of an underwater canon."

"Hey, Clark. Listen. You've done a lot more hard-core diving than me. Have you ever seen this happen to anyone before?"

He made a huffing sound of dismissal. "You'll be fine."

I reached toward the shape I knew was him and clenched the fabric of his shirt in my grip. "Have you ever seen anyone go blind like this?"

I heard him take a deep breath. "Yeah, I've seen blindness a couple times, but we got you into a chamber within minutes of the accident, so I'm sure you'll be fine."

"Tell me the truth, Clark. How did they turn out?"

"You're in good hands here. You've got nothing to worry about. These guys know what they're doing. That doctor is a former DMO for the SEALs, for God's sake. You couldn't be in better hands."

"I don't care if he was the dive medical officer for Jacques Cousteau. I want to know how the cases of blindness you've seen turned out."

"It's not the same, man. We were remote, and there was no way to deco the guys other than putting them back in the water."

His refusal to answer my question directly was exactly the answer I feared.

"Help me up. I have to know if I can stand."

He instantly began to argue. "You need to stay—"

I didn't let him finish. "Next time you feel inspired to start a sentence with the words *you need*, consider some other phrase. I don't respond well to those words."

I tossed back the clinical white sheet that was supposed to help keep me warm and swung my feet over the edge of the gurney. "I'm going to stand up. I'd like for you to either catch me or shove me back toward the gurney if I start to go down."

The deck was cold to my bare feet, but the world didn't immediately spiral out of control when I pushed myself up. On the other hand, the heart monitor had a fit. It screeched and blared its disapproval, but I didn't fall. I could stand, even if my heart didn't enjoy it.

Clark's hands gripped my biceps as I eased myself back onto the gurney. As expected, a hoard of clinical types galloped to my aid in response to the heart monitor's tantrum.

A cacophony of voices echoed disapproval, but I shut them down. "Relax. I'm fine. I just needed to know if I could stand up without falling. I can. Next, I'll probably experiment to see if I can walk across the room without hurting anyone or myself. I promise to let you in on the plan before I go for a stroll."

The disapproval continued, but this time Dr. Shadrack called for order in the court. "Well, it seems like you were right, Mr. Johnson. He is going to be a handful."

I could almost hear Clark rolling his eyes.

The doctor patted my leg. "Well, that was quite an adventure, huh?"

"I had to know," I said.

"Of course you did. But next time, get us involved. I want to see you walk, and we'll do that as soon as you're ready, but your vision is going to be an issue."

"I need to talk to the captain," I blurted out.

"The captain is a very busy man."

"Not as busy as he's going to be if I don't brief him. Things around here are about to get very ugly very soon."

The gaps in my memory had begun filling to overflowing. I remembered what I believed to be almost everything leading up to the explosion.

Muffled by the constant ringing in my ears, I heard the doctor and Clark murmuring.

"Now that he's got his wits about him, he's in charge," Clark said.

My vision was improving. Formerly blurry-edged objects had some definition, and I could almost tell the difference between a human and an IV pole.

"All right, then," Dr. Shadrack said. "If you feel up to it, we'll go see the captain."

Someone rolled a wheelchair to my bedside, and then as if I could see it, I turned my head toward the chair. "I believe I'll walk. If you wouldn't mind, block for me so I don't plow over anyone."

Clark actually laughed. "You're one stubborn S-O-B."

The doctor disconnected me from the heart monitor, removed my catheter, and I stood again. It required less effort than the first attempt, and I reached for Clark's arm. I've never been good at being dependent on anyone or anything, but without my eyes, I was at the mercy of the sighted.

Walking hurt, but I tried to pretend it didn't. I could pick out doorways and changes in lighting, but little else. Stairs were another issue altogether. There was no way to hide the pain of climbing. By the time we'd reached the bridge deck, I was exhausted and pouring sweat.

"I'll bet now you wish you would've let us wheel you up here."

"How would you have wheeled me up those stairs?"

"Oh, we have an elevator," the doctor said, "but you seemed insistent on walking."

"Point taken," I groaned. "I'll behave."

"Yeah, right," Clark mumbled.

"Captain, our guests of honor would like a word with you if you have time," Dr. Shadrack said.

The captain had a gruff voice I didn't recognize. "Yeah, all right. I'll be down in a little while. How's the dead guy doin'?"

Instead of letting the doctor have all the fun, I spoke up. "There's no need for you to come down, Captain. We came to you. Oh, and if I'm the dead guy, I'm a lot tougher than most dead guys who show up on your ship unannounced."

"Well, I'll be damned. Get in here and sit down. I'm Captain Stinnett. I guess I should officially welcome you aboard the research vessel, *Lori Danielle*. It's good to see you without an inch of glass between us."

"Thanks, Captain Stinnett. It's nice to meet you. I'm Chase Fulton, and I think you've already met Clark Johnson."

"Indeed, I have," he said, "but I didn't expect to see you up and about so soon."

"I'm a little stubborn," I confessed. "Are we alone?"

Someone else moved to my right.

The captain said, "Give us the bridge, Tommy. I'll call you when we're done."

Tommy shuffled past us and out the hatch.

The captain's tone softened just a little. "Now it's just Dr. Shadrack, Mr. Johnson, you, and me."

"I don't know how much you know, Captain, but—"

"I know who and what you are. I vaguely know what you're doing in this country, but not the specifics. Honestly, I don't want to know. I assume you aren't responsible for that big-ass boat sitting on the bottom of the Miraflores Locks and all hell breaking loose in Bahia de Panama."

"Before we go any further," I said, "is the doctor under an NDA?"

Being given access to classified information requires three distinct elements: the person must possess the proper level of security clearance, have a need to know, and be bound by a non-disclosure agreement.

"Dr. Shadrack is third in command. He can hear anything I can hear," said the captain.

"In that case, no. We're not responsible for any of the mayhem out there, but we do have a man on that ship who we have to retrieve. Are there any frogmen about?"

"At this moment, I'm afraid your partner there and my doctor are the closest things to SEALs there are in this part of the world. We could probably get a team here in eight hours or so if you can convince SOCOM to dispatch them."

I doubted I could convince Special Operations Command to dispatch a telegram, let alone a SEAL team.

"We do have an air asset," I said. "We've got a Huey and one of the best pilots I've ever seen."

"Yeah," said the captain, "I know Leo. That old coot had already been shot down a dozen times before you were born. He's definitely an asset."

I could feel the ship rolling beneath me. "Are we underway?"

"We are," he said. "When you two showed up, it was obvious that there was far more going on in the mouth of the canal than I wanted to get wrapped up in, so I lit the fires and spurred the old mule out of the barn. We aren't fast, but we're making about sixteen knots. We're far enough beyond the fray to avoid getting any of that

bullshit on us. Besides, I figured you boys might need a little plausi-
ble deniability when people start asking questions about Americans
in the water while Chinese ships are sinking."

"I appreciate that," I said, "but we have to get our man off that
boat. No matter how badly I screwed up the rest of the op, I won't
leave him behind."

"I can appreciate that," he said. "I'll tell you what I can do. I can
put us well within chopper range of the canal and still stay out of
sight. I'll get our coordinates to Leo, and he can put his Huey on
my helipad. Meanwhile, you come up with a plan to exfiltrate your
man and do what the doctor says. That's an order."

"I don't take orders very well," I said.

"No problem," said the captain. "I'll have the bosun drop your
dinghy back in the water, and you two can be on your merry way.
But as long as you're on my damned ship, you'll follow my damned
orders."

I'd apparently met my match. "Aye, Captain. I'll do what the
doctor says . . . within reason."

The return trip to sick bay was much more pleasant than the
trek to the bridge, primarily because it included an elevator ride.

"When should I expect my vision to return to normal?"

"It's impossible to say for sure," said Dr. Shadrack, "but I plan to
send you back into the chamber for another dive either this evening
or first thing tomorrow morning."

"Another chamber ride?"

"I'm afraid so. Hyperbaric medicine isn't an instant fix for anything. We'll continue the treatments until you stop showing im-
provement. Your condition is complicated by your physical injuries.
We simply don't know what percentage of your symptoms are related to the concussion of the explosion, and what percentage is
strictly due to the rapid decompression you experienced."

The feeling of dread over being shoved back in that big glass coffin sent my heart rate soaring.

"We've got a lot of work to do," I protested. "I don't have time to lie in that chamber when we've got a man out there relying on us to get him out."

"I don't think you understand," he said. "Your going back out there to recover your man isn't an option right now. You can't even climb a flight of stairs without nearly passing out. What good do you think you're going to be out there trying to rescue anybody?"

I surrendered. "Fine, put me back in the chamber now."

20

On a Leash

The most bizarre things happen in the human mind when it's removed from its natural environment. My ears popped and my sinuses protested as I headed back to simulated depth in the chamber I so loathed. I was imprisoned, encapsulated, and infuriated.

The dive, as they called it, consisted of a somewhat rapid pressurization until I'd reached a pressure equivalent to that of being one hundred fifty feet underwater. After that, I'd spend the allotted time before beginning my ascent. That bottom time was the arena in which my brain refused to relax. While confined to the chamber, I thought about every problem that could arise.

What if the boat sinks? What if there's a fire on board? What if the doctor forgets I'm in the chamber?

That's when I remembered my water bottles. Therein lay the solution for my anxiety. I squirted a long swallow into my throat and tried to relax, but relaxation required three more squirts.

I wondered who'd arrive during my psychedelic trip this time. *Would it be Anya again? Or maybe my father.* I knew enough about the mind to know the hallucinations weren't real, but I still wanted them to come.

My eyes became heavy, and I watched the fields of blurred white fade to black. When I opened my eyes, I didn't recognize the apparition standing just beyond the glass. He was holding a clipboard in one hand and a pen poised just above the paper in the other. He stared at me and pursed his lips.

"Who are you?" I asked.

He simply continued to stare.

"Who are you?" I demanded.

Still no answer.

His hair was short, almost as if he were military, but his posture and stance made me doubt he was a soldier. I pounded on the glass with my fist. "Answer me! Who are you?"

The man flinched and took a step back. He turned as if to check whether anyone else had seen me beating on the glass. I followed his gaze into the empty room. He and I were alone, but he had an enormous advantage. He could leave. I was stuck.

Instead of scurrying away, he picked up the handset. "Mr. Fulton, are you all right?"

"No, I'm not all right. I'm stuck in this coffin and trying to figure out who you are."

"I'm Benny Collins. I'm a nurse. How are you feeling?"

"I can see you. Am I awake, Benny Collins?"

He continued staring at me, and then his eyes narrowed into a slow, deliberate squint. I could see the lines around his eyes and the tiny hairs of his eyebrows.

"Yeah, you're awake. Can you tell me how many fingers I'm holding up?"

"Three," I said. "And the back of your clipboard reads, research vessel *Lori Danielle*, National Oceanic and Atmospheric Administration."

He turned the clipboard and studied the back. "Yeah, that's right. It does. I think I should go get the doctor."

"Yes, I think you should," I replied.

A few minutes later, Dr. Shadrack appeared beside the chamber with an eye chart in his hand.

"I hear you're trying to convince Benny that you can see," he said.

"Yep, that's me," I said. "Always pretending to have superpowers like being able to read, Dexter Shadrack, M.D."

The doctor looked down at the embroidery on his lab coat and tossed the eye chart aside. "I guess we won't be needing that."

"Dexter? That must have been hell in high school."

He smiled. "Yes sir, it was. That's why I went to medical school. Doctor sounds a lot better than Dexter."

"Tell me something there's no way I could know," I said.

"What?" He furrowed his brow.

"I think this might be a hallucination, so I need you to tell me something my brain doesn't know. I can't learn new information from a hallucination—only from a source beyond my own psyche."

"Psych major?" he asked.

I nodded.

"Okay, then, psych major. The serial number of the chamber you're in is RSI3200561, and my middle name is Rosenblum."

"Dexter Rosenblum Shadrack? Are you serious?" I tried not to laugh.

He pressed his Florida driver's license against the glass.

"Whatever was causing your vision to fail was clearly associated with your decompression sickness, and this second dive seems to have resolved it. That doesn't mean you'll be able to see when we bring you up, but it's a very good sign."

"Well, get me out of here, and let's find out. Besides, I need to go to the bathroom."

"I can't just yank you out of there," he said. "I have to bring you back up slowly, and you're out of luck for a bathroom. You should've thought of that before you insisted on going for a walk. If you'd stayed in bed, you'd still have your catheter, but now you'll have to wait at least an hour for me to resurface you."

I lifted my black plastic water bottle and removed the lid. There was, perhaps, three or four ounces of the narcotic-laced water left in the bottle. I deliberately inverted the cylinder, poured the water into the chamber, and then refilled his bottle. "Take all the time you need, Doc. As long as I don't get this bottle and the fresh one confused, I can stay here for a while."

He shook his head and went to work turning dials and recording readings from the gauges. According to the clock on the wall, which I could clearly see, it took fifty-two minutes to depressurize the chamber and return me to the atmospheric pressure of the world around me.

The doctor pulled my gurney from the chamber. "How do you feel?"

"Much better than before I went in," I said.

I tossed him the bottle I'd filled, and he swatted it from the air with the back of his hand, sending it rolling across the floor.

He held up the eye chart ten feet in front of me. "Now, read the smallest line you can."

I made out all the letters on the 20/40 line, but that was the best I could do.

"That's great," he said. "I was afraid I'd have to deal with you being blind *and* an asshole, but now my workload has been cut in half."

I endured a battery of pokes and prods from the doctor and discovered I wasn't badly injured. I was just bruised, beaten-up, and extremely sore. There were no broken bones, and all the parts that were supposed to be on the inside still were.

"I don't have to go back in that chamber, do I?"

Dr. Shadrack grimaced. "You don't have to do anything, but if there are residual symptoms from your DCS, continued recompression is the only method of remediating them. Continued recompression will not hurt you. There are no potential risks; only potential benefits. If you choose not to get back in the chamber, the DCS symptoms you're currently experiencing, if there are any, aren't going to improve."

"Since we now know my blindness was part of the DCS, will it continue to improve if I go back in?"

"I've been practicing hyperbaric medicine for a long time, and I've learned one very important thing. Sometimes we just don't know, but more important than that, we do know how to find out. We simply shove you back in there after a few hours of rest and watch what happens."

"When can I go back in the chamber?"

"I think we should wait at least eight hours, maybe more, but that's not a hard-and-fast rule. Our bodies aren't designed for compression and decompression. It's unexpected stress that our body doesn't know how to handle. I can put you back in now, but it would be better if you get a good night's sleep and some nourishment before another treatment."

"Okay," I said. "One more treatment in the morning. Do you know where Clark is?"

The doctor checked his watch. "It's just past six, so he's probably having dinner in the crew mess. Follow that corridor. You'll see and hear the crew mess amidships. Eat whatever they're serving, and I'll get the quartermaster to set you up in a berth. I'm sure you're tired of sleeping down here in sick bay."

"Thanks, Doc."

I rinsed off in the sick bay head and wondered why the shower on a ship that size was smaller than the one on my catamaran. Clark had said our gear was somewhere aboard the ship, but I had no idea how to find it, so I searched through a locker and borrowed a pair of scrubs that almost fit.

I found Clark in the crew mess devouring what I later learned was his second plate of chicken and dumplings, green beans, and cornbread.

"Looks like Cracker Barrel is catering tonight," I said.

Cornbread crumbs clung to the corners of his mouth. "Hey! How you feeling?"

I took a seat beside him. "I'm doing okay. My vision's returning. I'm up to twenty-forty, which isn't good, but it's better than this morning."

"Hang on. I'll get you a plate." Clark hopped to his feet, then he came back with a heaping plate for me and a third one for him. "These dumplings are really good. It's good to see you up and about."

"Where are we?" I forked the first mouthful.

He looked around, presumably to make sure no one was within earshot. "We're on Isla Cebaco, south of Santiago."

In my mind, I drew the map of the peninsula west of Panama City and tried to calculate how far we'd traveled. "That's got to be two hundred miles from the canal."

Between bites, he said, "Yeah, something like that. Captain Stinnett thought it would be a good idea to get us as far away from the action as possible."

"What's his story?"

"I don't know, but I think he's an old agency guy who'd rather be running boats than playing spook. I can't quite figure him out, but there's more to him than meets the eye."

He was right about the dumplings. They were amazing. It felt good to get some real food in my stomach. I was still a little groggy from the narcotics and sore from the explosion, but I was steadily improving.

"Any word from Leo?"

Clark wiped his chin with what was left of his napkin. "Oh, yeah. He'll be here just after daybreak tomorrow."

"Is he bringing that lying Javier with him? I owe that guy a few more broken fingers . . . at least."

"I've been thinking about that," he said. "I don't think he was lying. I think he told us what he knew, but his knowledge of the overall operation was pretty limited."

"You may be right," I admitted, "but if you were the one who'd been blown up and stuck in that tube for six hours, you'd want to break some fingers, too."

Clark sighed deeply. "I don't think I can eat another bite, but, man oh man, that was good."

I glanced at the serving line. "Are you sure? That looks like peach cobbler they're serving up."

Clark turned his head. "Well, like Skipper says, there's always room for a little dessert."

"I'll get it," I said. "You might burst if you try to move."

He didn't protest, and I returned with two bowls of cobbler that quickly disappeared.

"I don't know who the cook is on the tub, but something tells me he's from the South."

"I think you may be onto something."

A young woman in jeans and a tight-fitting black T-shirt strode into the mess hall.

"Oh, there you are, Mr. Fulton. I'm Christine Billings. I'm the quartermaster. Dr. Shadrack wants me to make sure you're comfortable for the night."

Clark's eyes lit up. Christine wasn't the typical seagoing quartermaster. She was petite with deep brown eyes and long, dark hair pulled back into a ponytail. Her olive complexion made it impossible to determine if she was South American or maybe a Pacific Islander.

"I'm sure the doctor wants me to be comfortable, too," said Clark, standing and extending his hand.

Christine smiled. "Nice try, Mr. Johnson. Tonight's not your night, but stick around. You never know what tomorrow might bring."

How does he do that?

I stood and offered my hand. "Thank you, Christine. Anything is fine. I just need somewhere soft for a few hours."

"I have just the spot," she said. "The executive officer is ashore working on a grant proposal for an upcoming research project, so his cabin is available. You'll be very comfortable up there. The cabin is next door to the captain's. It's quiet, so you'll be able to get some sleep. My cabin is on deck four amidships port side. Come find me when you're finished here, and I'll show you to the XO's cabin."

Her accent didn't match her look. She was undoubtedly American.

"Deck four, port side, amidships," Clark said.

She pointed a finger at him. "You behave and stay down here. I'll come find you if I run out of ways to amuse myself."

He pretended to pout. She pretended to ignore him.

"We're finished," I said. "Let's go take a look now. Oh, and I could use some clothes. Do you know where our gear is?"

We returned our plates to the galley and followed Christine into the passageway.

"I'll have someone bring your gear to your cabin," she said. "And *he* can come, but only if you keep him on a leash."

"I'll do my best, but he chews through every leash I put on him."

Christine keyed her radio and spoke into the mic in a language I didn't recognize.

"Your gear will be here soon. Make yourself at home. The doctor will be up to check on you in a bit. And you"—she paused and stuck her finger in Clark's chest—"you can stop by later if you have any questions about the ship . . . or whatever."

Clark turned his head and exaggeratedly chewed on an imaginary leash. The gorgeous young quartermaster tried not to laugh.

21

Are You on My Boat?

Clark backed into the passageway outside my cabin. "I'll make sure Christine kicks me out in time so I can wake you up before Leo arrives in the morning."

"Feel free to sleep in," I said. "I'm taking another ride in Dr. Shadrack's magic coffin bright and early tomorrow. I'll come find you when I resurface. Oh, and don't hurt your back. I have a feeling we're going to need our strength."

"I've never hurt my back."

"Yeah, well, before yesterday, you'd never had the bends either, Romeo."

Clark offered a mock salute. "Aye aye, XO." He disappeared down the passageway.

A deckhand arrived with two rolling Pelican cases. "Is there anything else you need, sir?"

I laughed at being called *sir.* "No, thank you. This is all I need. Did you happen to take the other two cases to my partner down on deck three?"

"No, sir, but I'm headed down there next."

"Do me a favor and tell him the quartermaster said she's sorry, but she has to stand watch tonight."

He scratched his temple. "Okay, sir, I'll tell him. You can ring three-three-four on the XO's phone if you need anything overnight. I'm on watch until oh-four-hundred, and my name's Cricket."

Had he been a bellman, I would've tipped him, but I doubted that was proper protocol on a ship skippered by a former CIA agent.

The doctor arrived just as Christine said he would. He gave me pills to help me sleep and then rechecked my vision. 20/30. Improving. It must've been the peach cobbler.

"I've got a lot of work to do tomorrow," I told him. "I'd like to get in the chamber as early as possible."

The doctor looked at his wristwatch. It was a Vostok Komandirskie, a Russian naval officer's watch, nearly identical to Dr. Richter's.

"Nice watch," I said. "I have a friend who has one just like it."

Dr. Shadrack smiled. "I'm sure you do."

Is everyone a spook?

He pulled the sleeve of his lab coat down over his watch. "I'll be in sick bay at oh-three-forty-five."

I set a windup alarm clock for three thirty and fell asleep almost instantly.

* * *

Dr. Shadrack pulled me from the chamber after two hours, and I resurfaced to find Clark pacing the deck and incessantly checking his watch.

"It's about time," he said. "Leo will be here just after sun-up. That's less than ten minutes."

"It's not even six a.m. yet. How was your night with Christine?"

He huffed. "Nonexistent. She had to stand watch."

Cricket was definitely getting a tip, even if it wasn't protocol aboard Captain Stinnett's boat.

I pulled on my cargo pants and T-shirt. "Let's grab some breakfast and see if Leo can land on a ship as well as he can land in a hole in the jungle,"

"Just hold on," Dr. Shadrack interrupted. "I need to take your vitals and recheck your vision before you go."

I sat on the edge of the gurney and offered him my arm. He wound the blood pressure cuff around my bicep and listened for my pulse.

"One twenty-four over seventy-seven," he whispered as he made a note in my chart. "Now read me the data plate from the chamber." He pointed toward a brass plate screwed to the chamber's panel of controls.

Without looking at the plate, I said, "It's RSI3200561, Dr. Dexter Rosenblum Shadrack."

He scribbled something in my chart then turned the clipboard around. "Read this."

I read the tiny block letters he'd printed on the paper. *Your friend, Dr. Richter, earned his watch. I bought mine.*

I locked eyes with him, and he nodded almost imperceptibly. "Be careful out there, Chase. There's a lot riding on what you're about to do. Just don't go too far and end up back in my chamber . . . or in someone else's."

I inhaled a long, deep breath and thought about Dr. Richter. He'd not only been my favorite psychology professor at UGA, but he was also the man responsible for recruiting me into the world of covert ops. To me, he would always be so much more than just an American hero—he'd become the father figure I'd so desperately needed after losing my family.

"Only those who risk going too far can possibly find out how far one can go. I think T.S. Eliot said that, but I think it applies to what we do, as well," I said. "Don't you think so, Doctor?"

He shook my hand then squeezed Clark's shoulder. "Keep an eye on him. If he starts doing things that make sense, get him back here as quickly as possible."

"Thanks, Doc," said Clark. "We appreciate what you've done for us. You saved our lives . . . especially his."

"When evil calls, men of honor not only stand to face it, but they rise above it and beat it into whimpering submission," Dr. Shadrack said.

I searched my memory for the quote. "Did General Patton say that?"

"Nope, it wasn't Patton. It was Captain Stinnett. He said that about you two last night."

Clark and I headed for the helipad.

The Huey came thundering over the Gulf of Montijo, making the sound only a Huey can. Leo came to a hover just above the helipad and performed a three-hundred-sixty-degree turn, then gingerly brought the skids to rest on the pad as if he were trying to touch down on fine china.

I punched Clark's shoulder. "Can you do that?"

"Ha! I could probably hit the helipad, but I doubt the chopper would be usable again."

Cricket and another deckhand secured the Huey to the deck with heavy chains then welcomed Leo aboard.

Leo knelt beside the skid and ran his hand along the aluminum tube. "You didn't scratch my skids with your ship, did you?"

"Is that the best you can do, old man?" Cricket said.

The two embraced, then Leo came skipping down the ladder from the helipad. "Cricket is my baby sister's kid. He did a stint in the navy and then came to work for these folks. He's a good kid. He'll probably be in command of this old tub someday."

As Cricket came down the ladder, I slid a hundred-dollar bill into his palm. "Thanks for your help last night. I appreciate everything you did."

He grinned. "No problem, sir. Glad I could help." He glanced at Clark and couldn't suppress a smirk.

Clark's eyes grew wide, and he shoved me almost hard enough to send me sprawling to the deck. "You dirty little . . . You put him up to that, didn't you?"

"I have no idea what you're talking about. I was just thanking him for bringing my gear to my cabin."

"You'll pay for that one, college boy. You'll pay."

"I hate to break up this little party of yours," Leo said, "but we've got work to do. Is there someplace we can talk privately?" He held up his laptop case and raised his eyebrows.

"We can go to my cabin," I said.

In my cabin, Leo set up the laptop and connected with Ginger, the analyst. When she appeared on the screen, I recognized the background.

"Are you on my boat?" I demanded.

She looked around. "Oh, I guess I am."

"Who let you aboard?"

Skipper stuck her head into the frame. "Hey, Chase. How are you? Where are you?"

"Skipper, did you seriously just let some strange woman come aboard and set up shop on my boat?"

"You said it was my home, too. And besides, she's not just some strange woman. Dominic said I should give her whatever she needs."

"Oh, Dominic said that, did he?"

"Yeah, he did," she said. "And that's not all. Do you know what she does? It's freakin' amazing. You wouldn't believe the things she can do with a computer. It's badass."

"Okay," I said. "We'll talk about this later. Right now, we need to talk with Ginger."

Ginger rolled back into frame. "Okay, guys. Brief me up. What's going on down there? You've been silent way too long. You've got to keep me in the loop. I can't help you if I don't know what's going on."

"We had a little incident," I said.

"Yeah, that's one way to describe it," Clark said. "He got himself blown up, got both of us a case of the bends, and he made me sleep alone last night."

Ginger bit her lip in an apparent attempt to avoid laughing. "Aw, I'm sorry, Clark. Maybe he'll snuggle with you when this is all over."

"No!" insisted Clark. "That's not what I mean. I don't want to . . . oh, forget it."

I briefed her on the explosion, and she filled us in on what was happening in the Miraflores Locks.

"They've put up a temporary dam at the north end of the locks just in case the upstream gates are rigged, but the *Pearl* is still on the bottom. She's stuck in the intermediate gates and listing. There seems to be minimal effort to float her. The Chinese are blocking all local efforts and demanding that only a Chinese salvage team can recover her. No one wants to piss off the Chinese down there, so the canal is essentially closed until the salvors arrive. I have my doubts that they're coming, but that's beside the point."

"That's exactly what I'd expect them to do," I said. "How about Diablo? Have you heard anything from him?"

"No. And I won't hear anything from him until you get him off that ship. He can't risk sending any outbound signals because there's enough monitoring equipment to hear a mouse sneeze. You've got to get him out of there."

I closed my eyes and sent my brain into overdrive. "Ginger, can you get me a schematic of the *Pearl* and the most recent high-def satellite imagery?"

"Sure," she said. "I'm sending it now."

"Do you have any idea where Diablo will be when we get aboard?"

"Hey, hang on," ordered Leo. "You're not going aboard that boat while she's sitting on the bottom. There'll be armed security all over that thing. You wouldn't be able to get near it even if you were invisible."

"That's what I'm counting on," I said. "Invisibility is overrated."

"Hello? Remember me?" came Ginger's voice. "The *Pearl* is all over the news up here. The whole world is watching. Unless something more dramatic than one of the world's biggest freighters sinking in the Panama Canal happens, you guys are going to be getting a ton of unwanted attention. Whatever you do, keep it off the evening news. We don't need an international incident stamped on our foreheads."

"You got it, Ginger. Is there anything else?"

"Yeah. Get that cute little devil out of there alive for me, okay?"

"We will. I promise." I reached to disconnect the feed.

"Wait," Ginger said. "There's one more thing I need to know. How much can I tell Elizabeth and Penny?"

"Those are two vastly different questions. Skipper, eh, Elizabeth doesn't have a clearance, but she knows what we do. Use your best judgment there. Penny is a different story. She doesn't have a clearance either, but she doesn't really know what we do. I mean, she knows we do some secret squirrel stuff, but she's never asked, and I've never volunteered."

"Gotcha," she said. "Be careful, guys. And no more explosions, please."

Leo pressed a key, disconnecting the feed, and detailed schematics of the *Pearl* replaced Ginger's face.

I used the mouse to scroll around, exploring every inch of the ship. "I'm not seeing any spaces that have the kind of room they'd need to set up a sophisticated electronic monitoring operation. All of the interior spaces big enough for something like that contain engines and machinery. That's no environment for a listening lab."

I switched to the satellite imagery and zoomed in as closely as possible. The resolution was astonishing, but no matter how much I scanned the ship, I couldn't figure out where they would've set up shop.

"She probably sent infrared as well," mumbled Leo.

I scrolled through the shots and watched the screen light up with a message sent from Heaven . . . or perhaps more appropriately, sent from the devil.

"Bingo!" I said.

Leo and Clark leaned in.

"That little devil really is something, ain't he?"

"Yes, Leo. He sure is."

Glowing like a beacon in the night was a strip of infrared reflective tape shaped into a bullseye on top of one of the containers in the center of the deck. Barely visible antennas jutted out from the four corners of the top of the container, and the entire box glowed a few degrees warmer than the rest.

"We could've searched that ship for days and never found that container," said Clark.

"You're right, but thanks to Diablo, we don't have to. All we have to do is get on board, find him, and get him out of there alive."

"Oh, sure, that sounds like a piece of cake," he said. "How do you propose we pull that off?"

I brought the visible satellite imagery back up and continued zooming and scanning the ship for any possible means of ingress.

"There." I poked my finger against the screen.

Clark leaned in closer. "What is that?"

I zoomed in as far as the software would allow. "It's Rapunzel."

"I'll be damned," said Leo. It's a knotted rope. Diablo built you a stairway to Hell."

"How long has it been since you've flown a sling load, Leo?" I asked.

"What do you have in mind?" His eyes were wide with excitement.

"It'll take over twelve hours to get there on this ship," I said, "but your big, beautiful Huey can get us there in under two hours."

Clark's crooked smile showed his instant approval of my crazy plan. "We'll rig the boat. You brief the captain."

22
Air Assault, Baby

"It sounds like a trap to me, son, but it's your op. I'm sure Leo can put you right down their stovepipe if that's what you want," said Captain Stinnett.

"Even if it is a trap, it's a way onto that boat," I said. "We're not easy to kill even if we're unlucky enough to get captured."

He raised a coffee cup to his lips and took a long swallow. "It ain't the worst plan I've ever heard, and I've known better plans that got shot all to hell, so I'll just wish you Godspeed. I don't know what that means, but it sounds fast to me."

I shook his hand and thanked him for the hospitality. "Send us a bill for the gas."

"Oh, don't worry, you'll be getting a bill. Doctors and ships like this one don't come cheap. Good luck, kid. I hope to see you again someday."

"Something tells me this won't be the last time our paths cross, Captain Stinnett."

I left the bridge and found Leo, Clark, Cricket, and three deckhands standing beside our RHIB on the aft deck. They were all looking up and shaking their heads.

"How's it coming?" I asked, then turned to see what everyone was looking at.

Leo spoke up. "Well, we can do it, but not without putting the boat back in the water. I'll blow those antennas to hell and back if I try to pluck it off the deck. How much does it weigh?"

"I don't know." I turned to Clark, hoping he might have a good guess.

"We've got an automated scale on the crane," Cricket said. "I'll pick it up and tell you exactly what it weighs."

Two crewmen rigged the boat for lifting, and she was hovering above the deck in less than two minutes.

"Thirty-two thirteen!" Cricket yelled down to the deck.

Clark and I immediately turned to Leo.

He winked. "No problem."

"Load our gear and put her in the water," I said. "I'm going to see the doc one last time before we go. I'll meet you on the stern."

I wound through the halls of the ship until I found sick bay.

"Doc, I want to thank you again for all you did for us. We owe you one."

He stood from his desk. "Don't mention it. Just go save the world or something."

"Will do," I said, "but I need to ask you something before I go."

"Sure. What is it?"

"Is it going to kill me to get back in the water for, say an hour, at maybe twenty feet?"

"No, of course not. In a few weeks, you'll be fine to get back in the water. There's no evidence that one case of decompression sickness makes a diver more prone to getting bent again."

I frowned. "No, I don't mean in a few weeks. I mean in a couple hours."

He pulled off his glasses, closed his eyes, and rubbed his knuckles into his eyelids. "Chase, as a DMO, I can't tell you it's okay to get back in the water anytime soon, but I understand what you're doing, and it's up to you whether you think it's worth the risk. Your body has been through a lot of trauma over the last few days. You're not at full strength, and you're about to subject yourself to an unpredictable and potentially dangerous environment. I have to recommend against it, but I know you're going to do it anyway, so just be careful and stay as shallow as you can. And for God's sake, keep the bottom time short. An hour is a long time for your body at any depth right now."

"I thought you'd say something like that. Thanks again, Dr. Shadrack. You're a lifesaver . . . literally."

I made it back to the deck and found Cricket almost ready to drop our boat back into the water. "Can you put a couple men in the boat to rig it for the lift, and then have somebody pick them up?"

"Sure. No problem. I've got a Force Recon Marine and a former combat diver. They'd love to get involved in whatever this is."

"Thanks, Cricket. I appreciate it."

"Say, before you go . . . Was your buddy trying to hook up with the quartermaster last night?"

I laughed. "Yeah, something like that. But I needed him well rested."

"That's cold, man . . . really cold."

I chuckled in acknowledgment, knowing Clark would return the favor at his earliest convenience.

I headed to the helipad where I found Clark and Leo already on board and waiting for me. Cricket attached a sling load rig to the belly hook and removed the chains holding the Huey to the ship. He then backed away and gave the universal signal for engine start. The Huey's jet engine whistled to life, and soon the rotors were turning overhead. Cricket turned to the bridge where Captain Stinnett flashed a series of lights, letting Cricket know we were clear for takeoff. He gave the hand signal and saluted as we lifted off. I looked into the cockpit and saw Leo returning the salute. Clark was on the controls.

We circled the ship and came to a hover over the RHIB. As we descended toward the water, the rotor wash blew the boat from beneath the helicopter. If we couldn't get the sling rig close enough to allow the two men to make the connections, our mission would be over before it ever got started.

I was lying facedown with my head and shoulders outside the chopper and watching the action below. One of the men in the boat went to the helm, started the engine, and signaled that he was going to motor into the wind. I relayed the information and Clark responded, "Roger."

As the RHIB picked up speed, Clark maneuvered the Huey to follow and slowly overtake the boat. The revised plan was working. As the sling rig swung into position above the boat, the first crewman reached up with a discharge pole and touched the hook dangling overhead. A shower of static electric sparks flew from the hook, and the crewman made the first connection of the rear straps and shackles. In seconds, he had the forward straps connected and secured. He then gave the signal to climb, taking the slack out of the sling rig. Inch by inch, Clark climbed the Huey until the hull of the boat was barely touching the water. The crewman shut down the engine and offered a crisp salute, which I returned, then both men rolled backward out of the boat and into the water. A plume of orange smoke rose from between the two crewmen, and a recovery boat piloted by Cricket approached from astern.

I watched our RHIB leave the surface of the ocean and begin to spin beneath us. Water trailed from the hull, leaving a misty white tail behind. The boat finally found equilibrium and stopped spinning as we continued to climb and pick up speed.

Through my headset, I heard Leo say, "Tell us if you see it start to oscillate. We're going to continue picking up speed until it misbehaves, and then we'll back off, but we need to make up all the time we can."

"Roger." I kept my eye on the boat, but it never oscillated. It trailed beneath and slightly behind us.

"One-ten. How's she look, Chase?"

"Solid," I said.

We headed east out over the Pacific and toward Bahia de Panama with our beloved boat along for the ride. I strapped into one of the net seats and slept until Clark emptied a canteen of water on my face.

I sputtered and swatted at him. "So, now we're even?"

"Not even close, buddy. Not even close."

I wiped my face and sat up. "Where are we?"

"About ten minutes out. We're going wet near Isla Otoque. That'll give us about twenty miles in the RHIB."

I stared out the door. "Perfect."

"Are you sure you're up for this one, Chase? I can go it alone."

"No chance, Baby Face. I'm not letting you have all the fun. I'm good to go."

We donned masks, fins, and snorkels before sitting in the door-way with our fins hanging over the skid.

From the cockpit, Leo gave the "okay" signal. I didn't see any other boats, so I flashed the thumbs-down, telling him to put her in the water. He descended and decelerated until the hull of the boat bounced across the tops of the waves. I gave him the release signal, and he cut away the sling with a disconnect lever in the cockpit. As the boat settled into the water, I turned to Clark and yelled, "Air-borne!"

He shook his head. "Air assault, baby!"

We pushed off and immediately covered our masks and snorkels with our hands to ensure they didn't get knocked off when we hit the water. As we fell, my body turned slightly, and my feet rose in front of me. I hit the water butt first, and it knocked the wind from my lungs. When I surfaced, Clark had one hand on my collar and was pulling me toward our boat bobbing on the waves. I caught my breath and nodded silent gratitude. We swam clear of the rotor wash and climbed aboard.

"Well, that was fun, huh?" Clark said as he threw his mask and snorkel to the deck.

"Yeah, a real joy ride."

"You gotta keep your feet underneath you, or else . . . well, you know."

"Yeah, I know," I said, "but that wasn't bad for my first time."

"Your first time?"

"Yeah, I've never done that before. I'm a college boy, remember?"

"Well, you never forget your first. Let's get to work."

He started the engine and eased the throttle forward. The impressive craft accelerated and soon settled into her rhythm, darting across the waves. Leo was heading back to the northwest. We hoped the next time we saw Leo was after we'd successfully extracted Diablo from the *Pearl*.

The closer to the canal entrance we got, the more ships we saw at anchor. The closure of the Miraflores Locks was causing dozens of ships to stack up and wait their turn. I wondered what the ships in Gatun Lake would do. I imagined they were just as stranded as the *Pearl*.

As the Bridge of the Americas came into view, I got an uneasy feeling in my gut. Nothing good had ever happened to me within sight of that bridge. I hoped I was about to break that cycle.

Clark yelled, "How close do you think we can get before somebody stops us?"

"I don't know, but I'd rather swim than risk getting stopped!"

We pulled up just off Farfan Beach and anchored in the brown water. The entrance to the canal was littered with boats displaying flashing lights of every color. It was like the Macy's Thanksgiving Day Parade. The work ahead of us would be nothing like a parade, but when it was finally over, we hoped we'd be able to disappear like Santa back up the chimney, leaving nothing but cookie crumbs and an empty milk glass behind.

We opened our cases and began gearing up for the long swim.

"Oh, Chase, I forgot to tell you. I scored a couple DPVs from the divers on the *Lori Danielle*."

Diver propulsion vehicles are small electric motors with plastic propellers that pull divers through the water without wasting the energy of finning.

"I could kiss you right now."

"Go ahead and try that and see where it gets you," he said.

"Okay. A raincheck, then?"

We packed our dry bags with every piece of gear we thought we'd possibly need for the mission and attached them to the DPVs. As much as I hated the thought of getting caught in Panama with a pistol, we couldn't risk going unarmed, so a pair of suppressed forty-fives also went into the bags.

"I had the gear technician on the ship refill the O2 and service and repack our scrubbers. We should be good for at least five hours or so."

Clark had been busy while I'd been riding Dr. Shadrack's magic carpet.

We donned and tested our rebreathers and communication equipment. Surprisingly, my gear hadn't been destroyed in the explosion, and the commo gear still worked just as advertised. We clipped the DPVs to our harnesses and rolled overboard.

To get an accurate reading of our position, our GPS equipment required that we float a buoy every few minutes. The buoy was small and brown, but it still could've been easy for a pair of vigilant eyes to see it on the surface. We marked our position when we entered the water and stored it in the GPS's memory. This way, we could find our way back to the boat, no matter what the conditions. We each plotted a course to the Miraflores Locks and agreed to meet at the stern of the *Pearl* in ninety minutes. We couldn't risk swimming together and both getting caught and detained. I'd swim the western side of the canal, and Clark would cross and swim the eastern side. Our DPVs could make the four-mile run in just over an hour if everything went perfectly, but nothing ever went perfectly.

"What's the contingency plan if one of us gets busted?"

I didn't hesitate. "We'll wait twenty minutes at the rudder and then continue the mission solo. We have to get Diablo off that boat."

"Agreed," Clark said in his best Green Beret voice.

When I swam over the spot where the explosion had occurred, I felt a cold chill, but I pushed it to the back of my mind and kept heading north. I floated the buoy and found that I was just off the navy base where we'd bought our new favorite toy from Pablo. I was making great time. I hoped the same was true for Clark.

I entered the narrow channel leading into the locks and slowed down to give Clark a little time to catch up. His swim was longer than mine since he had to cross the canal. I floated the buoy once

194 · CAP DANIELS

more to reconfirm my position and found that I had less than one mile remaining to the stern of the *Pearl*. I could make that in less than fifteen minutes with the DPV.

I recoiled the buoy line and pulled the trigger on my DPV. Nothing happened. I yanked the trigger a dozen more times and got the same response. Nothing. I beat on the side of the housing and shook the machine, but it was dead. My sub-fifteen-minute DPV ride had just turned into a half-hour swim.

Wasting no time, I unclipped my dry bag from the now useless DPV and reclipped it to my harness. Unwilling to let the device be discovered, I opened the housing and flooded it with seawater, sending it to the bottom of the canal. After taking a compass bearing, I started kicking.

My body soon reminded me that I wasn't at peak performance level. By the time I made it to the rudder of the *Pearl*, my heart was pounding like a drum, my ears were ringing out of control, and I was tired, but not exhausted. I discovered Clark's DPV tied to the rudder, and I was relieved to know he'd made it that far. God only knows what he was thinking had happened to me. Because his gear was still in the water, but he wasn't, I had to assume he'd arrived more than twenty minutes ahead of me.

I caught my breath, let my heart rate calm down, and then I slowly swam for the surface. My head barely broke the surface, and I scanned the area for onlookers or guards. I saw neither.

The knotted rope I'd seen in the satellite imagery was exactly where it was supposed to be, and tied to its end was a plastic devil figurine. I was starting to like Diablo.

Confident that I'd rested long enough to muster the strength to climb the rope, I secured my rebreather, mask, and fins to the rudder, and I started up.

After making the long climb with relative ease, I stowed the rope in a space beneath a bench and started my search for Clark and Diablo. When I rounded the port stern quarter of the ship, I saw a single forty-five caliber shell casing lying on the deck. A splatter of blood was on the bulkhead. Unless the Chinese were using Colt forty-fives, the shell casing was Clark's, and the blood was someone else's. With my pistol held close to my side, I crept forward, replaying the schematics of the ship in my head to avoid getting lost on the massive vessel. Several sets of stairs led me to the cargo deck. Clark would be moving toward the cargo container we'd seen with the bullseye and antennas.

Every sound froze me in my tracks. A few voices were speaking what I assumed was either Mandarin or Cantonese, but I couldn't tell the difference. The conversations sounded routine, so I continued my search.

I paced off the distance I'd memorized until I reached the walkway between the stack of containers they'd constructed as the listening lab and the next stack. There was enough rigging on the containers that would make the climb easy when I was ready.

I reached the center of the deck, still having encountered no resistance. Something didn't feel right about the absence of security personnel as I started making my way up the containers. There should've been a sentry at every walkway and on every stairwell, but it almost felt like the ship was abandoned.

Someone yelled in broken, Chinese-accented English. "Why you here? Why? What your name?"

The yelling was followed by a long silence and punctuated by the unmistakable sound of fists striking flesh, then Clark groaned.

"Why you here? What your name?"

I moved silently across the containers until I was confident which one contained my partner and his captors. I retracted the slide on my forty-five a fraction of an inch to reconfirm what I already knew. There was, indeed, a round in the chamber ready to be fired.

A rough door had been cut into the side of the container, and a clumsy attempt at installing a knob had been made. That was a one-second obstacle at most. The problem was I didn't know what I'd find inside.

How many targets are waiting inside? How are they armed? How prepared are they for my inevitable arrival?

Clark would be tied to a chair or table and wouldn't be able to move. I'd heard at least two angry voices, but there could've been more observers or additional guards waiting to take their turn at Clark. There were eight rounds in my pistol and fourteen more in my two extra magazines. I could make the first three or four shots count, but if there were more men than that, I'd be badly outgunned. There had to be a way to get a look inside the container without giving away my position.

I approached the makeshift door and pressed my face to the hot metal. To my surprise and delight, I could see through the slit where the door didn't quite mesh with the wall of the container. Clark was shirtless and strapped to a wooden rack on the wall. Blood was trickling from his mouth, but his eyes were open. Two interrogators had their backs toward me. I listened for sounds that didn't coincide with the movement of the two interrogators, hoping to get an accurate count of the bad guys.

That's when it happened. I was spotted.

But it wasn't the Chinese interrogators who'd seen me. Clark's eyes met mine, and he yelled, "Four! Eleven and One!" He ducked his head and closed his eyes against the delivery of the last punishing blows his captors would ever deliver.

In one blinding motion, I grabbed the door and threw it open. I sent a pair of hollow-point rounds into the faces of the two men at Clark's eleven and one o'clock positions, and then two more into each of the men moving to inflict their blows on my partner. I was too fast. They never got to deliver those blows. Clark opened his eyes just as I released the magazine from my pistol, letting it fall to the ground. I slammed another in its place, rechambering a round a millisecond before the slide closed.

Clark spat blood from his battered lips. "Okay, now maybe we're even. But I would've given Christine a night she'd never forget."

"Next time I see her, I'll tell her I'm sorry for robbing her of that pleasure," I said as I cut him free.

"What took you so long?"

"You gave me a lemon," I said. "I had to swim the last mile."

"I'm sorry about that, but under the circumstances, I think I'd have been glad to trade DPVs with you."

He'd taken a nasty beating, but he was far from out of the fight. I took a look at the cuts on his cheeks and around his eyes. "It looks like Baby Face may have just become Scarface."

He spat another mouthful of blood to the deck and forced a smile. "I'm still prettier than you, college boy. Now let's go find ourselves a water devil."

23

Runnin' with the Devil

Clark grabbed a pair of handheld radios from two of the bodies and recovered his pistol.

"That was a pretty good entry," he said, "but I had them right where I wanted them. It was all part of my plan. I was on the verge of handing them their butts on a platter."

"Yeah, but I can't let you have all the fun. Did you have any luck figuring out where Diablo is before you implemented your grand plan to get captured?"

"No, other than the IR tape, there's been no sign of him. I put down four Chinese gunmen before I ended up in here. The one on the stern went overboard, but I stashed the other three."

I tried to piece together a search grid to find Diablo, but I kept coming back to the fact that there was no sign he'd been aboard. "We have to find a way to let Diablo know we're here. We're never going to find him unless he wants to be found."

Clark nodded. "I thought he might react to the gunfire if I could ever get one of the Chinese guards to squeeze off a round. They're all carrying unsuppressed AKs, but he never would've heard the rounds we fired unless he was next door with his ear pressed to the container."

"That's it!" I said. "He may not be next door, but wherever he is, we know he'll be listening in to everything that's happening in that container. If we can get inside of it and cause some general mayhem, he'll know we're here, and hopefully, he'll reveal himself."

He holstered his pistol and pulled on his shirt. "I'm in." Blood was still trickling from his face, but the determination in his eyes made it clear he was feeling no pain.

We started our agonizingly slow climb up the mountain of containers, moving a foot or two at a time as we covered each other's movement. There was no way to know where they might have posted guards or installed monitoring cameras, and while we could deal with the guards, the cameras were another issue. We had to avoid being detected by an overwatch. If they had time to plan and dispatch a force to stop us, we'd be badly outnumbered and even more outgunned.

After climbing, crawling, and trying to remain invisible, we arrived near what I'd labeled "the listening lab."

"Let's take out the antennas and see if they send somebody out to investigate," I whispered.

"I'll knock out the two on the forward section."

Crawling across the neighboring container, Clark moved like a cat silently stalking his prey, but still not as stealthily as Diablo. I wanted to take out the four antennas as close to simultaneously as possible, so I slinked into position and waited for Clark to arrive at the front of the container. Two minutes later, he made eye contact and snapped the first antenna off at its base. His movements toward the second were less furtive and more rapid, never slowing down as he passed the corner of the container and broke the metallic whip like a twig.

I did the same, and we took up positions on diagonal corners of the container so we could see every exterior surface. We needed to know the egress points so we could make entry when the time came.

It didn't take long for our bait to attract a rat. A spiky-haired, twentysomething Asian in flip-flops, shorts, and a filthy T-shirt poked his head out of a well-camouflaged hatch near the front right corner of the container, and then he started climbing. When our flip-flop-clad techno nerd reached the broken antenna, he quickly turned, looking in every direction for the source of the damage. Confusion looks the same on everyone's face, regardless of the language they speak.

Clark and I ducked behind the corners of the container to avoid being seen, but in the end, it wouldn't have mattered if the man had seen us and taken our pictures.

As the tech threw one leg over the top of the container and began to pull himself up, a small figure fell from the sky, grabbed the tech's spiked hair, and yanked him from the container. As they fell, Diablo torqued the man's neck, releasing an audible crack. Our little devil then released the tech from his grasp, letting him fall some fifty feet to the deck below. In a swift, silent motion, Diablo kicked the side of one stack of containers, forcing his body toward the next stack. He grabbed the rigging and drew his body against the wall of the container, making no more than a slight brushing sound as he came to rest.

Where did he come from? How could he have been watching from above without Clark or me seeing him?

Knowing there would be a second technician emerging from the hatch at any minute, I moved to the top of the container and crept to the front corner. Clark joined me as Diablo climbed back to a position above our heads. As soon as the tech had reached the top of the container, I grabbed his right arm and threw him facedown, twisting both of his arms behind his back and pinning him to the hot surface. Clark folded the man's legs, pinning his feet to his butt, then sat on the man's shins and pressed a pistol to the base of his skull. In that position, the man could neither kick with his feet nor pound with his hands on the container to warn his comrades inside.

Clark leaned in close to the man's ear and whispered in Chinese.

In terrified English, the trembling man said, "Six."

"Six including you and the first guy, or six still inside?"

The man's face showed confusion. Clark switched to Chinese, and the man replied with something I didn't understand.

Clark wove his arm beneath the man's chin and squeezed until the technician fell limp and his breathing became deep and rhythmic. "Four inside."

I held up four fingers to Diablo then pointed into the container. He nodded and began climbing down the stack.

Four unarmed surveillance technicians weren't going to be a problem, but if the man had lied, we'd be in for a fight. We had to be prepared for every possibility when we breached the hatch.

I whispered the plan in English for Clark and Spanish for Diablo. "Clark, you go right. I'll go left. Diablo, you go low. Only shoot to avoid getting shot. There's no reason to kill these guys if they're unarmed."

Diablo grimaced at my mention of letting the men inside the container live.

I met his eyes. "Don't hold back. Tell me what you're thinking."

I was quickly learning how challenging bilingual tactical operations could be.

In rapid-fire Spanish, Diablo said, "They will destroy the data when we breach. They have to be stopped before they can do that. They will die to protect that data."

I agreed. "Okay. In that case, if they make any moves toward the equipment, we'll put them down. If not, we'll take what they have, disable and secure them, and get out. Agreed?"

"Agreed," said Clark.

"Sí," came Diablo's staccato response.

We made our way down the stack and took up positions outside the hatch. Clark and I had not only practiced tactical entry together countless times, but we'd made more than one real-world assault on confined spaces. However, this would be our first with Diablo. I didn't doubt his ability, but I was concerned with his ability to operate with restraint. If he had the opportunity to kill them, I doubted he would let anyone live.

I raised three fingers and began the countdown. Two. . . . One. . . .

Clark threw a powerful kick to the hatch, sending it flying inward. Diablo was first through the door and hit the deck like a cockroach, scampering left and right with astonishing quickness. With my left hand on Clark's shoulder, I followed him through the hatch. He broke right as I peeled off to the left.

Clark yelled what I assumed was some variation of "Don't move," then I heard his suppressed forty-five spit twice. I was tempted to turn and see who he'd shot, but I kept my focus on my sector as a mortified face appeared just beyond the front sight of my pistol. The man's hands flew above his head, and he whimpered in Chinese. Out of my peripheral vision, I saw another man stand, draw something from his waistband, and take up a fighting position.

Diablo leapt from the deck to face the man who was holding a glistening, curved, Kali-style fighting knife.

Short of being blown to the surface eighty feet above by thirty pounds of plastic explosive, there were few things I dreaded more than a knife fight. It ensured only one thing—you were going to get cut. Diablo obviously didn't share my concern. He propelled himself forward and delivered a powerful side kick to the man's knee, sending him melting to the deck. With his pinky laced through the finger hole, the man still had a firm grasp on the knife. Diablo stepped on his opponent's wrist with his left foot, and in a lightning-fast delivery, landed his right heel just beneath the man's chin. He exhaled a guttural groan and gave up the ghost.

I refocused my attention on my target whose hands had moved from directly over his head to his waist.

I yelled, "Hands up! Now!"

He followed my instructions, but this time his hands weren't empty. Dangling from his index finger was a metallic pin on a ring. Just leaving the fingertips of his other hand was the body of a Russian F1 anti-personnel grenade beginning its slow arc toward the center of the container. Diablo was right. They would die to protect the data. The spoon released a metallic click, and the fuse began to burn. Depending on the variant of the grenade, we had between three and five seconds before the container would be full of count-less shards of shrapnel flying through the air.

I yelled, "Grenade!" and dived toward the baseball-sized explo-sive sailing through the air. I caught it in my palm like a baseball and hurled it toward the hatch, hoping to get it outside the con-tainer before it detonated. To my horror, my throw was off the mark. The grenade clanged off the frame of the hatch and rico-cheted back onto the deck of the container. I had landed in front of the man who'd thrown the grenade, so I wrapped my arm around his knees and rolled with all my strength toward the grenade that was less than a second away from sending us and the data to the great beyond. Just as I'd hoped, the man's body collapsed toward mine as I continued my roll. He landed squarely on top of the grenade, and I allowed his momentum to carry me with him.

I experienced a second explosion in one week, but this one was inches away with a Chinese techie between me and the source of the blast. The sound was deafening, the shock wave was horren-dous, and we were lifted off the deck before falling back into a bloody heap of misshapen flesh. I couldn't tell how much of the blood was mine, but the shock reawakened every pain my body ex-perienced from the underwater explosion days before.

Clark had taken cover behind an overturned table full of com-puter equipment, and Diablo was crawling from beneath the body of the knife fighter. My ears rang from the thunder of the grenade coupled with the residual tinnitus from my bout with the bends. I doubted if I'd ever hear again. Clark rolled me off the corpse of the grenadier and felt my abdomen and chest for shrapnel and open wounds. After the examination, he collapsed to the deck beside me.

There was relief in his muffled voice. "I know you're willing to die for your country, but it's so much better making the other guy die for his."

He offered a hand and pulled me to my feet. Though temporar-ily nearly deaf, we were unharmed, and the data was intact. We bagged the data storage devices and made it through the hatch. I led the way with Diablo behind me carrying the bag, and Clark covering our six as we ran for the stern.

We emerged at a sprint from between two stacks of containers just as two armed guards leveled a pair of AK-47s at us. I downed each of them before they could get off a shot, and Clark stripped a rifle from one of the fallen guards. Every soul on that ship knew we were aboard, and covering our retreat with a thirty-caliber fully automatic rifle would be far more effective than doing so with his forty-five.

We descended the stairwells on the port side, backtracking the route I'd taken when I'd come aboard. At the base of the stairs, we picked up our pace, running with every ounce of speed we could muster. The unmistakable sound of rifle fire was behind us, but with my diminished hearing, it was impossible to tell if they were firing at us, or if we were firing at them.

Time slowed down as Clark, Diablo, and I dived from the stern toward the waiting water, and Van Halen's "Runnin' with the Devil" thundered in my head.

24

Ginger or MaryAnn

White ribbons of air followed the bullets through the water as they chased us downward toward the rudder. Clark and I knew we had air and rebreathers waiting for us fifteen feet below the surface, but Diablo didn't have that intimate operational knowledge. He was blindly following us toward certain death if we couldn't reach the rebreathers before one of the bullets found its mark.

We reached our gear, and I caught the slightest hint of a smile from Diablo as I poked a regulator toward his mouth. The three of us inhaled our first breath in over a minute and watched the full metal jacketed AK-47 rounds sinking harmlessly all around us.

We weren't out of the woods—or the water—just yet, but our ticket to relative freedom was less than four miles away . . . as long as someone hadn't helped themselves to our boat.

Clark and I donned the rebreathers and suited Diablo up with a mask, regulator, and cylinder. We had plenty of air for the water devil, but our problem wasn't air—it was electricity. The single remaining DPV was designed to pull one two-hundred-pound diver through the water at just over five knots. There were three of us. That was far too much load to expect the DPV to drag us at any meaningful speed. Fortunately, the Pacific tide was receding, and our adrenaline was still pumping. We clipped ourselves into a single line behind the DPV and headed south. I was in front, tucked in as tightly as possible behind the motorized housing with Clark in my wake, and finally, Diablo in the rear where his limited surface area would do little to diminish our speed through the water. We kicked at a moderate pace, adding propulsion to the tug of the DPV.

After forty-five minutes, I floated the buoy to take a GPS position. We were less than a mile from the boat. I was tempted to surface to sneak a peek back upstream, but I remembered the Bible story of Lot's wife turning to a pillar of salt when she looked back as they were fleeing Sodom and Gomorrah.

Twenty minutes later we were climbing aboard the RHIB and doffing our dive gear. Diablo checked the seal on the dry bag to make sure the data wasn't swimming in salt water, while Clark hauled the anchor aboard. Just as she had done at every turn of the key, the engine purred her reassuring rumble, and we roared southward, away from Farfan Beach and toward the island of Bona.

Clark made the sat-phone call, and I was relieved to see Leo and his trusty Huey racing barely above the waves from the north. He easily beat us to Bona and was waiting on the beach, ready to roll out the red carpet. We climbed from the boat, thankful to be feet dry on the beach.

"What happened to you, Baby Face?" Leo said. "You look like hell."

Clark dabbed at his face with the tips of his fingers. "Oh, this? It's nothing. I just cut myself shaving this morning."

"It's good to have you guys back. You, too, Diablo. I've been missing your world-famous roasted turtle."

Since Leo had chosen to welcome us home in English, Diablo stared at him with his trademark empty expression. "*Llévame a Ginger.*"

"Even I understood that," said Clark. "The little devil wants to see his girlfriend, and I think he's earned it. I've always been more of a Mary Ann kinda guy myself, but I can understand how he feels."

"Yeah, about that," said Leo. "I guess you guys haven't had a chance to catch the news."

"No, we've had our hands full this morning. What's going on?" I said.

"Well, it seems that a bunch of Muslim extremists hijacked four planes in the States this morning."

"Okay," I said. "What do they want?"

"It's not so much what they *want* as what they've *done* that's the problem," he said.

"Come on, Leo. Spit it out. What did they do?"

He dug at the sand with the toe of his boot and bit the corner of his bottom lip. "They seized control of two airliners and flew them into the Twin Towers of the World Trade Center in New York."

"My God," I said.

"How many dead?" asked Clark.

"We don't know yet, but that's not all. They also flew one into the Pentagon and dumped one in a field in Pennsylvania. There were minimal casualties at the Pentagon, and except for the passengers, crew, and hijackers, no one was hurt on the ground in Pennsylvania."

I was at a loss for words, so I busied myself tying our boat to a twisted tree.

When we'd finished briefing Leo on the success of the operation and extraction, I noticed Diablo was missing . . . again. I caught a whiff of a fire and found him cooking a peacock over a small, smoldering pit.

For someone who was barely half my size, food certainly seemed important. The four of us ate ravenously, and I contemplated the dramatic events back in the States.

"I can get you to Cuba, or Bimini, or maybe even Nassau," Leo said, "but there's nothing flying in the States. And I mean nothing."

I turned to Clark. "What do you think?"

"Elizabeth and Penny can get the boat to Bimini in two days," he said.

I still had trouble thinking of Skipper as Elizabeth, but he was right. "I'll get on the phone and get them headed that way."

Leo said, "I'll find you an airplane."

"Us?" questioned Clark. "You'll find *us* an airplane? Aren't you coming?"

"Not if you're going to Bimini. I'm persona non grata on that particular rock in the ocean for another few years," he admitted.

"What did you do to get thrown out of Bimini?"

"Well," he began, "I was *allegedly* involved in the reacquisition of a particular flying machine on behalf of someone I believed to be its rightful owner. I may have been slightly underinformed on the exact details of the whole situation."

"You stole an airplane?" I said.

"I prefer to think of it as mistakenly relocating it to a little island whose people tend to roll the best cigars in the world."

"You stole an airplane and flew it to Cuba?"

"Allegedly," he reiterated.

"Did you at least get paid?" I had to know.

"Allegedly."

"Don't feel bad," I said. "We're not exactly welcome back in Cuba."

"Oh really?" Leo raised his eyebrows.

"Yeah, I *allegedly* shot a Russian mafia kingpin in the shoulder and chopped up a legendary assassin with a borrowed outboard motor in Havana Harbor."

"That was you?" There was a hint of admiration in his tone.

I smiled. "Allegedly."

"How about you, Clark? Why don't the beautiful and friendly people of Cuba want you back on their little island?"

"The people don't have a problem with me. It's the government who isn't rolling out the red carpet for us. We, also allegedly, relocated a mini spy sub from the harbor one dark night."

"You boys get around, don't you?"

Clark and I echoed, "Allegedly."

* * *

Skipper answered on the seventh ring. I've come to believe that rings on a satellite phone have no correlation with actual rings, so I never hang up early.

She wasted no time with hello. "Chase, you're never going to believe this. Somebody hijacked two airplanes and—"

"Yeah, I heard, but listen . . . I need your help."

"My help?"

"Yes. I need you and Penny to get the boat to Bimini as quickly as possible. Leave right now if you can."

"Sure," she said, "but can we bring Ginger? She's awesome."

"Yes, absolutely bring Ginger. I don't know if she can sail, but we need her there. Do not leave her behind."

Before hanging up, she said, "Woo-hoo! Girls' cruise!"

Clark chuckled. "That was quick."

"They're leaving today. They should be there by Thursday morning."

Leo returned after a lengthy phone conversation. "Okay, guys. Here's the deal. I got you an airplane. It's a C-47."

"A DC-3?" I said, a little concerned about the range and speed of the old cargo plane.

"Yeah, a DC-3. The military called them C-47s, same-same. Anyway, we . . . well, *you* will pick it up in Puerto Jimenez tomorrow morning. You'll need a fuel stop, but she'll make the total trip in eight hours or so."

Clark was beaming with excitement. "Do we get to keep the airplane?"

"No, Clark," said Leo. "You can't keep the plane. It's part of my penance. It'll need to stay in Bimini."

"We never get to have any fun."

Leo huffed. "Yeah, Russian mafia boss, chopped-up assassin, stolen spy sub, air assault amphibious raid on a sunken Chinese freighter in the Panama Canal. . . . You guys never get to have any fun."

"Okay, okay," Clark relented. "We'll leave the plane in Bimini, but I'm pissing out the door when we fly over Castro's house in Havana."

Leo laughed. "I would expect nothing less."

We humped our gear to the chopper and left the key in the boat. Somebody was going to have a good time with our little toy, and I was going to miss her. I'd definitely be adding one just like her to my Christmas wish list.

The flight back to Puerto Jimenez was uneventful except that I got to do the flying. I had very little helicopter time, so it was a good opportunity to refresh my limited skill as Clark put me and the Huey through a battery of challenges. The chopper did well. Me? Not so much. But I had fun, and the landing was far better than I'd expected. Leo and Diablo slept through the whole thing.

The DC-3 looked like a pile of miscellaneous airplane parts taped and riveted together. I wasn't sure it would make it to the end of the runway, let alone fifteen hundred miles to Bimini over open ocean.

"*That's* your penance?" I said.

"Yeah, she ain't pretty, and she's old, but just like me, she still flies like the day she came off the assembly line."

I scoffed. "Oh, she's far worse than not pretty."

"Don't worry, Pretty Boy. It ain't the paint that makes 'em fly. It's the nuts and bolts, and she's got good bones."

Clark and I did an extensive preflight inspection and found Leo to be quite correct. She was mechanically sound, even if she was uglier than a bowling shoe.

"Well, boys. It's been fun. Thanks for taking an old man on an adventure with you. Maybe I'll send you a Christmas card sometime."

I shook his hand. "Thanks, Leo. Take care of yourself, and don't forget to send us a bill."

"Yeah, I'll get around to it. Fair winds and following seas."

With that, he and his Huey vanished across the canopy of trees and into the millions of acres of Central American rainforest.

Clark had a couple dozen hours in the DC-3, so he climbed into the left seat, and I settled into the co-pilot's perch. He walked me through the start-up procedures, and the old radial engines sputtered to life with clouds of smoke pouring from each.

"They do that," he said. "It's perfectly normal."

The gauges were all in the green as we taxied out, and the old workhorse lumbered into the sky just like she'd been doing for sixty years. She had two VHF radios, but it didn't seem possible to make either of them work for more than a few minutes at a time. The only navigation equipment was a compass that didn't point toward anything consistently, and an ancient automatic direction finder that was supposed to point toward nondirectional beacons and a.m. radio antennas. I couldn't make it do either one. As we leveled off at three thousand feet over the rainforest, I climbed out of the cockpit, rummaged through our dive gear, and pulled out our GPS units.

I returned to the cockpit. "Here you go. Now we're GPS equipped."

Clark laughed. "I was just hoping to get close enough to George-town to smell the fried grouper or maybe jerk chicken if we happened on Jamaica."

We settled in for the three-and-a-half-hour flight, and everything went perfectly.

My landing at Georgetown didn't qualify as textbook, but I kept us on the concrete, and none of the big pieces fell off the old plane. We cleared customs without any issues. Surprisingly, Diablo had a diplomatic passport, but he wouldn't let us see it.

I called my old friend at the Cayman International Bank, and he arranged for transportation and a suite at the Ritz-Carlton. It's good to have friends.

On the beach, we had grilled snapper on paper plates, using plastic forks, and washed it down with Hammerhead Lager. It was quite a change from Diablo's gourmet grilling, but it was welcome.

Every conversation we overheard was about the hijackings in the States. Everyone seemed to have a friend or relative who'd been in one of the Twin Towers. The unimaginable footage played endlessly on every television screen. As I watched those buildings burned and finally collapsed, and my blood boiled at the audacity of the terror-ists to attack thousands of innocent civilians who were simply going about their lives, feeding their families, and not hurting anyone.

The attack on Pearl Harbor in 1941 had been terrible, but at its core, it was a military attack on a military target. These animals had used our hospitality and our civilian aircraft to deliver a coward's blow against an unarmed, defenseless target. Someone was behind the attack. Someone planned, funded, and orchestrated the atrocity. Those were the people who'd pay with their lives, and it would become my pilgrimage to send as many of those bastards to meet Allah as I could. They had no idea what hell they'd just called down upon themselves, and I'd make sure I delivered as much of that hell as I could carry.

25
Amigo

Back at the Ritz, we turned in early. Clark claimed the room with the best view of the pool. His justification for it was "just in case a fair maiden needed to be saved from drowning overnight."

Diablo made a nest of one sheet, a blanket, and a pillow on the floor just inside the door. What a strange little devil he was.

I crawled into a luxurious king-sized bed and was asleep in no time, confident that Diablo wouldn't let anyone through the door —not that I had any reason to fear we'd befall attack at the Ritz-Carlton. Of course, I suppose the victims of the brutal and senseless attacks in the States also believed they were safe.

I heard Diablo whisper, "Amigo. Amigo."

Blinking, I pulled myself from my dream of Penny's arm draped across my hip and her breath on my neck. I was so looking forward to seeing her again.

"Yeah, what is it?" I asked, trying to figure out why he would wake me up at four fifteen.

"I have to tell you about the men who killed your family." He spoke in accented but otherwise flawless English. I thought I was dreaming.

"What are you talking about?" I mumbled in my barely-awake voice.

"Your parents, Archie and Jean, and your little sister. I'm sorry. I don't know her name." He spoke just above a whisper, presumably to avoid waking Clark.

I sat up. "What do you know about my family's killers?"

"I was there that night, amigo. I saw what they did."

"Why didn't you stop them?" I almost yelled.

He put his finger to his lips. "Shh. This is for you to know. There will be too many questions if we wake him." He raised his chin toward Clark's room.

"Okay, but why didn't you stop those people from killing my family?"

"I wasn't supposed to be there. I was young then. I was not yet in a position to make decisions. I did only what I was told . . . at least until that night."

"Tell me what happened."

"General Noriega was a bad man. He was using the orphanage to hide contraband."

"What kind of contraband?"

"Drugs and money. Lots of both. That's why your parents were there. They were moving the children to someplace safe so they wouldn't be harmed when the raid happened."

"Go on," I encouraged him, unable to believe what was happening.

"They came to take one more small bus of children away when six of Noriega's fighters discovered what they were doing. They killed everyone on the bus, amigo. Five children, including your sister, and both of your parents. They shot all of them, but your mother and father fought bravely. Your mother shot one of the men in the shoulder and then again in the face. Your father fought with them like a wild animal, amigo. Like I fight . . . just the same. He hurt them badly and even killed the man who had murdered your sister. Your father tore the man apart like a paper doll. I saw it happen from maybe a thousand meters away through a spotter's scope. I had no rifle and no way to get to them in time, but I took a mental photograph of every man who was there, and I burned those pictures into my mind. When they finally killed your father, he was swinging a machete like a sword. He died fighting like a warrior . . . like *you*, amigo. When I first saw you in the helicopter in the jungle, I knew immediately who you were. And when I saw you fight on that ship, I knew your father had not died. His spirit is in you. You look like him and move like him. He is very proud."

I couldn't process everything he was telling me.

Is this all a dream, just like Anya's story when I was in the recompression chamber? Can any of this be true?

"What about the men from that night? Where are they now?"

"They are in hell, amigo. I sent them there. I killed them with the same machete your father held as he died."

"When?"

"Not long after they murdered your family. I followed them and found them sleeping. I woke each of them so they would spend all of eternity knowing they had died by your father's knife. That is how I became this animal that I am. That is when I stopped living as a man and became a weapon against men like them."

"Why are you telling me this now? Why didn't you tell me before?" Confusion dripped from my every word.

"It was not the time before. There was much work to be done, and this is too much to think about in times like those. I hope you understand."

"I do," I whispered. "Thank you, my friend."

* * *

The rays of the morning sun filtered through the windows and cast shapes and shadows on the western wall of the suite. Knowing that my family's killers had paid the ultimate price for what they'd done should've brought me some degree of closure and satisfaction, but it didn't. To me, it closed and locked a door on a scene I could never reopen. I had wanted to find the men who'd murdered my family and cut them down one by one. I wanted them to look into my eyes as they drew their last breath and beg for their lives. That had been done on my behalf, and I would have to live with the knowledge that their murder had been avenged, but not by me.

* * *

Clark came out of the restroom wiping his bruised face with a towel, then pointed backward. "That guy is taking a bath in about an inch of water. He is one weird little dude."

"He's all right," I said. "I'm glad he's on our team."

"We need to get moving. We don't want the girls to beat us to Bimini."

I showered and shaved in the other restroom. When I came out, room service had arrived. There was an enormous breakfast spread on the table, and we ate like civilized humans from glass plates and with real silverware. It was a nice change.

Diablo didn't speak another word in English that morning, and he ignored us when we spoke. Clark was right—he was one strange bird, but I had a lot of respect for Diablo de Agua.

We landed in Bimini just before noon and shut down on the ramp. Two men from the customs and immigration office climbed aboard the plane before we unbuckled our shoulder harnesses.

One of the men extended his hand. "Passports, please."

We handed them over, and he promptly stamped each of them. "Welcome to Bimini. Enjoy your stay. You can leave our airplane here, and someone will take it away later."

"We have a passenger in the back," I said. "He'll need a stamp, too."

Both men laid eyes on Diablo.

"Do you see any passengers?" the first man said.

"No, just an empty cargo plane," said the other.

They climbed out and disappeared back into the terminal.

"That was weird," I said.

"What was weird?" asked Clark. "I didn't see anything."

We hired a truck to take us and our gear to the marina on the south side of Port Royal and waited for my catamaran to sail into the marina.

It wasn't long before I saw the top of the mast and the brilliant white sails to the west.

"There they come," I said, unable to hide my smile.

In English, Diablo asked, "That is your love?"

Clark jerked his head toward Diablo. "You speak English?"

"Yes, of course. Everyone speaks English. You just assumed I could not because I did not."

Clark playfully pulled a knife from the bar and shook the blade toward Diablo. "You're a sneaky little dude. I'm keeping my eye on you now."

Diablo smiled and struck Clark's wrist with the back of his fist, sending the knife clanging to the ground. "Never bring a knife to a fight with the devil."

I laughed at the exchange and finally answered Diablo's question. "Yes, that's my love. She's a fifty-foot custom sailing catamaran."

He smiled. "No, amigo. Not the boat. Your love is aboard the boat. I see it in your smile. Penny or Elizabeth?"

"Elizabeth is like my little sister. And Penny, well, she's nothing like a sister. She's . . ."

Diablo put his hand on my arm. "It is okay. I understand. My love is on that boat, too."

We met my boat at the dock and helped the girls tie up.

Skipper was the first one off and bound into my arms. "It's good to see you. Welcome home!"

"It's good to be home, sort of," I said. "How was the sail over?"

"Fine." she said, turning to Clark. "Oh my God. Clark, are you all right? What happened to you?"

He hugged her. "Let's just say I learned my lesson about buying American. Chinese razors suck."

Skipper turned to Diablo and stuck out her hand. "I'm Elizabeth."

"I'm sorry, Skipper. This is Diablo de Agua. He worked with us on this operation."

"It is nice to meet you, Elizabeth. I have heard many great things about you. Please call me David . . . David Ruiz."

"Seriously?" Clark said. "Your name is David? I'm going to kill you in your sleep."

Diablo laughed. "What makes you think the devil ever sleeps, *Cara de Bebe?*"

Penny came bouncing down from the helm station. Her hair danced wildly around her head in the midday breeze. She threw her arms around me and pressed her lips to mine.

"I missed you," she said. "I was worried."

I stole another kiss. "I missed you, too."

She hugged Clark and dabbed at his bruised face. "You're still pretty," she said, "but that looks like it hurts."

"And this is David," I said. "David, meet my love, Penny Thomas."

Diablo grinned. "It's nice to meet you, Penny. Chase has been pining for you for days. He could speak of nothing other than seeing your face again."

"Is that true?" she asked.

"Why would I lie?" Diablo said, feigning insult.

"There's somebody on board who's pretty excited about seeing you, too. She insisted on freshening up before we arrived."

Diablo blushed.

"Come on," I said. "Let's get aboard. I think we could all use a cocktail, and Diablo, I think you have a debriefing to endure."

He clasped his hands at his chest. "What torture that will be, being debriefed by a beautiful woman who insisted on freshening up."

I was pouring drinks and listening to Skipper tell us about crossing the Gulf Stream when one of the most beautiful women I'd ever seen came through the companionway. Her auburn hair breathed fire in the sun, and her radiant smile was impossible to ignore. Her green eyes were focused intensely on Diablo, and he quickly stood to greet her. They embraced, and then she took his face in her hands, which were no bigger than a child's. She was shorter than Diablo, and they looked as if they'd been made for each other.

"Hey, guys. I'm Ginger, and I'm not short. I'm fun-sized. Isn't that right, Diablo?"

"You're perfect," he whispered.

"I'm Chase."

"And I'm Clark."

"Oh, I know all about you guys. What wasn't in the file, I learned from Penny and Elizabeth. It's good to have you back, safe and sound," she said.

I poured her a drink, and we sat in relative silence, listening to the birds chirping and the wind blowing through the rigging.

Ginger had obviously waited longer than she could tolerate. "We have some talking to do and some data to dump," she said.

Diablo followed her into the main salon and closed the door behind them.

"I want to do what she does," Skipper said as soon as the door closed.

"What?" Clark and I asked.

"She's an analyst, and she's amazing. She can find anything on her computer, and she says she'll teach me. I know you were worried when I said I wanted to go to The Ranch, but now I can work with you and not have to do all that stuff. It's perfect, and it's what I want to do."

"I can't think of anyone I'd rather have watching over me than you," Clark said. "I think it's a great idea."

Skipper anxiously stared at me as if I had some standing to approve or disapprove her plan.

"Hey, I'm not in charge. If that's what you want to do, and if Ginger's willing to train you, I think you should go for it. I've never heard of an analyst getting shot."

Clark formed a pistol with his thumb and index finger. "And I've never heard of an operator not getting shot."

"I love you guys." Skipper squealed and hugged each of us as if she were trying to squeeze us to death. "Thank you, thank you. I'm going to be the best analyst, ever. Just wait. You'll see."

220 · CAP DANIELS

"I have no doubt," Clark said. "And speaking of getting shot, our hero here tried to get himself killed on this op, and almost pulled it off. He spent two days in the recompression chamber after blowing himself out of the water with about a ton of plastic explosive."

"It was thirty pounds," I protested. "And besides, you're the one who got himself captured and tortured by the Chinese."

"Touché," he said.

Penny crawled across the settee and nestled between my legs. Her body felt warm and welcoming next to mine.

She gently pinched my chin. "I'm glad you're okay."

I ran my fingers through her hair and kissed her forehead. "I'm glad I have you to come home to."

She slid her hand beneath my T-shirt and placed her hand over my heart. "I love . . . I mean, I love . . . that you come home to me. I know what you do is important, and I think it's kinda sexy. My boyfriend is like James Bond or something."

"Is that what I am?"

"Yeah, you're kinda like James Bond. Aren't you?"

"That's not what I meant. I meant, am I your boyfriend?"

"You're whatever you want to be, Mr. Bond."

Ginger and Diablo came through the door and back into the cockpit.

"Guys, this is the best intel on Chinese surveillance technology we've ever seen," Ginger said. "The NSA is going to wet their pants when they see this. You guys are amazing."

"It wasn't us," I argued. "We just gave him a ride in and back out. That little devil did all the work."

"*We* did the work." Diablo tapped his finger on his temple. "I just kept good records."

Clark poured more drinks and raised his glass. "Here's to keeping good records and coming home safely."

We all raised our glasses. "Cheers!"

26
They Lied

We grilled a wahoo Ginger caught on the crossing and some vegetables Skipper had bought at the St. Augustine farmers' market. We watched the sun melt into the ocean off toward Miami, and that made me think about Clark's dad.

"I need to check in with Dominic." I stood and headed for my cabin.

"Yeah," Clark said. "We should've done that this morning when we landed."

It was nice to lie on my own bed aboard my own boat without worrying about anyone shooting at me. I dialed Dominic's number and waited for the rings.

"It's about time you called," he said. "Tell me you're somewhere safe and that my son is with you."

"We're perfectly safe and sound in Bimini," I said.

"Good. How was the vacation?"

I cleared my throat. "Ginger tells us it was the best intel ever gathered on Chinese surveillance technology."

"Wow. Ginger isn't usually that forthcoming with praise. You guys must've done some fine work down there. How's the little guy?"

I laughed. "He's fine. I don't think you could kill that guy with a landmine. He's something else."

"Isn't he, though? Listen, Chase. I need to tell you something."

"Yeah, I already know about the hijackings and the World Trade Center."

"No, it's not that. I assumed you were already briefed on that. This is personal."

I sat up on my bed. "Personal? What is it?"

"It's Richter," he said.

"Dr. Richter?"

"Yeah, Chase. He's not doing well. It's his heart."

"Where is he?" I demanded.

"He's at UAB in Birmingham. It's one of the best cardiac units in the country."

"Can you get me a flight out of Miami? I can be there by morning."

"There are no flights, Chase. Because of the hijacking, all air traffic is grounded with very few exceptions, and getting you on a plane to Birmingham isn't going to fall into one of those areas of exception. You'll have to get a car in Miami and drive up."

"I'll be there tomorrow afternoon. Can I talk to him?"

"No, I'm sorry. He's in the cardiovascular ICU, and I only get to see him for a few minutes every day. Chase, it's serious."

"I'm on my way."

I hopped from my bed and noticed something lying on the sill beneath the portlight. It was the old, battered machete that had taken the lives of my family's killers—the machete my father held when he died. I lifted the weapon and sent up a silent prayer for David Ruiz—devil or not.

I grabbed a stack of cash and my go bag packed and stowed in a locker by my bed, and I headed up the stairs.

"Guys, I have to get to Miami. Dr. Richter is in the ICU at UAB. There are no flights because of the hijacking, so I have to find a boat tonight that'll take me across to Miami so I can rent a car."

In a matter-of-fact tone, Penny said, "I'm going with you."

"There's no time. I have to go now."

She was already on her way down the stairs to my cabin, then emerged seconds later with a backpack of her own. "You're not the only one who keeps a go bag packed. Now let's find a boat. Do you have some cash?"

I smiled and took her hand. "Yeah, I've got everything we'll need. Clark can you—"

"Yeah, yeah," he said. "I've got this. You go. Call as soon as you know anything."

"Thanks," I said, and we stepped from the boat to the dock.

"Wait!" yelled Ginger. "Chase, you've got an airplane, right?"

"Yeah, sort of, but there's no way to get a clearance after the hijackings."

"That'd be true for most normal people, but we're not most people, and we certainly aren't normal," she said.

"Spit it out. I don't have any time to waste."

"Give me the tail number of your airplane and five minutes. Surely you've got five minutes."

"What are you going to do?"

"I'm going to trade the best collection of Chinese surveillance intelligence we've ever seen to the NSA for an air traffic control clearance from Bimini to Birmingham."

"But we gave the plane to the customs agents," Clark said.

"No, they *believe* we gave it to them, but I don't remember any such transaction. Do you, Diablo?"

"No, I was there the whole time, and there was no transaction. They just welcomed us to Bimini and stamped *your* passports."

"Give me the information. Who's the PIC? You or Clark?"

"Clark has to be the pilot in command. I'm not type rated in the DC-3 yet," I said, and I gave her the numbers.

We climbed back aboard, and Ginger soon returned with a piece of paper in her hand. "Here's your prior permission required number and your flight plan. Call Miami Center as soon as you're airborne, and give them the PPR. They'll clear you direct to BHM. It's seven hundred miles. Do you have the fuel for that?"

Clark hung up the phone. "She'll be fully fueled when we get there. Let's roll."

"Ginger, you're the best. Thank you. Diablo, do something nice for her as soon as possible, will you?"

He winked at me. "Oh, I plan to."

"I'm still coming," said Penny.

"I wouldn't have it any other way," I said, and we leapt to the dock. "Oh, I almost forgot. You guys will probably want to sail up to Freeport and check in with immigration or sail back to Florida. I don't think the local customs officers are going to be too happy in the morning."

We hailed a taxi at the marina entrance and were airborne in no time after reaching the airport.

Clark was on the controls, and I was trying to convince my underwater GPS that we could swim to Birmingham at two hundred knots. As we climbed through four thousand feet headed northwest, I tuned the radio and prayed it would work.

"Miami Center, this is November-seven-six-one-November-Alpha. We're a Douglas DC-3 off Bimini for Birmingham Shuttlesworth, Bravo Hotel Mike with a PPR."

I waited somewhat impatiently for the controller to answer. I'd spent a lot of time flying in Miami Center's airspace, and I'd never heard the radio silent. It was eerie.

Finally, a controller came on. "Calling off Bimini with a PPR, say again."

I repeated my request and read him my PPR number.

"November-one-November-Alpha, squawk-zero-six-four-one."

I dialed the code into the aged transponder, and the little yellow light flickered every time the radar signal bounced off the antenna beneath the plane.

"November-one-November-Alpha, you're radar contact one seven northwest of Bimini, and you're cleared direct Birmingham. Climb and maintain one zero thousand."

I read back the clearance and reported out of seven thousand for ten. It had worked. Ginger had pulled it off. If Skipper could learn to do that, there would be no limit to what we could accomplish.

On the flight, I left Clark in the cockpit and sat with Penny in one of the uncomfortable cargo net seats.

"Are you okay?" she asked.

"Yeah, I'm okay. There are just some things you need to know before we get to the hospital."

"Okay. You can tell me anything."

I spent forty-five minutes explaining how Dr. Richter had been my favorite psychology professor at UGA and how he'd recruited me into American covert ops. That was the easy part. Telling her about Anya was tough.

"So, this Russian agent lied about being your psych professor's daughter and pretended to be in love with you?"

"Yes, but it's more complicated than that."

Penny chewed on her lip. "But she's dead now, right?"

"Well, I thought so, but maybe not." I tried to make it make sense for her, but it didn't even make sense to me.

"Chase . . . are you still in love with her?"

That question hit me like a sledgehammer, and I tensed.

Penny hung her head. "You are."

I took her hand. "No. I was never in love with her. I was in love with the character she played. The person I thought I loved didn't exist. It was all a convoluted play to worm her way into U.S. covert ops. None of it was real."

"It was real to you when it was happening," she said.

"Yes," I admitted. "It was real to me back then, but not now."

"Okay. This is all pretty hard to swallow, but I'm going to trust you since I'm on what I assume is a stolen seventy-five-year-old airplane, in the middle of the night, going to see your dying spymaster who may also be the father of your former lover, who was, or maybe still is a Russian spy."

"Sixty," I said.

"Um. . . ."

"The plane is only sixty years old. Not seventy-five."

She broke into laughter and wrapped her arms around me. "You know, I don't just love that you come home to me. I also love—"

"Hey, Chase! Get up here. I need you. We're starting our descent into Birmingham."

I turned to Penny. "I know. Me, too."

The old DC-3 was a handful in the daytime with wind on the nose, but she turned out to be a bear at night in a crosswind. We touched down at three on Friday morning and finally wrestled the old girl to the ramp.

I pulled into the University of Alabama Birmingham cardiovascular unit parking garage just after four. There was no way they were going to let me see Dr. Richter before the morning visiting hours, but I wasn't going to miss my window of opportunity. Clark dropped us by the door and said he'd meet us inside. I suspected the truth was that he was going to go sleep in the back seat of the rental car until the sun came up. He had to be exhausted.

Penny and I passed through the glass doors of the hospital.

"You know, if your dead Russian girl shows up here, I'll scratch her eyes out."

I wanted to warn her that not even James Bond could protect her if she tried to scratch Anya's eyes out. Instead, I said, "I think that's pretty sexy that you'd fight for me, but let's not go to jail in Birmingham tonight, okay?"

She squeezed my arm. "No promises, remember?"

We found an abandoned information desk and waited for what felt like hours for an attendant, but it never happened. Finally, Penny vaulted across the locked half-door and settled in behind the computer. "What's his first name?"

"Robert," I said. "Robert Richter."

"He's in cardiovascular ICU, second floor, room two-one-one-four."

An angry, overweight, middle-aged guy in a rent-a-cop uniform waddled down the hall. "Hey! You can't be back there. What are you doing?"

"We waited for half an hour, and no one showed up. We couldn't wait any longer. My dad is in the CICU."

"Damn that Lois. She does this crap every night. She thinks because she brings me pound cake that I won't rat her out, but the pound cake isn't that good anyway. Okay, okay, just get out from behind there and go on up. Morning visiting hours start at seven. There's coffee in the waiting room up there." The guard unlocked the half-door and let Penny out.

Penny kissed the guard on the cheek. "I think it's cute that you call it pound cake. Thanks, officer."

He blushed. "Get out of here, you two."

We rode the elevator to the second floor and found the CICU waiting room. Dominic Fontana was asleep on the overstuffed sofa, and there was an infomercial trying to sell tape that could hold a boat together after they'd cut it in half.

I could use a roll or two of that.

I settled into a surprisingly comfortable chair, and Penny went to work brewing a fresh pot of coffee.

She giggled. "Maybe I should take some down to the guard so he can have it with his pound cake."

Dominic started to stir. "Hey, Chase. How did you get here so fast?"

"We found a flight. It's a long story. How's he doing, Dominic?"

"A flight? How'd you get a flight?"

"The NSA sort of owed us a favor. I'll tell you all about it in the morning. How's Dr. Richter?"

He sat up and pointed toward the coffee pot. "Is that fresh?"

"Yeah, I just made it. I'm Penny, by the way."

"Dom," he said. "Dominic Fontana. It's nice to meet you, Penny. Would you mind pouring me a cup?"

She handed him a paper cup with a little foldout paper handle.

"Who uses these?" he said. "Why can't we get a real coffee cup?"

"Dominic," I said, "how's Dr. Richter?"

"They let me see him last night right after I got off the phone with you. It doesn't look good, Chase. I told him you were coming, and he said he wanted to see you as soon as you got here."

"Did he have a heart attack?"

"Yeah, they think so. He's getting old, you know."

I nodded and took a paper cup from Penny.

"I'll let you two talk," she said. "I'm going for a walk."

I gave her a weak smile as she left the room. "Tell me what's going on, Dominic."

He looked down the hall. "Close the door and turn off the TV, will you?"

I did as he asked and then sat across from him.

"Let's hear it, Dominic. I'm tired. I've spent the last two days in the cockpit of a raggedy old DC-3, and the two days before that in a recompression chamber after getting blown out of the water. I've got no patience for this."

He squinted and shook his head. I could tell he wanted details, but so did I.

"It's this whole Norikova ordeal, Chase. It's done a number on him. When he was overseas in the seventies, that Katerina woman really got under his skin. He's spent the last three decades trying to get over her. He was never married. Did you know that?"

"No," I admitted. "I didn't know that."

"Yeah, he was hung up on Katerina. Anyway, when Norikova showed up pretending to be his daughter, he was twenty-one again and over the moon. To see that girl who looked so much like Katerina screwed him up. It's spooky how much they look alike, you know?"

"Yeah, I know. Colonel Tornovich picked precisely the right girl to play the part. If he couldn't have found their actual daughter, she was as close as anyone could ever be."

"Yeah," he said. "It's just spooky." He took a long drink of coffee from the paper cup. "This is ridiculous. I'm bringing my own cup tomorrow."

"You can go to the hotel and get some real sleep now. I'll stay here as long as necessary."

"I could use a shower and a shave. I may take you up on that after we see him in the morning. What time is it anyway?"

I glanced at my watch and couldn't even remember which time zone I was in. "I think it's almost five, but maybe it's almost four."

On a small table, a telephone's LED screen flashed four-fifty-seven. "I guess it's almost five."

"Visiting hours start at seven, but sometimes they let me in before that if he's awake. He's going to be happy to see you."

"It'll be good to see him, too," I said. "Dominic, is he going to make it?"

He drank the last of his coffee and crushed the paper cup in his palm. "I don't think so."

Penny came back with a pair of ceramic coffee mugs with "Waffle House" stenciled on the side of each. She poured both of us another cup and set them on the table in front of us.

Dominic smiled and inspected the mug. "Thank you, Penny. I didn't know you could buy these."

"You can't," she said, "but it turns out they'll give them to you to get you to stop telling the customers that the cook has gonorrhea and isn't wearing gloves."

Dominic looked at me. "I like her. Where'd you find her?"

"Ah, I picked her up about thirty miles east of Charleston."

"That's in the Atlantic Ocean," he said.

I smiled. "We all need a mermaid in our lives sometimes."

He raised his mug. "Here's to mermaids who can score Waffle House coffee cups at five in the morning."

"I'll drink to that," I said. "So, Clark is sleeping in the car. He'll be in after he wakes up if you want to wait for him. Otherwise, you're welcome to grab a hotel. I'll call you if anything happens here."

"I think I'll wait until we get to see him at seven. I'll see Clark for a few minutes, and then I'll get some rest."

At twenty past six, a nurse stuck her head in the waiting room. "Old grouchpuss is awake if you want to go in."

"He's developed quite a reputation around here already," Dominick said.

"That's our Rocket." I reached for Penny's hand. "Are you coming? I'd like for you to meet Dr. Richter."

"I'll wait here this time and go in later if that's okay. I think you two probably have a lot to talk about, and it would be easier without me."

I nodded and kissed her cheek.

We walked into his room, and it was all I could do to keep from falling apart. He'd always been thin with sunken eyes, but he looked like a skeleton with leathery skin stretched across his bones. I tried to smile, but couldn't, so I bit my lip and sat on the edge of his bed.

He reached for my hand, and I could swear he was trying to smile, too. I didn't know what to say, so I said the dumbest thing I could. "How are you?"

He actually did smile then. "Never better. Did you bring me any good scotch?"

"I'm sure I could round up a bottle."

"Thanks for coming. I'm glad you're here." The words came on a raspy, breathy voice that I never would've recognized as his.

He turned his hollowed eyes to Dominic. "Can you give us the room, Dom? We've got a lot to talk about."

"Sure," he said as he got up to leave. "I'm going to get some rest, and I'll see you this afternoon."

"Son, I'm serious about the scotch," he hissed. "I'm never leaving this hospital alive, and I'd like to have one last drink with you—and a cigar if you think you could pull it off."

I choked back the wall of tears threatening to flood my eyes. "When are the next visiting hours?"

"Who gives a damn what time visiting hours are? I'm an old man, and I'm going to be dead soon. You're a spy, for God's sake. You come and go as you please and put a bullet in anyone who tries to stop you."

He started coughing and wheezing. I poured him a cup of water from a plastic pitcher on the side table. He drank most of it, while the rest dribbled down his chin.

"I don't like you seeing me like this, son, but I'm glad you came. Did you hear about the damned Arabs flying into the Twin Towers?"

"Yes, sir, I heard."

"Cut the *sir* crap. We're the same now—just sixty years apart. That's the only difference."

He wheezed until he finally caught his breath. An oxygen cannula dangled from the rail of his bed.

"Why don't you wear your oxygen?"

"I hate that thing," he said. "It makes me feel like an invalid."

"It didn't make you feel like an invalid when you were breathing oxygen in the Mustang," I said.

Dr. Richter had been a P-51 Mustang pilot over Brittan in World War Two, and he still owned a D-model Mustang named *Katerina's Heart*. I'd flown with him in the old warbird the weekend he and his friends recruited me into covert ops. I'd never seen him more alive than when he was at the controls of that Mustang.

"Humph. You're a pretty good psychologist. You must have had a good teacher."

He pulled the cannula from the bed rail and laced it across his ears and beneath his nose. The wheezing stopped, and the color returned to his cheeks.

"So, what have you been up to, son?"

I told him about the op in the Panama Canal.

He said, "Those Chinese are crafty little bastards. You've got to hand it to them . . . they'll try anything."

He pointed to his water pitcher. I poured him another cup, and he managed to keep most of it in his mouth.

"I knew that Leo, by the way. Crazy old coot. He's the best chopper pilot I ever saw."

"Yeah, I've never seen anything like it," I said. "He could stick that thing down a chimney if you bet him he couldn't."

"It sure is good to see you, Chase. It's been too long, and now this'll probably be the last time we ever get to sit and talk . . . just the two of us."

"Don't say that, Dr. Richter."

"I'm too old and sick to dance around the truth, son. Now listen. I've got some intel you need. I need you to just listen and not interrupt me. Can you do that?"

I nodded and poured him another cup of water. He held it up, and then leaned over the side of his bed and looked toward the floor.

"What is it, Coach?"

I started calling him Coach in college after I'd broken my hand and couldn't play ball anymore. I thought of him as my coach back then, and somehow, it just stuck.

He pressed the call button on the remote control hanging by his arm.

A dislocated voice came through the tiny speaker. "What do you need, grouchpuss?"

He tried to laugh. "The septic tank is full again."

"I'll be right there." The nurse came in, emptied the urine drainage bag attached to the end of Dr. Richter's catheter and recorded the amount in his chart. He sighed a sound of relief, and the bag began to fill again.

"Okay, so now are you ready to listen?"

"Yes, sir."

"They lied to us, son."

"Who lied to us?"

"I told you not to ask any questions. Just listen."

"Sorry."

"The CIA lied. Of course, that's what they do, but they didn't *have* to lie to us."

I was lost, but I'd promised to shut up.

He continued. "Nearly thirty years ago, Katerina Burinkova and I spent four days in Vienna. It was the most unforgettable four days of my life. Every night before we fell asleep, I'd brush Katerina's long hair and listen to her sing. Son, not a day of my life has gone by when I didn't close my eyes and relive those four nights. At the end of our time together in Vienna, Katerina left for Moscow in a hurry. She left behind almost everything she'd brought with her. I was due in London, but there was no particular rush, so I packed up everything she'd left behind and took it all with me. I had no way to know that would be the last time I'd ever see her."

He paused to catch his breath and have another drink of water. "Boy, some nice scotch sure would be good." He coughed, struggled to catch his breath again, and continued. "Anyway, when you brought Anastasia to the house in Athens . . . you remember that day, don't you?"

I'll never forget that day. Dr. Richter had played right into Anya's hand and let himself believe she was his daughter. It had all been part of Colonel Tornovich's diabolical plan, and it worked nearly flawlessly.

I nodded.

"So, when the two of you were at my house for those two days, there hadn't been a woman in there for years. Anastasia asked if I had a hairbrush, and I dug around and found a brand-new one still sealed up in the plastic."

I couldn't hold my tongue any longer. "Where's this going, Dr. Richter?"

"Patience, my boy. Patience. I promise not to die until I finish the story. So, anyway, the brush. She used it and left it behind when we went back to Florida. After all that horseshit from the CIA came out about Anastasia being a double agent and not really being our daughter, I got to thinking about that hairbrush and the time I'd spent in Vienna with her mother all those years ago . . . and about brushing Katerina's hair."

I leaned in closer to him.

"I have no idea why, but I'd kept that old hairbrush I'd spent hours pulling through Katerina's long, beautiful hair. I'd sent the bag where I'd kept it all those years and the brush Anya had used to some people I trust at a lab. They're not only some of the best in the world, but they're also some of the best at keeping secrets. You know, son, trust is a hard thing to earn, but damned easy to lose."

He raised his eyebrows above the rim of his glasses and looked down his nose at me. "I waited around a few weeks, and finally, one of the guys from that lab called me and said I should come down there. So, I went, and he took a DNA sample from me and did whatever those guys do under their microscope or whatever they have back there in those clean rooms. A few days later, he called and said there's no chance Anya is anybody's baby girl other than mine and the woman whose hair was in that old brush."

"So, she *is* your daughter?"

He coughed again, and I poured more water. I was bursting with questions.

After what felt like an eternity, he said, "I don't know anything about the science of DNA testing, but if that girl was somebody named Captain Ekaterina Norikova, I'll eat your shorts. That girl is Anastasia Robertovna Burinkova, and she is my daughter, just as sure as you and me are spies, boy."

I pulled open the curtains in front of the oversized window and watched the first shadows of the morning cover a gazebo and court-yard I hadn't noticed when we'd arrived.

"She's still alive, isn't she?" I heard myself ask the question, but it sounded as if someone else had spoken the words.

He licked his thin lips and tried to clear his throat. "Listen to me, son. I'm never going to leave this hospital bed, and I'm not go-ing out with the taste of that rancid water in my mouth. Go find us a bottle of good scotch. We're both going to need a drink before I have the courage, and before you have the gut, for the answer to that question. Can you do that, Chase?"

I could count on one hand the number of times he'd called me by my first name.

"Yeah, I can do that. I'll be back as soon as I can. Do you need anything else before I go?"

He tried to smile. "I just need to have one more drink with the only son I'll ever have before. . . ."

I squeezed his bony shoulder, refusing to let him see me cry. "I'll be right back."

I found my way back to the parking garage. Clark was sound asleep in the back of our rental car, and Penny was sitting in the front seat, braiding strands of hair into a long cord across her shoul-der. She stared off into the distance as if she were lost in thought, or perhaps worry.

I pulled open the driver's door and slid onto the seat beside her. I half expected Clark to spring awake with his pistol drawn, but he didn't budge.

"Are you okay?" Penny asked through a frown.

I turned the key and swallowed the lump in my throat. "No, I'm not okay. Dr. Richter isn't going to make it. He insists that I find a good bottle of scotch for one last drink."

"Chase, you can't take scotch in there. There's no way they're going to let you—"

"Who's going to stop me? That rent-a-cop with the pound cake addiction? That man lying in there dying has done more for me than anyone else on Earth. If he wants scotch, or anything else for that matter, I'm going to see to it that he has it."

She forced a brief smile and placed her hand on my thigh. "In that case," she said, "let's go find the man some scotch. I have an idea. Turn left out of the garage."

I followed her directions and turned north onto a two-lane street lined with restaurants, bars, and mom-and-pop shops.

"What's your plan?" I asked.

"Just trust me. Turn right at the next stop sign and go slow. How much cash do you have?"

"Maybe a thousand bucks."

We turned east onto a one-way street lined with delivery trucks.

She stuck out her hand. "Stop here and give me what you've got. I'll be right back."

Penny had never disappointed me. After all, she had scored two coffee cups from the Waffle House. I pulled to the curb and handed her a wad of cash. She disappeared down an alley just as I heard Clark start to stir.

"What's going on?" he asked in his barely-conscious voice.

"Penny's scoring some scotch for Dr. Richter."

He mumbled, "Oh, okay," and fell back asleep.

I watched delivery drivers come and go, and I kept checking my watch every thirty seconds. Finally, Penny skipped around the corner of the old brick building and slid back onto the seat beside me.

She held out a bottle of twenty-five-year-old Macallan. "Will this do?"

"That'll do just fine," I said, "but how did you . . ."

She winked. "Your girlfriend's got skills."

"Is that what you are? My girlfriend?"

She kissed me on the cheek. "At least. Now let's get back to the hospital before the daytime rent-a-cops take over."

The maze of one-way streets took longer to navigate than I'd expected, but I finally found a vacant parking spot beside the gazebo I'd seen from Dr. Richter's window.

Penny and I stepped from the car.

"Don't you want to park in the garage?"

"No, his room is right up there." I pointed toward the window, and what I saw through the thick pane of glass sent the hair on the back of my neck standing on end. I froze in my tracks.

A woman was standing beside Dr. Richter's bed. Her long, golden-blonde hair shined as she bent over and kissed him on the forehead.

"Who is that?" asked Penny.

"That's Anya!" I broke into a sprint toward the hospital door.

I bounded up the stairs to the second floor and burst through the heavy oak door, slamming it against the wall. Still at a sprint, I rounded the corner by the nurses' station and saw a horde of nurses running nearly as fast as I was. They poured into Dr. Richter's room in a chaotic rush, and I didn't slow down. When I'd shoved my way through the door and into his room, the scene unfolding in front of me was beyond comprehension.

The heart monitor displayed a long, flat line, and a continuous tone blared into the antiseptic air of the room. A young nurse had one knee on the side of Dr. Richter's bed and both hands planted firmly in the center of his chest. I watch the nurse's shoulders rise and fall rhythmically as his hands compressed my mentor's chest. Another nurse pumped air from a respiration bag into Dr. Richter's mouth while the bevy of nurses scurried about, all intent on saving his life.

The world in front of me fell from focus except for the gaunt, pale face of the man who'd molded my mind into that of a psychologist, and who'd delivered my body into the service of my country; the man who'd been the greatest influence of my adult life. His gray-blue eyes drooped lifeless and bleak.

Suddenly aware of my own heart pounding in my chest, I gasped for air. A thin, delicate hand slipped into mine, and I squeezed the familiar flesh.

"Clear!" the doctor ordered.

The body of the man I loved so dearly arched upward in rigid response to the shock of the defibrillator.

"Clear!" he commanded again.

Once more, Dr. Richter's body lurched violently, stiffened, and fell back to the sheets.

At my side, the woman whispered, "I'm so sorry, Chase."

She was the woman I knew I could depend on. The woman I so desperately needed and desired. The woman I loved.

The doctor placed the paddles back on the cart and looked at his watch. "Time of death, seven twenty-four a.m."

Penny pulled me into her arms and held me tight as the room fell silent and my body succumbed to the exhaustion and despair I'd held at bay.

About the Author

Cap Daniels

Cap Daniels is a former sailing charter captain, scuba and sailing instructor, pilot, Air Force combat veteran, and civil servant of the U.S. Department of Defense. Raised far from the ocean in rural East Tennessee, his early infatuation with salt water was sparked by the fascinating, and sometimes true, sea stories told by his father, a retired Navy Chief Petty Officer. Those stories of adventure on the high seas sent Cap in search of adventure of his own, which eventually landed him on Florida's Gulf Coast where he spends as much time as possible on, in, and under the waters of the Emerald Coast.

With a headful of larger-than-life characters and their thrilling exploits, Cap pours his love of adventure and passion for the ocean onto the pages of The Chase Fulton Novels series.

Visit www.CapDaniels.com to join the mailing list to receive newsletter and release updates.

Connect with Cap Daniels

Facebook: www.Facebook.com/WriterCapDaniels
Instagram: https://www.instagram.com/authorcapdaniels/
BookBub: https://www.bookbub.com/profile/cap-daniels